AS A MAN GROWS OLDER

Italo Svevo was the pen name of Ettore Schmitz, who was born in Trieste in 1861. Educated primarily in Bavaria, Svevo wrote in Italian, but had to work as a French and German correspondence clerk in a Trieste bank. At the age of thirty-one he admitted his artistic drive and wrote and published, at his own expense, his first novel, *Una Vita* (*A Life*), whose hero, like himself, was not happy in the business world. It was followed four years later by *Senilità* (*As a Man Grows Older*), but both books were such failures that he gave up writing for twenty years and tried to settle down to a business career.

During this long period, while he was working as a partner in his father-in-law's business, he made friends with James Joyce, then making a living as an English tutor in Trieste. Joyce was very impressed with Svevo's work and when *La coscienza di Zeno* (*Confessions of Zeno*) was published in 1923, Joyce engineered that a translation be published in Paris some years later. Svevo immediately won fame and recognition in France and, through Joyce's influence, the rest of Europe, but he was only beginning to be known in his own country when he was killed in a car accident in 1928.

ITALO SVEVO

As a Man Grows Older

Translated from the Italian by
Beryl de Zoete

PENGUIN BOOKS

in association with Martin Secker & Warburg

Penguin Books Ltd, Harmondsworth, Middlesex, England
Penguin Books, 625 Madison Avenue, New York, New York 10022, U.S.A.
Penguin Books Australia Ltd, Ringwood, Victoria, Australia
Penguin Books Canada Ltd, 2801 John Street, Markham,
Ontario, Canada L3R 1B4
Penguin Books (N.Z.) Ltd, 182–190 Wairau Road, Auckland 10, New Zealand

—

Senilità First published 1898
This translation first published by Putnam 1932
Published by Martin Secker & Warburg 1962
Published in Penguin Books 1965
Reprinted 1977, 1983

—

—

Made and printed in Singapore by
Richard Clay (S.E.Asia) Pte Ltd
Set in Linotype Baskerville

I

A T once, with his very first words, he wanted to make it perfectly clear that he had no intention of beginning anything in the nature of a serious flirtation. For this reason he addressed her more or less as follows: 'I love you very much and it is for your sake that I feel we ought to agree to behave with great prudence.' His words sounded, indeed, so very cautious that it was hard to believe the sentiment which inspired them was altogether disinterested; had he been able to speak a little more frankly he would probably have said something of this sort: 'I am very much in love with you, but it is impossible that I should ever consider you as more than a plaything. I have other duties in life, my career and my family.'

And his family? An only sister who made no claim at all on him, either physically or morally. She was small and pale, several years younger than himself, but older in character, unless it were perhaps that the conditions under which she had lived so long made her appear so.

Of the two it was really he who was the egoist. She was like a mother to him in her unselfish devotion, but this did not prevent him from speaking as if his shoulders were weighed down by the burden of another precious life bound to his own, and of acting as if this weight of responsibility obliged him to go cautiously through life, avoiding all its perils, but also renouncing all its pleasures and all hope of earthly felicity. At the age of thirty-five, the desire for pleasures he had never tasted, for love he had never known surged up in his heart, but with a sense of bitterness and frustration at the thought of all he might have enjoyed; and he was conscious at the same time of a great mistrust of himself, and of the weakness of his own character which hitherto he had had occasion rather to suspect than to prove by actual experi-ence.

Emilio Brentani's career was a more complicated mat-ter, because at that time it consisted of two distinct occu-pations, with completely diverse aims. His official career was a quite subordinate post in an Insurance Society, which was just sufficient to provide for the needs of his small family. His other career was literary, and apart from a mild degree of fame, which flattered his vanity rather than satisfied his ambition, it brought him in nothing, but also took nothing out of him. For many years now, in fact since the publication of a novel on which praise had been showered by the local Press, he had written nothing at all, not from any mistrust of his own powers, but from sheer inertia. His novel, printed on bad paper, had turned yellow on the shelves of the bookshops, but Emilio, who at the time of its publication had been spoken of only as a literary star of the future, had by degrees come to be looked upon as a solid literary asset who had some weight in the petty artistic scales of the city. The original estimate had never been revised, it had merely developed with time into something else.

He had too clear a perception of the insignificance of his own work ever to boast about the past; but in art as in life he regarded himself as being still in a preparatory stage, secretly considering his genius to be a powerful machine in process of construction but not yet function-ing. He lived in a perpetual state of impatient expecta-tion of something which was to be evolved for him by his brain, namely art, and of something which was to come to him from outside – good fortune, success – as if he had not already passed the age when his vitality was at the full.

Angiolina walked beside him. She was a tall, healthy blonde, with big blue eyes and a supple, graceful body, an expressive face and transparent skin glowing with health. As she walked, she held her head slightly on one side, as if it were weighed down by the mass of golden hair which was braided round it, and she kept looking

6

down at the ground which she tapped at each step with her elegant parasol, as if she hoped there might issue from it some comment on the words that had just been spoken. When at last she was sure she had heard aright, she murmured: 'How strange!' and looked at him from under her eyelids. 'No one ever said such a thing to me before.' She could not understand him, but somehow felt flattered at seeing him assume a responsibility that was not really his, that of warding off a danger from her. It made the affection he offered her seem of a tender, brotherly nature.

Having stated his conditions, Emilio felt that he had set his mind at rest, and could allow himself to resume a tone more in keeping with the occasion. He rained down on her fair head the lyrical effusions which the desire of all these long years had ripened and refined, and as he uttered them, they seemed to him to have been born afresh at that moment, under the inspiration of Angiolina's blue eyes. It seemed to him that it was years since he had really tried to compose, since he had drawn ideas and words from his inner consciousness; and this discovery endowed the humdrum tenor of his life with a rare and unforgettable quality of peace and suspended movement. A woman had come into his life! The glamour of her youth and of her beauty was over it all, banishing from his mind the memory of his sad and lonely past, full of unsatisfied desires, and holding out to him the promise of a joyful future which could not, he felt sure, be compromised by her.

He had approached her with the idea of a brief and easy intrigue, such as he had so often heard described, but had never yet experienced, at least hardly in such a form as to be worthy of the name. She had dropped her sunshade just in time to provide him with an excuse for accosting her, and now that he was thus cunningly entangled in the pretty web of the young girl's life he felt no desire to free himself from it until he should have advanced much farther into her intimacy.

But the amazing purity of her profile and her incomparable health – are not good health and corruption always assumed by the rhetorician to be incompatible? – had subdued the ardour of his first onset and, overcome with a sudden reluctance to go farther, he now found all his delight in marvelling at the mystery of her face, with its clear and delicate chiselling and infinite sweetness of expression. His happiness was complete, he was at rest.

She had told him very little about herself, and he was so much preoccupied with his own feelings that at the time he did not even listen to the little she told him. She was obviously poor, very poor even, but for the moment, as she related to him with a certain amount of pride, she had no need to earn her living. This added a certain charm to the adventure, for to carry on a flirtation with someone who is on the brink of starvation has a disturbing influence on one's enjoyment. Emilio had therefore not much information to go on, but it seemed to him on the whole that such conclusions as he was able to draw were sufficiently reassuring. If the girl were honest, as her limpid gaze seemed to suggest, he should certainly not be the one to deprave her. If, however, her profile and that clear eye of hers belied her real character, so much the better for him. In either case he had a fair prospect of enjoying himself, and in neither did there seem to be any danger.

Angiolina had not understood a great deal of what he was saying, but there were plenty of small indications to enable her to interpret the rest. Even the words she found most difficult to comprehend were spoken in a tone of voice which left no doubt as to how they should be interpreted. Her colour rose, and she did not withdraw her shapely hand when Emilio impressed a chaste kiss upon it.

They remained standing a long time on the terrace of S. Andrea, looking out over the calm sea with the glow of sunset still upon it under a clear, starry sky. Though there was no moon the night was not dark. A cart drove by on the road below, and in the great silence which surrounded them the distant sound of wheels over the uneven ground reached them long after it had passed. They amused themselves by trying to catch the sound as it became more and more distant, till it melted at last into the universal silence, and it pleased them that they both lost the sound at the same moment. 'Our ears agree well together,' said Emilio with a smile.

He had said all he had to say and did not feel inclined to talk any more just then. It was only after a long interval that he broke silence by saying: 'I wonder whether this meeting will bring us good luck.' He was quite sincere. He felt the need to express aloud the doubt he entertained as to his own future happiness.

'I wonder,' she replied, trying to convey in her own voice the emotion she had felt in his. Emilio smiled again, but thought it more becoming to hide his smile. Given the premises from which he had started, what sort of good luck could come to Angiolina from knowing him?

At last it was time for them to part. She did not want him to be seen with her in the town, so he followed slowly at a distance, unable wholly to tear himself away from her. How charming she looked, as she walked along in all the assurance of her splendid youth, never faltering, though the pavement was covered with a slippery mud! There was something of a wild beast's beauty in her strong and graceful carriage.

As luck would have it, the very next day he learned a good deal more about Angiolina than she had told him herself.

He met her by chance in the Corso, at midday, and greeted her with all the enthusiasm of delighted surprise, almost sweeping the ground with his hat in a magnificent gesture of salutation: she replied with a slight inclination of the head, enhanced however by a brilliant glance of her flashing eyes.

Someone named Sorniani, a thin, shrivelled little creature, reputed to be a great ladies' man and also a malicious gossip, touched Emilio on the arm and asked him where on earth he had got to know that girl. They

9

had been friends since childhood, but it was several years since they had spoken to each other and it was only the sight of a pretty woman that had made Sorniani feel the need for renewing their former acquaintance. 'I met her at some friends of mine,' replied Emilio.

'And what is she doing now?' asked Sorniani, in a tone which implied that he knew all about Angiolina's past, and was quite injured at knowing nothing about her life at the moment.

'I have no idea,' answered Emilio, adding, with well-feigned indifference: 'She strikes me as being a very nice sort of girl.'

'Don't be too sure,' exclaimed Sorniani emphatically, as if he would have liked to assert the contrary; it was only after a short pause that he corrected himself. 'I know nothing at all about her now, and at the time I knew her everyone seemed to think her quite respectable, though once she had been in a rather equivocal situation.'

It needed no encouragement on Emilio's part for him to relate that the poor girl had been within an ace of a great stroke of good fortune which, perhaps by no fault of her own, had turned out very badly for her. When she was scarcely more than a child, a certain Merighi had fallen madly in love with her. He was an extremely handsome fellow, that Sorniani was obliged to admit, though he had never liked him personally, and he was a very prosperous man of business. His intentions towards her were perfectly honest. He had removed her from her family, of whom he did not think very highly, and had insisted on his own mother adopting the girl. 'His own mother!' cried Sorniani. 'As if the idiot could not have enjoyed the girl outside his own house, but must needs do it under his mother's very nose.' He was bent on proving the man to be a fool and the woman dishonest. In a few months time Angiolina returned to her own home, which she ought never to have come out of, and Merighi and his mother left the town, giving out that they had lost a good deal of money over an unlucky speculation. But some people gave a rather different account of what had happened. Merighi's mother was said to have discovered that Angiolina was carrying on a disgraceful intrigue with someone else and to have turned her out of the house. Sorniani volunteered, unasked, other variations on the same theme.

He took an evident pleasure in enlarging on so spicy a subject, and Brentani only paid attention to such of his words as seemed to be worthy of credence, facts which must be notorious to everyone. He had known Merighi by sight and remembered very well his tall, athletic figure, obviously the perfect mate for Angiolina. He remembered having heard him favourably spoken of as an idealistic businessman, rather too daring in his conceptions; a man who was convinced that he could conquer the world by his energy alone. He had also heard from people connected with him in business that Merighi's lofty ideals had cost him dear, and that he had in the end been obliged to liquidate his knowledge under the most unfavourable conditions. But Sorniani might as well have talked to the winds, for Emilio was now sure that he knew exactly what had happened. Merighi, impoverished and discredited, had lacked the courage to embark on matrimony, and Angiolina, who was to have been made into the respectable wife of a rich bourgeois, had ended by becoming a plaything in his own hands. He felt a profound pity for her.

Sorniani had himself witnessed various incidents in Merighi's love-making. He had often seen him on Sunday at the door of Sant' Antonio Vecchio, waiting patiently while she knelt before the altar, saying her prayers; he had watched him gazing with all his soul at that fair head shining in the twilight of the church.

'Two adorations,' thought Brentani, deeply moved. He found it easy to understand the tenderness which held Merighi spellbound on the threshold of the church.

'What a fool!' wound up Sorniani.

The result of Sorniani's communication was to make his own adventure seem more important in Brentani's eyes. He awaited Thursday, when he was to see her again, in a state of feverish impatience, and his impatience made him communicative.

His most intimate friend, a sculptor named Balli, was told about his meeting with Angiolina the very next day. 'Why shouldn't I amuse myself as well as everyone else, when it costs me so little?' Emilio inquired of him.

Balli listened to his story with an expression of utter amazement. He had been a friend of Brentani for more than ten years, and this was the first time he had ever seen him excited about a woman. He at once saw the danger which threatened his friend, and took a grave view of this adventure.

Emilio protested. 'What danger can I possibly run, at my age and with my experience?' He was fond of talking about his experience. What he was pleased to call so was something he had absorbed from books: a considerable mistrust of his fellow-men and a great contempt for them.

Balli had turned forty-odd years to better account, and his experience enabled him to judge that of his friend. He was less cultivated, but he had always exercised a sort of paternal authority over him, which Emilio accepted only too gladly; for although his lot was rather drab and perfectly ordinary, and though his life was entirely devoid of unforeseen happenings, he did not feel safe without a few hints as to its conduct.

Stefano Balli was a tall, powerfully built man, with one of those smooth, bronzed faces which never seem to grow old, and youthful blue eyes. His beard was neatly trimmed, his appearance correct and his expression somewhat unbending. The only sign of age about him was that his chestnut hair was turning slightly grey.

When animated by curiosity or pity his piercing look became almost tender; but if his antagonism was aroused, even during the most trivial discussion, he could assume an expression of great severity.

Fortune had not favoured him either. Various juries, when rejecting his designs, had praised certain details, but no work of his had found a place on any of the numerous piazzas in Italy. Yet he had never allowed himself to be depressed by his want of success. He was satisfied with the praise of a few individual artists, convinced that his very originality must prevent him from having a wider and more popular appeal, and he had continued to pursue an ideal of spontaneity, a certain wilful ruggedness, a simplicity, or, as he preferred to say, perspicacity of idea from which he thought his artistic 'ego' must emerge purified of all that was not original either in form or idea. He would not admit that one could be discouraged by the success or failure of one's work, but it is doubtful whether he would really have escaped discouragement if his enormous personal success had not brought him a certain solace which he was at pains to hide, and always denied, but which certainly went a considerable way towards keeping his handsome figure erect and confident. The attraction which all women felt for him did more than satisfy his vanity, although ambition being the prime instinct of his being, he was not capable of falling in love. He tasted success, or something very like it, in the love of women; loving the artist, they loved also his art, though it would have seemed to have in it so little that could appeal to them. So that his conviction of his own genius, added to the love and admiration which others felt for him, made it possible for him to continue to play the part of a superior being. In matters of art his judgement was severe and uncompromising; in society he made no effort to create a favourable impression. He was, on the whole, not at all popular with men and never sought their company unless he knew that they already had a certain admiration for him.

About ten years before, Emilio Brentani, then quite a young man, had been at his feet. Balli had recognized in him an egoist less fortunate than himself and had taken a fancy to him. At first he only sought his company because he felt himself to be an object of admiration. As time went on, Brentani's society became so familiar that he could no longer do without it. Their friendship bore witness to Balli's influence at every point. It became, like all the rare friendships of the sculptor, more intimate than Emilio, from motives of prudence, might perhaps have desired. Their intellectual relations were confined to the representative arts, and here they were in complete agreement, because Balli's absorbing idea reigned therein supreme, namely, the necessity of discovering afresh for ourselves the simplicity or naïveté of which the so-called classicists had robbed the arts. Agreement was easy: Balli taught and the other had nothing to do but learn. Never a word passed between them of Emilio's complicated literary theories, because Balli loathed everything that he could not understand, and Emilio was influenced by him even to the point of walking, speaking, and gesticulating like him. Balli, who was a man in the true sense of the word, submitted to no outside influence, and in Brentani's company had almost the sense of being with one of the many women who were entirely dominated by him.

'Yes,' he said, after listening carefully to every detail of Emilio's story. 'I don't think you ought to run any danger. The nature of the affair is sufficiently indicated by the sunshade slipping from her hand at such a very convenient moment, and by her immediately giving you an appointment.'

'That is true,' Emilio agreed, though he did not add that up to this moment he had paid so little attention to those two details that, now that Balli mentioned them, they struck him as two quite new facts. 'Do you think, then, that what Sorniani says about her is true?' When listening to Sorniani's revelations he had certainly not taken those two facts into account.

'You must introduce me to her,' said Balli cautiously. 'Then I shall be able to judge better.'

Brentani could not keep his secret even from his sister. Amalia had never been pretty. Tall, thin and colourless – Balli used to say that she had been born grey – the only quality of youth that remained to her was her slender, white, exquisitely shaped hands to which she devoted infinite care and attention.

It was the first time he had ever spoken to her about a woman, and Amalia listened in surprise and with a sudden change of countenance to words which, as he spoke them, he felt to be innocent and above reproach, but which on his lips became fraught with passionate desire. He had in reality told her nothing, but she was already murmuring Balli's warning: 'Do be careful not to do anything foolish.'

But then she wanted him to tell her everything, and Emilio thought he might safely confide in her the wonderful happiness he had felt that first evening, though he instinctively hid from her the proposal he had made to Angiolina and all the hopes he had based on it. It did not occur to him that what he had told her was really the most dangerous part. She sat listening to him at supper, continuing all the while to supply his every need silently and attentively, so that he never needed to interrupt his story to ask for this or that. It was with just such an expression that she had read the several hundred novels ranged on the shelves of the old cupboard which served as a library; but the fascination which Emilio's story exercised on her was, as she herself recognized with surprise, something quite different. She was no longer merely a passive listener, it was not the fate of some outside person which fascinated her, but her own fate which suddenly assumed for her a new and vivid interest. Love had entered the house and was there beside her, restlessly at work. A single breath had sufficed to dissipate the stagnant atmosphere in which she had lived blindly up to that moment and she was astonished, when she came to examine her own feelings, that being made as she was she could have been content to live like that, without being conscious of any desire to suffer or enjoy.

Brother and sister were embarking together on the same adventure.

2

DARK though it was he recognized Angiolina the moment he turned into the Campo Marzio. To recognize her he only needed by now to see her shadow moving forward with that smooth, unaccentuated gait peculiar to her, as if she were being securely and tenderly borne along. He hastened to meet her and at the sight of her brilliant colouring, so strangely vivid, so flawless in its perfection, he felt his heart leap for joy within him. She had come, and as she leaned on his arm he felt that she had given him the whole of herself.

He led her down towards the sea, away from the main road where a few people still passed from time to time; once on the beach they were completely alone. He wanted to kiss her at once but did not dare, though she continued to smile at him encouragingly, without however uttering a word. The very idea that if only he had dared he might have touched her eyes or her mouth with his lips, moved him so deeply as to take his breath away.

'Oh, why are you so late? I thought you were never coming.' That was what he said, but he had already forgotten whatever resentment he had felt. Like certain animals when under the influence of love, he felt the need of uttering a complaint. And a moment later it seemed to him that his discontent was fully explained when he said gaily: 'I can't believe that I have really got you here beside me.' This reflection gave him a complete sensation of his own happiness. 'And I thought that it was impossible to spend a more perfect evening than we spent together last week.' He felt so much happier now that he could even rejoice in his coming conquest as if it were already won.

They came all too soon to kissing, seeing that after the first impulse to clasp her suddenly in his arms he would have been content just to gaze at her and dream. But she was even less capable of understanding Emilio's feelings than he was of understanding hers. He had ventured timidly to caress her hair, which seemed to him so much pure gold. But her skin was golden too, he said, she was all made of gold. To him it seemed that in doing so he had expressed everything in saying this, but Angiolina was far from thinking so. She remained thoughtful for a few moments, and then complained that one of her teeth was aching. 'This one,' she said, opening her delicious mouth for him to see, and displaying her red gums and strong white teeth, which seemed like a casket of precious gems chosen and set there by the incomparable artificer – health. He did not laugh, but gravely kissed the mouth she held out to him.

Her vanity did not worry him since he profited by it so much; indeed, he was scarcely even aware of it. Like all who have never come into contact with the facts of life, he had believed himself stronger than the most exalted spirit, more indifferent than the most confirmed pessimist, and now he looked round him at the silent witnesses of this night's great event.

The moon had not yet risen, but far out at sea an iridescent radiance hung upon the water as if the sun had but lately left it and everything were still reflecting its light. But on either side of the bay the distant blue headlands were already hidden in deepest shadow. Everything seemed enormous and without boundary; the only thing which moved in that vast solitude was the colour of the sea. He felt that in the whole of nature at that moment he was the only active force, he alone was in love.

He spoke to her about what Sorniani had told him and ended by questioning her about her past. She at once put on a very serious face and talked in a dramatic tone about her adventure with Merighi. Abandoned by him? That was hardly the way to put it, seeing that it was she who had spoken the decisive word which had released the Merighis from their obligation towards her.

It was true that they had worried the life out of her by making it plain that they looked on her as a burden on the family. Merighi's mother, horrid, grumbling, jealous old cat that she was, had certainly not minced matters; she had let her have it plain: 'You are a perfect plague,' she had said; 'if it wasn't for you my son could be looking about for someone with a fortune.' At that she had left their house of her own free will, and gone home to her mother, (she pronounced the sweet word 'mother' in a softer tone), and she was so unhappy that she fell ill very soon after. Her illness was a relief, for if you are in a high fever you forget all your worries.

Then she wanted to know who it was had told him all this. 'Sorniani.'

At first she seemed unable to remember his name, but then she burst out laughing and exclaimed: 'Why, that horrible, bilious-looking creature who is always about with Leardi!'

So she knew Leardi too, a youth who had only just come to the fore, but who was already living at a pace which had made him notorious among the young voluptuaries of the town. Merighi had introduced him to her many years ago when they were all three scarcely more than children; they had often played together. 'I am very fond of him,' she wound up, with an engaging frankness which gave a colour of sincerity to everything else she said. Even Brentani, who was already beginning to tremble at the mention of that formidable young Leardi with whom he could not dream of competing, had his suspicions laid to rest by her last words. Poor child! She was honest and disinterested.

Would it not have been better to teach her to be less honest and a trifle more calculating? He had no sooner asked himself this question than he conceived the splendid idea of educating the girl himself. In return for the love he hoped to receive from her he could only give her one thing, a knowledge of life and the art of making the most of it. His would also be an inestimable gift, for such beauty and such grace as hers, under the guidance of an experienced person like himself, were bound to be victorious in the struggle for existence. Thanks to him, then, she would win for herself the fortune he was unable to give her. He wanted to tell her on the spot some of the ideas which were passing through his head. He stopped kissing and flattering her, and as a preparation for her initiation into vice he assumed the severe aspect of a professor of virtue.

Adopting an ironic tone which it often amused him to assume towards himself, he began by pitying her for having fallen into the hands of someone like him, who had very little money, and at the same time very little courage or energy. For if he had had more courage, and his voice trembled with emotion as he made her his first serious declaration of love, he would have taken her in his arms, clasped her to his breast, and never let her go while life lasted. But he had not sufficient courage. It was bad enough to be poor if one was alone, but together it was horrible; it was the most wretched form of slavery. He dreaded it for himself and still more for her.

But here she broke in with: 'I should not be afraid. I should be quite happy to live with the man I loved, no matter how poor he was.' He had the feeling that she was going to take hold of him by the neck and fling him into the condition he most dreaded.

'But I never could,' he said, after a moment's pause which was meant to give the impression that he had hesitated before making his decision. 'I know myself too well.' And after another pause he added in a grave, deep voice the one word 'Never!' while she gazed seriously at him, her chin resting on the handle of her parasol.

Having thus put everything in its proper place, he observed by way of introducing the subject of the education he intended to give her, that it would have been better for her if she had been approached by any one of the five or six other young men who had agreed with him in admiring her that day, rather than by him: the *richard* Carlini, the feather-headed Bardi, who was amusing himself by throwing away the last dregs of his youth and of his immense fortune; or the financier Nelli, who was piling up more money every day.

Each and all of them, for one reason or another, were more worth while than he was.

For a moment she succeeded in adopting the right tone. She took offence. It was, however, only too obvious that her anger was feigned and exaggerated, and Emilio could not fail to be aware of it. But he did not blame her for playing a part. She began twisting herself about as if she were trying to escape from his embrace and get away, but she contrived that her efforts should not extend to her arms by which he was holding her. These she continued to leave lying passive in his grasp, till at last he gave up holding them tight and ended by stroking them and covering them with kisses.

He asked her to forgive him, he had expressed himself badly, he said, and then he went boldly on to repeat in other words exactly what he had said before. She did not make any comment on this fresh insult, but continued for some time to speak in an injured tone. 'I don't want you to think that it would have been all one to me whichever of those young men had accosted me. I should not have allowed them to speak to me.' She reminded him that at their first meeting they had vaguely remembered meeting each other in the road about a year ago. So that, as she explained, he was not just anyone. Emilio gravely replied that he had only meant to say he would have got what he deserved.

At that point he began to instruct her on some of the assets in which her education seemed to him to be lacking. He said she was not calculating enough, and he blamed her for it. A girl in her situation ought to look after her own interests better. What was honesty in this world? Why, self-interest! An honest woman was one who looked out for the highest bidder and took care not to fall in love unless she could make a good thing out of it. As he spoke, he felt himself to be a superior being, an immoralist, who sees things as they are and is content that they should be so. He suddenly felt that his thinking-machine, which had so long been inactive, had begun functioning again and was in perfect order. His bosom swelled with pride, he was a man once more.

She listened to him with profound attention and in some bewilderment. She evidently thought he intended her to believe that an honest woman and a rich woman were one and the same thing. 'So this is what those grand ladies are like?' Then when she saw him looking somewhat surprised, she at once denied that that was what she meant to say; but if he had really been as acute an observer as he imagined himself to be, he would have seen that she no longer understood at all the line of argument which had caused her so much astonishment a short while before.

He repeated and developed his idea. An honest woman knows her own value, that is her secret. If you are not honest you must at least seem to be so. It was bad enough that Sorniani should allow himself to speak lightly of her, worse still that she should announce she was fond of Leardi – and here his jealousy got the better of him – that odious little Don Juan whom no nice woman would care to be seen with. It was better to do wrong than to look as if one were doing it.

She at once forgot the general ideas which he had been explaining so carefully, and began to defend herself vigorously against his accusations. Sorniani didn't know anything against her, he had no business to talk about her, and as for Leardi, he was a perfectly nice young man, whom no girl would mind being seen with.

He had finished his lesson for that evening; so potent a medicine, he thought, had better be administered in small doses. Besides, he felt he had already made a sufficient sacrifice in snatching all those moments from love-making.

He had a certain literary prejudice against the name Angiolina. He called her Lina; but when this abbreviation did not please him he turned her name into French and called her Angèle; or, if he wanted to be more tender still, he changed it to *Ange*. He taught her how to

21

say in French that she loved him. When she knew what the words meant she refused to repeat them, but at their next meeting she volunteered without his asking her *'Je tem bocù.'*

He was not really at all surprised to have made such rapid progress. It was exactly what he had hoped. She had found him so reasonable that she felt she could trust him completely, and for a long time he did not even give her the opportunity of refusing him anything.

They always met in the open air. They had made love in all the suburban roads of Trieste. After their first few meetings they deserted Sant' Andrea because it was too frequented, and for a certain time after that they favoured the Strada d'Opicina, which was a broad, lonely road, leading almost imperceptibly uphill, and bordered on each side by dense horse-chestnuts. They always halted by a low, jutting wall which came to mark the limit of their walk, because they had sat down on it to rest the first time they went that way. They remained folded in a long embrace, with the city at their feet, as silent and dead as the sea which, from that height, seemed one vast expanse of colour, mysterious, undefined. Motionless there in the silence, city, sea, and hills seemed to be all of one piece, as if some artist had shaped and coloured all that matter according to his own strange fancy, and dotted the intersecting lines with points of yellow light which were really the street lanterns.

The gradually increasing moonlight did nothing to change the colour of the landscape. Certain objects whose outlines had become more distinct, could rather be said to be veiled in light than to be illuminated by it. A snowy brilliance overspread it, motionless, while colour slumbered within a shade of secret immobility even on the sea, whose external movements one could just discern in the silver play of water on its surface; colour was lost in sleep. The green of the hills and all the many colours of the houses were darkened, while the light which saturated the outer air seemed to be suspended in white incorruptible purity, inaccessibly removed from contact with the objects of our vision.

The moonlight seemed to have become incarnate in the girl's face so near to his own, and to have stolen the youthful rose of her cheeks while leaving intact that golden glow which it seemed to Emilio that he could actually taste with his lips. Her face had become grave, almost austere, and as he kissed it he felt himself to be more than ever a seducer. He was kissing the pure virginal moonlight.

Later on, they preferred to this place the thickets on the way up to Hunter's Hill, as they felt more and more the need to be alone together. They would sit side by side under a tree, and divide their time between eating and drinking and kisses.

By now he had almost given up taking her flowers, he bought her sweets instead, but soon she refused these as well, they were bad for her teeth, she said. Their place was taken by cheese and sausages, bottles of wine and liqueurs, all of which made a considerable hole in Emilio's slender purse.

But he was only too willing to sacrifice to her the small savings he had accumulated during all the long years of his uneventful bachelor life; he would begin to economize again, he thought, when his small store began to run out. He was much more occupied for the moment by another question. Who had taught Angiolina how to kiss? He could not remember now anything about the first time she had kissed him; he had been so much occupied in kissing her that the kiss she had given him in return had only seemed to him to be the necessary complement of his own; but he could not help thinking that if her mouth had really been so ardent in returning his kisses he must have felt a certain amount of surprise. Was it he then who had initiated her into an art in which he was himself but a novice?

And now she confessed. It was Merighi who had taught her to kiss. She laughed when she related how many kisses he used to give her. Emilio must surely be joking if he pretended to doubt whether Merighi would have taken advantage of his position as her fiancé at least to kiss her as much as he wanted.

Brentani did not feel in the least jealous of Merighi who had, after all, so much better claim to her than himself. But he was distressed that she should speak about him so lightly. He felt she ought rather to have shed tears each time she mentioned him. When as sometimes happened he let her see how hurt he himself felt at her showing so little feeling, she would force her lovely face to put on a very dismal expression, and conscious that she was being in some way reproached, she would try to justify herself by reminding him that she had been made quite ill by Merighi's desertion. 'Oh, if I had died then I should not have cared.' A few minutes later she would be laughing loudly in the arms which he had opened to receive and comfort her.

She seemed to regret nothing, and this surprised him as much as it did to discover how deeply he pitied her and sympathized with her. Was he really in love with her? Or was it only that he felt so grateful to the sweet creature for behaving as though she existed solely for his delight? For she was an ideal mistress in that she did all that he wanted without making any demands upon him.

It would be late when he got home, still in a state of pleasurable excitement, and quite unable to talk about anything else to his pale-faced sister, who left whatever she was doing to keep him company while he ate his supper; unable even to feign the smallest interest in all the petty affairs of the household which made up the whole of Amalia's life, and about which she had always been accustomed to tell him. She would go on again at last with whatever she was doing, while he continued to eat his supper in silence, and they would both remain there in the same room, each occupied with their own thoughts.

One evening she sat gazing at him for a long while without his noticing it, and then, with a forced smile, she asked: 'Have you been with her all this time?'

'Who do you mean by *her*?' he said, and suddenly

burst out laughing. Then, because he felt he must talk to someone, he confessed. It had been such an unforgettable evening. He had loved her in the moonlight, in the warm evening air, with all that boundless lovely landscape spread out before them, existing, as it seemed for them alone and for their love. But he could not explain what he was really feeling. How could he give his sister an idea of what that evening had been, without telling her about Angiolina's kisses?

But while he kept on repeating: 'What a light there was, what a delicious air!' she divined on his lips the print of those kisses which really filled his thoughts. She hated that unknown woman who had stolen away her companion and her only comfort. Now that she saw him in love like all the rest of the world, she felt she could not bear to be left without that one example of voluntary resignation to the same sad fate as her own. How dreadfully sad it was! She began to cry, at first shedding silent tears which she tried to conceal in her work and then, when he saw her tears falling, bursting out into violent sobs which she attempted in vain to repress.

She tried to explain away her tears. She had not been well all day, she had not been able to sleep all the night before, she had eaten nothing, she was feeling very weak.

He did not question the truth of what she said.

'If you are not better tomorrow, we will send for the doctor.' Then Amalia's grief changed to anger that he should allow himself to be so easily deceived as to the cause of her tears; it proved how completely indifferent he was to her. She lost all self-control, and burst out that he need not bother to send for the doctor; it was not worth while getting better, only to lead the sort of life she led. What had she got to live for? What point was there in going on being alive? Then seeing that he still persisted in understanding nothing she confessed the real cause of her grief: 'Not even you have any use for me.'

He still did not understand, and instead of sympathizing with her, he got angry in his turn. All his youth he had been so lonely and sad; he surely deserved some distraction from time to time. Angiolina was of no importance in his life; it was only an adventure which would last a few months and no more. 'It is very unkind of you to reproach me for it.' He only began to pity her when he saw her go on weeping silently in a state of helpless despair. To comfort her, he promised to come home more often and keep her company, he said they would read and study together as they used to do, but she must try and be more cheerful, for he did not like to be with unhappy people. His thoughts flew at once to *Ange*! She knew how to laugh! How wonderful her laughter was, so gay and so infectious, and he could not help smiling when he thought how strangely her laughter would have echoed in his sad house.

3

ONE evening he had arranged to meet Angiolina punctually at eight o'clock; but half an hour before the appointed time he had a message from Balli to say that he would be waiting for him in Via Chiozza just at that time, and had something very important to tell him. He had several times refused a similar invitation, because he suspected it of being only a pretext for getting him away from Angiolina; but on this occasion he seized the opportunity of paying a visit to her house on the pretence of putting off his appointment. He wanted to continue his study of someone who already played such an important part in his life, by observing the things and people among whom she lived. Although he was already quite blind in any matter where she was concerned, he still played the part of someone whose sight was perfect.

The house where Angiolina lived was on the outskirts of the town, a few yards beyond Via Fabio Severo. It was a tall, barrack-like house, standing by itself out in the fields. The porter's lodge was closed and Emilio, not without a certain amount of trepidation, for he was uncertain what reception he would meet with, went straight up to the second floor. 'It certainly does not look very sumptuous,' he muttered aloud, in order to give himself confidence. The staircase looked as if it had been built in a great hurry, the stonework was badly finished, the banisters were made of the roughest iron, the walls were whitewashed; you could not say it was dirty, but it was mean and poverty-stricken.

The door was opened by a little girl about ten years of age, dressed in a long, clumsy, cobwebby sort of garment. She was fair like Angiolina, but her eyes had a lifeless expression, and her face was yellow and anaemic-looking. She did not seem at all surprised to see a new face; she only lifted her hand to her bosom to hold together her ragged little jacket, from which all the buttons were missing. 'Good evening,' she said. 'What can I do for you?' She treated him with a ceremonious politeness which contrasted oddly with the childishness of her appearance.

'Is Signorina Angiolina at home?'

'Angiolina!' called out a woman who had advanced meanwhile from the end of the passage. 'There is a gentleman asking for you.' She was probably the sweet mother to whom Angiolina had so longed to return after she had been deserted by Merighi. She was an elderly woman, dressed like a servant, in colours which had once been bright and now were somewhat faded. She had on a large blue apron, and the handkerchief, which was tied round her head in peasant fashion, was blue too. Her face still bore traces of former beauty and her profile reminded him of Angiolina, but her long, impassive face, with its small, black, haunted-looking eyes, had something in it of an animal on the look-out to avoid the blows of a stick. 'Angiolina!' she called again; then announced in a tone of great politeness: 'She will be here in a moment,' and repeated several times over, but without ever looking him in the face while she spoke: 'Please walk in, and wait till she comes.' With a nasal voice like hers it was not possible for her to create a favourable impression. She hesitated before each sentence, like a stammerer at the beginning of a speech, but once she had started all the words came pouring from her mouth in one jet, entirely without any warmth or expression.

But now Angiolina appeared, running from the opposite end of the passage. She was dressed for going out. When she saw him she at once began laughing, and greeted him very warmly. 'Oh, it is Signor Brentani. What a pleasant surprise!' She introduced him without any further ceremony: 'My mother, my sister.'

So that really was the mother she had described as being so sweet! Emilio, delighted at being so well received, at once put out his hand, and the old woman, who was unprepared for such condescension on his part, showed a certain delay in holding out her own. She seemed hardly to understand what was expected of her and she fixed him for a moment with her uneasy, wolf-like eyes in obvious and instant mistrust. After her mother had shaken hands with him, the little sister stretched out her hand too, while still holding her dress carefully together over her bosom with her left hand. Then, when she had received that great favour from him, she said gravely: 'Thank you.'

'Come in here,' said Angiolina, hurrying towards a door at the end of the passage, and opening it.

Brentani was radiant when he found himself alone with Angiolina; for the mother and the sister, after showing him politely in, had remained on the other side of the door. And directly the door was shut he forgot all about his resolution to play the part merely of an observer. He drew her to him.

'No,' she protested. 'My father is asleep in the next room; he is not very well.'

'I can kiss you without making any noise,' he declared, and he pressed his lips against hers and held her mouth a prisoner, while she continued to protest; so that his kiss was broken into a thousand fragments, couched deliciously on her warm breath.

28

She broke away from him at last, exhausted, and ran to open the door.

'Now you sit down and behave yourself, for they can see us from the kitchen.' She was still laughing, and often when he thought of her afterwards it was with that expression of a happy teasing child, who has just played a successful trick on the person it loves most. Her hair was all ruffled up on her forehead by his arm in which, as usual, he had imprisoned her fair head; and he continued to caress with his eye the traces of his real caress.

It was not till a few moments later that he began to take stock of the room in which he found himself. The wallpaper was none too fresh, but compared with the staircase, the passage and the clothes worn by her mother and sister, the furniture was surprisingly sumptuous. It was a complete bedroom set made out of walnut; on the bed was a broad fringed bedspread, in one corner of the room stood an enormous vase filled with magnificent artificial flowers, and on the wall above it a number of photographs were arranged with evident care. It was, in fact, quite luxurious.

He began looking at the photographs. There was an old man who had struck a statesmanlike attitude, and was resting his arm on a pile of papers. Emilio could not help smiling. 'That is my godfather,' Angiolina explained. There was a young well-dressed man, but looking rather like a navvy out on holiday, with an eager expression, and a good deal of character in his face. 'That is my sister's godfather, and this is the godfather of my youngest brother,' and she pointed to the portrait of another young man, smaller in build and of a more refined appearance.

'Are there any more of them?' asked Emilio lightly. But the joke died on his lips, for among the other photographs he suddenly caught sight of two faces that he knew: Leardi and Sorniani! Sorniani, who even in the photograph looked as grim and jaundiced as ever, appeared, from his post on the wall, to be still saying horrible things about Angiolina. Leardi's photograph was the best; the camera had fulfilled its true function in reproducing every degree of light and shade, and Leardi was as handsome as if he had been portrayed in the natural hues of life. He was standing very much at his ease, not leaning against a table, but with his gloved hands slightly extended as if in the act of entering a lady's boudoir for an intimate *tête-à-tête*. He looked down on Emilio with an almost protective air, very becoming to his handsome young face, and Emilio was obliged to turn away his eyes in order to hide his vexation and envy.

Angiolina did not immediately comprehend why Emilio's brow had become so overcast. It was the first time that he had so crudely betrayed his jealousy. 'I don't at all like finding all these men in your bedroom.' Then when he saw the look of bewilderment that his reproof produced on her innocent face, he softened the severity of his remark. 'It is just what I was saying to you a few nights ago. It makes a very bad impression for you to be seen with people like these round you, and it may do you a great deal of harm. The very fact of knowing them is compromising in itself.'

At once a look of great amusement lit up her face, and she declared she was delighted to have made him jealous. 'Jealous of people like that!' she cried, then she became serious again and said with a reproving air: 'But I should like to know what opinion you have of me!' He was just about to reassure her when she made a false move. 'Listen, I will give *you* not only one but two of my photos,' and she ran to the chest of drawers to get them out. So all of them already had a photograph of Angiolina then; she had just told him so herself, but with such an air of ingenuous innocence that he did not dare to upbraid her with it. But worse was to come.

He forced himself to smile, and began looking at the two photographs which she held out to him with a playful curtsey. The first one, which was in profile, was taken by one of the best photographers in the town. The other was an excellent snapshot, but what had come out best in it was the very smart dress, trimmed with lace, which she had been wearing the first time he had met her; her face was rather screwed up by the effort she was making to keep her eyes open in the strong sunlight. 'Who took this one?' asked Emilio. 'Leardi perhaps?' He remembered having seen Leardi walking along the street one day with a camera under his arm.

'No, no!' she said. 'You jealous old thing! It was taken by a perfectly serious married man: Datti, the painter.'

Married perhaps, but hardly serious! 'I am not jealous,' said Emilio, in a low, deep voice, 'but sad, very sad indeed.' Then he caught sight of a photo of Datti himself, among the other photos – a man with a great red beard, whose portrait all the artists in the town loved painting – and on seeing him Emilio recalled with acute pain something he had once heard him say: 'The sort of women I have to do with don't deserve that my wife should be jealous of them.'

He had no need to hunt for proofs; they were showered upon him, they weighed him down, and Angiolina seemed to be clumsily doing her best to draw attention to them and force him to take them up. Feeling hurt and humiliated, she tried to justify herself by saying in a low voice: 'I got to know all these people through Merighi.' She was obviously lying, for it was impossible to believe that a hard-working businessman like Merighi should have numbered among his acquaintance all these fast young men and artists, or that even if he had known them he should have introduced them to his future wife.

He gave her a long, searching look, as if he were seeing her for the first time, and she understood quite well the significance of that look; she became rather pale, and waited, keeping her eyes fixed on the ground. But Brentani suddenly remembered how little right he had to be jealous. No! he said to himself, he was not going to humiliate her or make her suffer; he never would do that. Very gently this time, in order to show her that he still loved her – he remembered that he had approached her quite differently only a few minutes earlier – he tried again to kiss her.

Her manner showed at once that he was forgiven, but she drew away from him and begged him not to try and kiss her any more. He was surprised at her refusing a kiss that to him meant so much, and he ended by getting even angrier than he had been before. 'I have so many sins on my conscience already,' she said very seriously, 'that I shall find it very hard to receive absolution today. It is your fault that I am going to confession badly prepared.'

A new hope awoke in Emilio's breast. What a blessed thing religion was! He had banished it from his own home and deprived Amalia of its comfort, but now that he found it again at Angiolina's side he welcomed it with indescribable joy. In face of an honest woman's religion all those men on the wall seemed to him less formidable, and as he went away he kissed Angiolina's hand respectfully, a homage which she accepted as a tribute to her virtue.

So that the only result of his visit was that he had found out the way to her house. He got into the habit of going there every morning to take her something nice to eat with her coffee. How much he enjoyed the hour he spent with her then. She had only just got out of bed, and he took her wonderful body in his arms and pressed it to him, still warm from sleep. He felt its warmth through her thin wrapper, and had the sense of immediate contact with her naked body. The spell of religion had vanished very quickly, for Angiolina's was hardly of the quality to protect anyone who had to rely on that alone for her defence; but Emilio's suspicions never returned to him with their former violence. When he was in that room he had no time to look about him.

Angiolina tried on another occasion to stimulate a religious feeling which had stood her in such good stead once before, but she was unsuccessful, and she soon began to make game of it in the most shameless way. When she had had enough of his kisses, she would push him away with the words: *Ite missa est,* thus sullying a mystic idea which Emilio in all seriousness had several times expressed at the moment of parting from her. She would ask a *deo gratias* when she had a small favour to ask of him, and cry *mea maxima culpa* when he became too exacting, or *libera nos, domine,* when he began saying something she did not want to hear.

Though he had never possessed her completely, his incomplete possession gave him perfect satisfaction, and if he tried to go farther it was really from lack of self-assurance, and because he was afraid of being an object of derision to all those men who looked down on him from the wall. She defended herself energetically. Her brothers would kill her, she said. Once, when he was more than usually aggressive, she burst into tears. He did not really love her, she said, if he wanted to make her unhappy. Then, pacified and happy, he gave up his offensive. She had not belonged to anyone and he could be certain of not being an object of ridicule.

But she solemnly promised to give herself to him if she could do it without getting herself into trouble or making difficulties for him. She talked about it as if it were the simplest thing in the world. One day she had an inspiration: they must find a third person on whom to put the burden of any complication that might arise from their relationship, and whom it would be great fun to deceive. He listened enraptured to her words, which he interpreted as a declaration of love for himself. There was small hope of finding a third person of the kind Angiolina imagined, but he felt now that he could rest assured of her feeling for him. She was in very truth all that he could have desired her to be, and she gave him her love without trying to bind him, without apparently endangering his independence.

It was true that his whole life was at the moment taken up by his love; he could think of nothing else; he could not work; he could not even attend satisfactorily to his office duties. But so much the better. His life had taken on a new aspect for a short while, and afterwards he would find it almost a distraction to return to his former untroubled state. His love of images led him to see his life as a straight, uneventful road leading across a quiet valley; from the point at which he had first met Angiolina the road branched off, and led him through a varied landscape of trees, flowers, and hills. But only for a short while; after that it dropped to the valley, and became again the straight high road, easy and secure, but less tedious now because it was refreshed by memories of that enchanting, vivid interlude, full of colour and perhaps too of fatigues.

One day she told him she was obliged to go and do some work at the house of some acquaintances of theirs, called Deluigi. Signora Deluigi was a kind woman; she had a daughter, who was a friend of Angiolina, and an old husband; there were no boys in the family. All the household were devoted to her, Angiolina said. 'I like going there very much, for I have a much better time than in my own home.' Emilio could not say anything against it, and resigned himself to seeing her only in the evening, though even then less often than before, for she got back late from her work and it would not be worth while to come out again.

So he found himself again with some evenings free, which he could devote to his friend and his sister. He still attempted to deceive them – as indeed he deceived himself – about the importance of his adventure, and he even went so far as to try and make Balli believe that he was glad Angiolina was sometimes engaged in the evening, so that he was not obliged to keep her company every day. But he blushed when Balli turned on him his calm scrutinizing gaze, and not knowing how else to hide his passion he began to make fun of Angiolina, confiding to Balli certain observations which he was engaged in making upon her, but which did not in reality in the least diminish his tender feeling towards her. He would laugh heartily at his own witticisms, but Balli, who knew him well enough to detect a false ring in his words, let him laugh alone.

She used to try and talk the Tuscan dialect, but in such an affected manner that her accent was more English than Tuscan. 'Sooner or later,' said Emilio, 'I must cure her of that habit; it is beginning to irritate me.' She had a way of carrying her head continually bent towards her left shoulder. 'A sign of vanity, according to Gall,' Emilio remarked, and with the gravity of a man of science engaged on an experiment, he added: 'Who knows whether Gall's observations were not much less inaccurate than is generally supposed?' She was greedy, he said, she liked plenty to eat and drink, and she must feed well; he pitied anyone who was saddled with her! In this he was lying shamelessly, for he liked just as much to see her eat as to hear her laugh. He made a point of mocking at all the little weaknesses which he specially liked. He had been much moved one day when, in talking about some woman who was very ugly and very rich, Angiolina had come out with the exclamation: 'Rich! Then she is not ugly!' She set so much store by beauty, yet she was ready to put it beneath the feet of that other power. 'A vulgar woman!' Now he could afford to laugh with Balli.

Gradually, between his way of talking to Balli and his way of talking to Angiolina, Brentani had come to build up two distinct individuals who lived quietly side by side, and whom he never made any effort to reconcile. At bottom he did not really lie either to Balli or to Angiolina. He could never confess to himself that he loved talking for its own sake, and he felt as safe as the ostrich who thinks he can elude the hunter merely by not looking at him. But when he was alone with Angiolina he gave himself entirely up to his own feeling for her. Why should he try to resist the strong and joyful impulse of his love? What danger could there be to him in loving her? What reason to stem his love? For it was not only desire he felt for her, but love. He almost felt within him the stirrings of paternal love, when he thought how weak, how unprotected she was, like some young tender animal. Her very lack of intelligence was but one weakness the more, and constituted one more claim on his tenderness and protection.

He had met her at Campo Marzio just as she, vexed at not finding him already there waiting for her, was on the point of going away. It was the first time he had ever kept her waiting, but he was able to prove to her, watch in hand, that he was really not at all late. When her anger had calmed down she confessed that she had been more than usually in a hurry to see him that evening, so that she had come rather early herself. Such strange things had happened to her, which she wanted to tell him all about at once. She leaned affectionately on his arm. 'I have cried ever so much today,' and she wiped away some tears, which in the darkness he was unable to see. She refused to tell him anything till they had reached the terrace, and they climbed arm in arm up the long, dark avenue leading to it. He was in no hurry to arrive. The news she had to tell him could not be very bad, since it had made Angiolina more affectionate than usual. He stopped several times to snatch a kiss from her.

When they reached the top he made her sit down on the low wall, rested one arm lightly on her knee and sheltered her with his own umbrella from the fine, penetrating rain which had not stopped falling for the last few hours.

'I am engaged,' she said, in a voice into which she attempted to put a touch of sentimentality, which was very soon banished by a strong impulse to burst out laughing.

'Engaged!' Emilio repeated the word. At first he was so incredulous that he at once began to try and discover her reason for telling him such a lie. He peered into her face, and in spite of the darkness he thought he could detect in her expression the sentimentality which had at once disappeared from her voice. It must be true then. Besides, what reason could she have had for telling him a lie? So they had at last found the third person they stood in need of!

'Will you be happy now?' she asked him in a cajoling voice.

She was far indeed from suspecting what was taking

place in his mind, and he was ashamed to speak the words which his lips were burning to utter. But by no possibility could he have feigned the joy she seemed to expect from him. His anguish was so acute that he remained there petrified, till he heard her reminding him that he had never minded before hearing her talk about that plan of theirs. But so long as it had been only a plan Angiolina's lips had seemed to turn it into a caress. He, too, had toyed with the idea, had dreamed of its becoming a reality and of all the happiness that would ensue from it. But how many other plans had not passed through his brain, without leaving any trace behind? In the course of his life he had dreamed of theft, murder, and rape. He had experienced imaginatively the criminal's courage, strength, and perverse desires, he had even dreamed the results of his crime, above all that he should invariably escape punishment. But then he had had the double satisfaction of indulging in his dream and of discovering all the things he had wanted to destroy still intact, so that his senses were satisfied and his conscience at rest. He had committed a crime without any harmful result. But now that what he had dreamed and hoped for had actually materialized, he was as much astonished as if the dream had never been his; he could not even recognize it as his, so different was its aspect now from that under which he had known it.

'Aren't you going to ask me who I am engaged to?' He pulled himself together with a sudden tremendous effort.

'Do you love him?'

'How can you ask me such a thing?' she cried in genuine astonishment. Her only reply was to kiss the hand which was holding the umbrella over her.

'Then don't marry him!' he commanded. To himself his words seemed quite intelligible. She was his already; he did not desire her in any other way. Why must he give her up to someone else just in order to possess her more completely? Seeing her increasing astonishment he tried to argue with her. 'You would never be happy with a man you did not love.'

But such scruples as his were unknown to her. For the first time she complained to him about her family. Her brothers did no work, her father was ill; how was it possible to make both ends meet? And it was none too cheerful at home. He had seen it in the most favourable light, when the boys were out. Directly they came home they began quarrelling among themselves, and finding fault with their mother and sisters. Of course she wouldn't have chosen the tailor Volpini for a husband if she could have got anyone better. But though he was forty, he was a decent man, kind and gentle enough, and she thought she might grow to be fond of him in time. How could she hope for anyone better? 'You love me, I know, don't you? But you never admit the possibility of marrying me.' He was very touched at hearing her allude to his egotism without the slightest resentment.

Yes, perhaps after all she was doing the best for herself. With his usual tendency to follow the line of least resistance, when he found himself unable to convince her he finally succeeded in convincing himself.

She told him she had got to know Volpini at the Deluigis. He was a tiny little man: 'He only comes up to here,' she said laughing, and pointing to her shoulder. 'He is a jolly little man. He says he may be small, but that his love is big.' Suspecting perhaps – but in this instance quite without cause – that Emilio might be feeling jealous, she hastened to add: 'He is fearfully ugly. His face is covered all over with hair the colour of straw. His beard reaches right up to his eyes, even up to his eyebrows.' Volpini's business was at Fiume, but he had told her that when they were married he would allow her to spend one day a week in Trieste, and till then, as he was away most of the time, they would be able to go on seeing each other in peace, just as before.

'But we must be very careful,' he insisted. 'Very careful indeed,' he repeated. If it really was a good thing for her, wouldn't it be better to give up seeing her altogether, then and there, so as not to compromise her in any way? He felt himself capable of any sacrifice which should quiet his uneasy conscience. He took her hand and held it against his forehead, and in that attitude of adoration told her all that was in his mind: 'I would give you up altogether rather than that any harm should happen to you through me.'

Perhaps she understood him; in any case she made no further allusion to the treason they had plotted together, and that fact alone would have made this evening one of the most charming they had spent together. For once only, and for one short hour, she seemed to have risen to the level of Emilio's feeling for her. She struck no false note, she did not even once tell him she loved him. He was able to nurse his grief secretly. The woman he loved was not only sweet and unprotected: she was a lost woman. She sold herself here and gave herself there. Oh – he could not forget how she had wanted to burst out laughing at the beginning of their conversation. If that was her attitude towards the most important step in her life, how would she behave when she was living with a man she did not love?

She was lost! He held her closer and closer to him with his left arm, laid his head in her lap and with a feeling of the deepest compassion rather than of love for her, he murmured: 'Poor child, poor child.' They remained thus a long while; then she bent over him, and certainly without intending him to be conscious of it, kissed him lightly on the hair. It was the nicest thing she had done during all the time he had known her.

Then suddenly everything changed and became brutal and horrible. The thin, monotonous, melancholy drizzle which had accompanied Emilio's grief with a faint undertone of pity, as it seemed to him at one moment, or of indifference at another, changed without warning into a violent downpour. A cold blast of wind from the sea shattered the rain-drenched atmosphere and hurled itself against them too, snatching them from the dream with which one sweet moment had blessed them. She was terrified at the thought of wetting her clothes, and set off running as fast as she could, refusing to take Emilio's arm; she needed both her hands to hold up the umbrella against the wind. Her struggle with the wind and rain put her so out of temper that she would not even fix their next meeting: 'It will be time enough to think about that when I have got home safely.' He watched her get into the tram, and from his dark corner saw her lovely, indignant face in the yellow lamplight, and her sweet eyes examining intently the extent of the damage done to her clothes by the rain.

4

OFTEN during their relationship torrents of rain would come like that, to snatch him violently from the enchantment to which he abandoned himself with such exquisite delight.

Very early next morning he was on his way to Angiolina. He could not tell yet whether he should avenge himself by some biting remark for the way in which she had left him the evening before, or whether, when he saw her living face, he would recover the tender feelings which his painful reflections during the night had threatened to destroy, but of which, as he realized by the anxiety which impelled him to come all this way to seek her, he stood at the moment so much in need.

Angiolina's mother opened the door to him and gave him the usual friendly words of welcome, which contrasted so strangely with her parchment-like face and harsh-sounding voice. Angiolina was dressing and would come almost immediately.

'And what do you think about it?' the old woman asked suddenly. She was alluding to Volpini's proposal. He was so surprised that the mother should want to have his approval of Angiolina's marriage that he hesitated to reply, and she, mistaking the nature of the doubt which she saw written on his face, began trying to convince him: 'You see, don't you, what a piece of luck it is for Angiolina? Even if she is not very fond of him it doesn't matter; she won't have to worry about anything, and he will make her happy, I'm sure, for he's very much in love with her. You should just see him!' She gave a short, harsh laugh which seemed to go no farther than her lips. Evidently she was well satisfied.

On thinking it over he felt quite gratified that Angiolina had made her mother understand how important it was to her that he should give his consent, and he expressed his unqualified approval. He was sorry, he said, that Angiolina was to marry someone else, but seeing it was for her good.... The old woman laughed again, but this time her mirth was more facial than vocal, and it seemed to him rather ironic. Did the mother know then about the pact he had made with her daughter? He would not have minded very much if she had. If that laughter was aimed at honest Volpini he had no reason to take it to heart. In this case it certainly could not be intended for himself.

Angiolina appeared fully dressed to go out; she must be quick, for she had to be at Signora Deluigi's by nine o'clock. He could not bear to leave her so soon, and for the first time they walked along the road together by daylight.

'We seem to make a fine couple,' she said with a smile, seeing that everyone they passed in the street looked around at them. It was indeed impossible to pass her by without looking at her.

Emilio turned to look at her too. Her white dress (which according to the fashion of the moment exaggerated the figure), with its pinched waist and wide sleeves, almost like inflated balloons, clamoured to be looked at, and existed for that purpose. Her face rose out of all that whiteness, in no wise overpowered by it, but flaunting its roses unabashed; the thin blood-red curve of her mouth was sharply outlined against her brilliant teeth, and her lips were parted in a gay, sweet smile which she seemed to fling upon the air for the passers-by to catch. The sunlight played among her fair curls, powdering them all over with golden dust.

Emilio blushed. It seemed to him that every passer-by cast an insulting glance at her. He looked at her again himself. It was unmistakable that her eyes gave a kind of greeting to every good-looking man they passed; she did not actually look at him, but there was a sudden lightening in her eye. There was a perpetual movement in the pupil which was continually modifying the intensity and direction of its light. The light in her eye literally seemed to *crackle*! Emilio clung to this word, which he felt to characterize so well its ceaseless activity. In the small, rapid, unforeseen movements of the light it was almost as if one heard a slight sound.

'Why do you keep on making eyes?' he asked, forcing a smile to his lips.

She laughed and replied unblushingly: 'Me? My eyes were given me to look about with!' So she was conscious all the while of what she was doing with her eyes; she was only deceiving herself in calling it 'looking about'.

Soon after they passed a small employee named Guistini, a handsome young man whom Emilio knew by sight. Angiolina's eye at once became animated and Emilio turned round to see who the lucky mortal was who had just passed. He, too, had stood still and was looking after them. 'He has stopped to look at me, hasn't he?' she asked, with a gay smile.

'Why does it give you any pleasure?' he inquired sadly. She obviously could not understand what he meant. Then she cunningly tried to make him believe that she did it on purpose to make him jealous, and finally, to pacify him, shamelessly, before all the world, she puckered her lips into what was evidently intended to be a kiss. No, she was incapable of deceit. The woman he loved, named *Ange*, was his own invention, he had created her by an effort of his own will: Angiolina had had no part in this creation, she had even, by the resistance she offered, prevented its completion. The dream vanished in the light of day.

'There is too much light,' he murmured, dazzled by it. 'Let us walk in the shade.'

She looked at him curiously, seeing his face so painfully contorted. 'Does the sun hurt your eyes? Fancy that! But I remember hearing it said that there are some people who cannot bear it.' It was she who was wrong to love the sun.

At the moment of parting, he said: 'Supposing Volpini were to hear about us walking together all through the town?'

'Who would be likely to tell him?' she answered with the utmost composure. 'I should say you were a brother or a cousin of the Deluigis. He doesn't know anybody in Trieste, so it is easy to make him believe whatever one wants.'

When he had left her, he felt the need of analysing his own impressions once more, and walked on alone without noticing where he was going. A sudden flash of energy quickened and intensified his thoughts. He set himself a problem which he solved immediately. The best thing he could do would be to leave her at once and never see her again. He could no longer deceive himself as to the nature of his own feelings. The pain he had just experienced, the shame he had felt on her account and on his own, revealed it to him only too clearly.

He sought out Stefano Balli, intending to make him a promise which he would be obliged to keep, so that there could be no question of going back on his resolution. But the very sight of his friend was enough to make him abandon it. Why could not he be like Stefano and just amuse himself with women? It came over him only too vividly what his life would be like without love. On one side would be Balli always trying to lead him on, on the other Amalia, with her perpetual gloom; and that would be all. He felt no less energy than he had felt only a short while ago; but now he wanted to live, to live and enjoy even if he had to suffer for it. He would display his energy in the way he treated Angiolina, not by a cowardly flight from her.

The sculptor welcomed him with a coarse oath. 'Are you still alive? I warn you that if you have come to ask a favour of me, as I rather gather from your contrite face, it is labour lost, and you will simply be wasting your breath. Rotter!'

He went on shouting comic threats into his ear, but Emilio no longer felt any doubt about the line he must take. His friend, by implying that he needed his help, had incidentally given him a good piece of advice. No one, after all, could be so useful to him as Balli in this emergency. 'Please listen to me,' he said. 'I want to ask your advice.'

The other burst out laughing. 'Of course, it's about Angiolina, isn't it? I refuse to hear anything about her. She has already come between us, and there let her stay; I won't be plagued by her any more.'

Even if Balli had been twice as savage, he would still not have been able to rid himself of Emilio, once he had resolved to ask his advice. For in that, Emilio felt, lay his salvation. Stefano, who knew so well all about it, could tell him what kind of life he must live in order to enjoy without suffering. In a single instant he fell from the height of his first manly resolve into the utmost dejection: to a consciousness of his own weakness and a state of perfect resignation. He was crying out for aid! He would have liked at least to keep up the appearance of someone who is asking advice merely because it would interest him to hear another person's opinion. But the mechanical result of Balli's shouting was to make Emilio assume a tone of entreaty. He felt an extraordinary desire to be treated tenderly.

Stefano took pity on him. He seized him roughly by the arm and dragged him along with him to the Piazza della Legna where he had his studio. 'Now, tell me all about it. If there is anything I can do to help you, you know I will do it.'

Emilio was touched by his sympathy and made a full confession. Yes, now he saw it all clearly. It had become a very serious matter for him, and he described his love, his longing to see her and talk to her, his jealousy, his doubts, the torment he suffered continually, and his entire forgetfulness of everything which was not in some way related to her or to the state of his own feelings. He went on to speak of Angiolina as he now saw her in consequence of her behaviour in the street, of the photographs she had hanging on the wall in her bedroom and her sacrifice of herself to the tailor; he told also of the pact they had made. He smiled from time to time while he told his story. He had evoked her image before his mind; he saw her gay and ingenuously perverse and he smiled back at her without resentment. Poor child! She was so proud of her photographs that she must always have them hanging up on the wall; she enjoyed so much being admired as she walked along the street that she even wanted him to see how many men made eyes at her. While he went on talking he felt there was really nothing in all this for anyone to take offence at; he had stated that he only looked upon her as a plaything. It is true that he omitted certain of his observations and experiences from the tale he told Balli, but any that did not find a place there had for the moment ceased to exist. He looked timidly at Balli from time to time, expecting to see him burst out laughing, and it was only his sense of logic which forced him to proceed. He had said he wanted to ask advice, and ask it he must. The sound of his own words continued to echo in his ears, and he tried to draw a conclusion from them as if they had been someone else's words. Very calmly, almost as if he wanted to make Balli forget the warmth with which he had spoken hitherto, he inquired: 'Don't you think I ought to give up my connexion with her, as I don't seem able to take up a right line about it?' Again he hid a smile. It would certainly have been comic if Balli had advised him in good faith to give up seeing Angiolina.

But Stefano soon gave proof of his superior intelligence by refusing to advise him at all. 'You will understand that I can hardly advise you to be made differently from what you are,' he said affectionately. 'I knew from

the first that this was not the sort of adventure for you.'
Emilio argued that since Balli could speak like that the
feelings he had been so alarmed about by himself a short
while before must be quite commonplace ones, and he
found therein a fresh source of consolation.

At that moment Balli's servant Michele came in; he
was an old soldier, well on in years. He stood to attention while saying something in a low voice to his master,
and went out after taking off his hat with a sweeping
gesture, while his body remained motionless.

'Someone is waiting for me in the studio,' said Balli
with a smile. 'It is a woman, and it's a pity you can't be
present at the interview. It would be very instructive for
you.' Then an idea struck him. 'Would you like us to
make up a party of four one evening?' He thought he
had found a way of helping his friend, and Emilio
accepted with enthusiasm. Of course! The only way to
be able to imitate Balli was actually to see how he set
about it.

Emilio had an appointment with Angiolina that evening at the Campo Marzio. During the day he had
thought out certain reproaches he intended to make her.
But she was coming to give herself wholly to him for one
hour at least; at that moment there would be no passers-
by to distract her attention from himself. Why should he
diminish his happiness by quarrelling with her? He
thought he could imitate Balli better by the sweet enjoyment of her love than by the renunciation which in a
moment of madness he had contemplated only that
morning. The only trace of his former irritation was a
kind of excitement which gave an added animation to
his words and to the atmosphere of the evening, which
during the first part at least was wholly delightful. They
decided to spend the first of the two hours they would
have together in going for a walk outside the town, and
the second in walking back again. It was he who suggested this plan, for he wanted to calm his nerves by
walking at her side. It took them about an hour to reach
the Arsenal, an hour of perfect happiness in the limpid

evening air, just freshened by the first touch of early autumn.

She sat down on the low wall which ran along the road, while he remained standing and looking down at her. He saw her head stand out against the dark background, lit up on one side by a street lamp. He saw the Arsenal stretching along the shore, and the whole city, which at that hour seemed dead. 'The city of labour!' he said, surprised at himself for having chosen that place in which to make love to her.

The sea had disappeared from view; it was shut out by the peninsula facing them. There were a few houses scattered over the shore like men on a chess-board, and farther off was a ship in process of construction. The city of labour seemed even bigger than it really was. Away to the left some distant lamps seemed to carry it still farther than its actual extent. Those lamps, he remembered, belonged to a great factory situated on the opposite bank of the valley of Muggia. Yes, work was going on there too; it was right that it should appear to the eye as a continuation of the city they were in.

She was looking too, and for a moment Emilio's thoughts were far removed from thoughts of love. In the past he had indulged in socialistic ideas, of course without ever stirring a finger to realize them. How far away those ideas seemed from him now!

He was stricken with remorse for having betrayed his early ideals and aspirations; for the moment the whole of his present life seemed to him to be a kind of apostasy.

But these faint prickings of conscience soon vanished. She was asking him questions about certain objects, especially that great monster hanging in mid-air. And he explained to her the nature of a crane. When he had lived as a solitary student he had never succeeded in making his thoughts and words intelligible to those to whom he sought to address them, and he had vainly tried, several years ago, to come out of his lair and mix with the crowd. It was no use; he had been obliged to retire discomfited from the unequal contest. He had only seemed ridiculous. But how sweet he found it now to avoid all difficult words and ideas, and make himself understood. It was quite easy for him now to break up his thoughts into fragments while he talked, and release it from the difficult, prisoning word under which he had first conceived it; and how happy he was when he saw a ray of intelligence light up her blue eyes!

But the music of that night was not without its discords. Some days ago he had heard a story which moved him deeply. A German astronomer had been living for about ten years in his observatory on one of the highest peaks of the Alps, among the eternal snows. The nearest village was about three thousand feet lower down, and his food was brought up daily by a girl who, when he went there first, was twelve years old. In ten years of going up and down those three thousand feet daily the girl had grown into a strong and beautiful woman, and the astronomer made her his wife. The marriage had been celebrated in the village a short while before, and for their honeymoon the couple had gone up to their home together. He thought of this story while lying in Angiolina's arms; that was how he would have liked to possess her: three thousand feet away from any living person. And so, granted that it were possible for him, as for the astronomer, to go on devoting his life for ever to the same end, he would have been able to bind himself to her for good and all, without any reservation. 'And you?' he asked impatiently, seeing that she had not understood why he had told this anecdote, 'would you like to stay up there alone with me?'

She hesitated – she clearly hesitated. One part of the story, the mountain part, she had grasped at once. He only saw the love in it; she, on the other hand, at once felt the boredom and the cold. She looked at him, saw what answer he expected of her, and just to please him, replied without any enthusiasm: 'Oh, it would be glorious!'

But she had already hurt his feelings too much. He had always believed that if ever he should make up his mind to marry her she would accept with enthusiasm whatever conditions he might impose. But no! At such a height as that she would not have been happy, even with him, and dark though it was he could read in her face the amazement she felt at his daring to propose that she should go and spend her youth among the snow in that terribly lonely place; all that made up her beauty too, her hair, her complexion, her teeth, everything she so much enjoyed seeing people admire.

Their roles were now reversed. He had proposed to marry her, though only as a figure of speech, it was true; and she had not accepted him; he was utterly dumb-founded. 'Of course,' he said with bitter irony, 'there would be no one up there to give you their photographs, and you would not find anyone standing still in the road to stare at you.'

She felt the bitterness of his words, but she was not offended by his irony because she agreed with him and at once began discussing the question. It was so cold up there, she said, and she didn't like the cold; in winter she always felt miserable even in the town. Besides, you can only live once on the earth, and up there you ran the risk of living a shorter time and of leading a less pleasant life, because you would never get her to believe that it could be very amusing to watch the clouds go by even if it was beneath your feet.

She was right, no doubt, but how cold-hearted and stupid she was! He refused to continue the discussion, for how could he ever hope to convince her? He looked away, trying to find an argument. He might have avenged himself and quieted his nerves by saying some-thing insulting. But he remained silent and irresolute, gazing out into the night, at the lights scattered over the peninsula opposite, at the tower which rose, a motionless, dim blue shadow above the trees at the entrance to the Arsenal, a shape which chance had fashioned and flung upon the air.

'I don't say I wouldn't,' Angiolina added, in the hope of pacifying him. 'It would be glorious, of course, but ...' She stopped suddenly; she reflected that since he was so anxious for her to enthuse about that mountain which they would certainly neither of them ever see, it would be foolish not to humour him: 'It would be absolutely lovely,' she repeated the phrase again and again in a crescendo of enthusiasm. But he went on gazing out into the night, without looking at her; he was more hurt than ever by her mock enthusiasm, which was so obviously unreal that it seemed as if she were just laughing at him, especially as she made no effort to draw him to her. 'If you want a proof,' she said, 'I will go away with you tomorrow, or now this very minute, and live alone with you for ever.'

His state of mind was now identical with that of the morning before, and in a flash he thought of Balli. 'Balli, the sculptor, wants to make your acquaintance.'

'Really?' she cried gaily. 'I should like it so much too,' and she sounded ready to run off on the spot in search of Balli. 'I have heard so much about him from a girl who was in love with him that I have wanted to know him for ever so long. Where can he have seen me to make him want to know me?'

It was nothing new for her to show interest in other men before him, but it always gave him a painful sensation. 'He didn't even know of your existence,' he said sharply. 'He only knows what I have told him about you.' He had hoped to offend her, but on the contrary she was very grateful to him for having talked about her. 'But I wonder now what you have been saying to him about me,' she remarked with a comic note of diffidence in her voice. 'I told him that you are a traitor,' he said with a laugh. His words made them both burst out laughing, which at once put them into the best of humours with each other. She let him kiss her again and again, and full of tenderness whispered in his ear: '*Je tem bocù.*' 'Traitor,' he repeated, but this time sadly. She laughed again noisily, but then she discovered something better. With an exquisite gesture which he could never afterwards forget, and in a sweet, imploring voice, richer than her ordinary voice, she put her mouth to his and in

50

the midst of kissing him breathed into his lips the question: 'It isn't true, is it, that I am what you said I was?' So that the end of their evening was delicious too. One movement invented by Angiolina was enough to cancel all his doubts and all his pain.

On the way back he remembered that Balli was going to bring a woman with him too, and he made haste to tell her. She did not seem to mind, but later she asked him with an air of indifference, which was certainly not put on, if Balli was very much in love with this woman. 'I don't think so,' he said in all sincerity, glad to notice that she seemed indifferent. 'Balli has an odd way of being in love with women; he loves them very much and all equally, supposing they please him at all.'

'He has had a great many, I suppose?' she inquired thoughtfully. And here he thought it his duty to lie, and replied, 'I don't think so.'

The party of four was to meet the following evening at the Giardino Pubblico. Emilio and Angiolina were the first to arrive. It was not very pleasant waiting out in the open, for though it was not actually raining the ground was damp on account of the sirocco. Angiolina tried to conceal her impatience under an appearance of ill-humour, but she did not succeed in deceiving Emilio, who was seized with an intense desire to win back this woman whom he felt he had already lost. The result was that he bored her; he felt it himself and she took care to let him feel it even more. Pressing her arm tightly in his own he asked her: 'Do you love me at least as much as you did last night?' 'Yes,' she replied sharply, 'but it isn't the sort of thing one keeps on repeating every moment.'

Balli appeared at last, coming from the direction of the Aqueduct, arm in arm with a woman as tall as himself. 'What a beanstalk!' said Angiolina, at once giving expression to the only judgement it was possible to form of her at that distance.

When they had come nearer, Balli introduced them: 'Margherita! Ange!' He tried to get a view of Angiolina in the dark and brought his face so near to hers that by putting out his lips he could have kissed her. 'Are you really *Ange*?' Nothing would satisfy him but he must strike a match and light up her rosy face, which with the utmost solemnity lent itself to the operation. Lit up thus in the darkness it seemed to shine with an adorable brilliance: the small yellow flame pierced her pale eyes like the clear waters of a pool and they shone back at him with their sweet, wild, bewitching lustre. Quite unperturbed, Balli lit up in its turn Margherita's face, a pale face, pure in outline, with great blue vivacious eyes which at once riveted the attention, an aquiline nose and masses of chestnut hair piled up on her little head. What struck one most in her face was the contradiction between her bold challenging eyes and the suffering, madonna-like air of her finely chiselled features. She took advantage of the tiny flame for studying Emilio rather than for displaying her own charms: then, as the match was still not quite burnt out she blew it out.

'Now you all know one another; and that fellow there,' said Balli, pointing to Emilio, 'you will soon have an opportunity of seeing in the full lamplight.'

He led the way with Margherita who had already put her arm through his. Margherita was too tall and thin for her figure to be really good; but they had both been struck by the mixture of liveliness and suffering in the expression of her face. She walked insecurely, and took very small steps in proportion to her size. She was wearing a short jacket of a flaming red colour, which lost all its dashing character on her modest unassertive-looking back, with its slight stoop; it had rather the air of a military uniform which a boy was dressing-up in, whereas the dullest colour which Angiolina wore took on a lively hue. 'What a pity!' whispered Angiolina, genuinely distressed. 'Such a lovely head stuck up on a maypole like that.'

Emilio felt a desire to say something. He caught up Balli and said to him: 'I think your young lady's eyes are so lovely that I should like to know what you think of mine.'

'Her eyes aren't bad,' declared Balli, 'but the modelling of her nose is not perfect; the line of the lower part is very sketchy; it needs a little retouching.'

'Really?' exclaimed Angiolina, much upset.

'I may be mistaken, of course,' said Balli, in the most serious voice. 'I shall be able to see for certain in a moment, when we get some more light.'

When Angiolina had got far enough away from her terrible critic, she said spitefully: 'As if that great gawk of his was perfect!'

When they reached the 'Mondo Nuovo', they went into a long room which was timbered at one end and had at the other a glass door opening on to a large open-air café. The waiter, who at once rushed to meet them, was quite young, and very much a peasant, judging by his dress and manners. He climbed on a stool and lit two gas-jets, which were a very insufficient illumination for so big a room; he was in no hurry to come down, but stayed up there rubbing his sleepy eyes till Stefano ran to pull him down, shouting out that he could not allow anyone to fall asleep so high above the ground. The lad leaned on the sculptor's shoulder and allowed himself to be lifted down, then ran off wide awake and in the best of humours.

Margherita had a sore foot and she sat down at once. Balli busied himself about her, full of solicitude, and told her not to stand on ceremony, but to take off her boot. But she refused, saying: 'It always hurts me more or less, and this evening I hardly feel it at all.'

How different that woman was from Angiolina! Chaste and affectionate by nature, her declarations of love were made silently and almost imperceptibly, while Angiolina, when she wished to signify that her sensibility was aroused, made a thousand preparatory moves like an engine which needs a long time to get under way.

But Balli was not satisfied. He had said that she was to take off her boot and he insisted on being obeyed, till at last she declared that she was perfectly ready to take off both her boots if he told her to, but that it would not do the slightest good, for the boots had nothing whatever to do with her pain. All through the evening he made a point of compelling her submission from time to time, because he wanted to illustrate his method of dealing with women. Margherita lent herself admirably to the part; she laughed at him a good deal, but she obeyed. Her manner of talking seemed to show that she was capable of forming her own judgement upon things, and this made her submissive attitude all the more salutary as an example.

At first she tried to get into conversation with Angiolina, who by standing on tiptoe was trying to get a view of herself in a distant mirror, in order to put her curls in order. She told her about the pains she had in her chest and legs; she couldn't remember the time when she had not suffered from some pain or other. Still intent on her image in the mirror, Angiolina commented, 'Really? Poor thing!' then added with extreme simplicity: 'I am always quite well.' Emilio, who knew her so well, could hardly help smiling, for he realized the complete indifference to Margherita's maladies which was conveyed in her words, and the entire satisfaction she immediately felt in her own well-being. Other people's misfortunes only made her more delightfully conscious of her own good fortune.

Margherita placed herself between Stefano and Emilio; Angiolina was the last to take her seat, facing Margherita, and before sitting down she cast one strange look at Balli. Emilio thought it was a look of defiance, but the sculptor knew better how to interpret it: 'Dear Angiolina,' he said unceremoniously. 'She looks at me like that in the hope that I may admire her nose too; but it is no good. Her nose ought to have this shape,' and he proceeded to dip his finger in the beer and to draw on the table the curve he wanted, a broad line which it would have been difficult to imagine on a human nose.

Angiolina looked at the line as if she would have liked to commit it to memory; then she touched her own nose:

'It is better like this!' she said almost to herself, as if she were no longer interested in trying to persuade anyone else.

'What bad taste!' cried Balli, unable any longer to keep himself from laughing. It was evident that from that moment he found Angiolina most entertaining. He went on saying uncomplimentary things to her, but he seemed to be doing it only in order to rouse her to defend herself. She obviously took a certain pleasure in it herself. When she looked at Balli her eye shone with the same affectionate interest as Margherita's. She seemed to be copying her, and Emilio, having in vain tried several times to attract a little attention in the general conversation, was beginning to ask himself what had induced him to get up such a party.

But Balli had not forgotten him. He was merely following out his system, which was apparently one of brutality even towards the waiter. First he shouted at him because all the dishes he proposed serving seemed to have veal in them. Then he resigned himself to ordering one, but almost before the waiter had left the room he would shout after him in a comic fit of unprovoked anger: 'You dog! you villain!' The waiter seemed thoroughly to enjoy being shouted at, and obeyed all his orders with extraordinary promptitude. When he had thus reduced everyone to subjection, Balli felt he had given Emilio exactly the lesson he intended.

But Emilio was incapable of applying such a system even in regard to the most insignificant matters. Margherita did not want anything to eat: 'Beware!' Balli said to her, 'or it is the last time I ever take you out to dine. I can't endure people giving themselves airs!' She at once let him order a portion for her too; her appetite returned so quickly that Emilio immediately reflected he had never received a similar sign of affection from Angiolina. Meanwhile she, too, after hesitating for a long time, finally declared that she could not eat any veal.

'Didn't you hear?' Emilio said, 'Stefano can't endure people giving themselves airs.' She shrugged her shoulders; she didn't care, she said, whom she pleased and whom she didn't, and to Emilio it seemed that her contempt was directed against him rather than Balli.

Balli, with his mouth full, then addressed himself to the other three: 'This veal repast,' he said, 'is not a very harmonious function. You two clash terribly together: you as black as coal, and she as fair as an ear of corn at the end of June – you seem to have been arranged by an Academy painter. As for us they might have given us the title: "Grenadier with wounded wife."'

To this Margherita replied with true feeling: 'We don't go out together in order to be looked at by other people.' Balli rewarded her by a kiss on the forehead, but even this token of affection was given with his habitual brusquerie and mock severity.

Angiolina, with sudden bashfulness, began looking at the ceiling. 'Don't pretend to be so virtuous,' said Balli fiercely to her. 'As if you two don't do much worse things than that.'

'Who told you so?' asked Angiolina, looking threateningly towards Emilio.

'I didn't,' Emilio rather feebly protested.

'And what do you do together every evening, I should like to know? I never see him now, so it must be with you that he spends all his evenings. Why did he need to fall in love at his age? Farewell billiards, farewell our walks together. I stay there waiting for him, or am obliged to put up with the first fool who comes along, to keep me company. We used to get on so well together. I, the most intelligent person in the town and he the fifth, for there are four places vacant immediately below me, and he comes directly after that.'

Margherita, to whom the kiss had restored all her serenity, cast an affectionate glance at Emilio. 'It is quite true. He is always talking about you. He is very fond of you.'

Angiolina, however, was thinking that the fifth intelligent person in the town was not worth very much, and reserved all her admiration for the first. 'Emilio told me you sing so well. Do sing a little. I should so much like to hear you.'

'I should be delighted. But I always rest after eating. I take as long to digest as a snake.'

Margherita alone guessed Emilio's state of mind. She looked severely at Angiolina, then turning to Emilio, she devoted all her attention to him, and went on talking to him about Stefano. 'Sometimes he is rude, of course, but not always, and even when he is there is really nothing to be afraid of.' Then in a low, sweetly modulated voice, she added : 'A man who thinks for himself is so different from all the rest who don't think at all.' It was clear that by 'all the rest' she meant the people she generally had to consort with, and for the moment he was able to detach himself from his own melancholy situation, and looked at her pityingly. She was right to love in others the qualities she lacked; such a sweet, gentle creature was incapable of standing alone.

But Balli called attention to him once more. 'How silent you have become!' Turning to Angiolina he asked : 'Is that what he is like all the time during those long evenings you spend together?'

She had apparently forgotten the hymns of love he had sung to her, and said rather crossly: 'He is a serious man.'

Balli good-humouredly tried to enhance Emilio's prestige; he began by drawing a mock picture of him. 'As regards goodness he comes first and I only fifth. He is the only man I have ever been able to agree with. He is my *alter ego*, my other self, he thinks as I do, and always accepts my opinion if I don't at once accept his.' By the time he reached the last sentence he had entirely forgotten the good intention with which he set out, and good-humouredly buried Emilio beneath the weight of his own superiority. Emilio was obliged to compose his features in a forced smile.

Then, feeling that it would not be difficult to divine the effort behind the smile, he determined to say something so as to appear more at his ease. There had been some talk, he could not remember exactly how it had arisen, of Angiolina's posing for a figure which Balli had in his head. He had no objection; it was only a matter of copying her head, he told Angiolina, as if he did not know quite well that she would willingly have offered far more. But without asking his opinion she had already accepted while he was engaged in conversation with Margherita, and she now burst in on his unnecessarily long and stilted speech with the exclamation: 'But I have already accepted.'

Balli thanked her and said that he should certainly call on her, but not for a few months, as he was at the moment too much occupied with other works. He looked at her for a long time, imagining the pose he would place her in for her portrait, and Angiolina grew quite pink with pleasure. One would have thought that Emilio would at least have had a companion in his suffering. But no! Margherita was not at all jealous, and she, too, looked at Angiolina with the eye of an artist. Stefano would certainly do something beautiful of her, she said, and she spoke with enthusiasm of the surprises art had given her, when she saw emerging from the docile clay a face, an expression, life itself.

Balli at once resumed his brusque manner. 'Are you really called Angiolina? A diminutive for a great, strapping girl like you. I shall call you Angiolona, perhaps only Giolona.' And henceforward he always called her that, emphasizing the broad vowels to the utmost, so that the sounds conveyed the maximum of contempt. Emilio was surprised that Angiolina showed no dislike for the name; she never got angry at it, and when Balli bellowed it in her ear she only laughed as if he had been tickling her.

On their way back together Balli sang. He had a voice of considerable volume and even tone, which he modulated with much taste and subtlety, though the popular songs he sang by preference hardly deserved such delicate treatment. He sang one that evening of which he was obliged, by the presence of the two young women, to leave out some of the words, but he supplied their lack by suggestive glances and a certain sensuality in his voice. Angiolina was enchanted by them.

When they parted, Emilio and Angiolina stood still a moment and watched the others walking away. 'He must be blind!' she said. 'How can he love a smoke-dried stick which can scarcely hold itself upright?'

Next evening she did not allow Emilio time to utter the reproaches which he had been turning over in his mind all day long. She had some surprising news for him. The tailor had written to her – she had forgotten to bring his letter along – to say that he would not be able to marry her for a whole year. A partner of his was preventing him by threatening to break up the partnership and withdraw his capital. 'It seems that the partner wants him to marry his own daughter, a hunchback, who would certainly match my fiancé very well. But Volpini swears that he will be able to do without the partner and his money in a year's time, and that then he will marry me. Do you understand?' He showed that he did not. 'There is something else,' she said softly and rather timidly. 'Volpini says he can't live a whole year with his desire unsatisfied.'

He understood at last. He protested that she could not expect him to consent to such a thing. But what objection could he raise? 'Shall you have any guarantee of his good faith?'

'Whatever I choose. He is ready to make a contract with a notary.'

After a short pause he asked: 'When?'

She laughed. 'He can't come next Sunday. He wants to get everything ready for the contract which he will make in a fortnight's time, and then...' She broke off laughing and kissed him.

She would be his at last! It was not thus that he had dreamed of possessing her, but he, too, embraced her effusively and tried to persuade himself that he was perfectly happy. He ought to be grateful to her, no doubt. She loved him, or rather she loved him as well. What had he got to complain of?

Besides, this was perhaps the cure he had been hoping for. Polluted by the tailor, possessed by him, *Ange* would soon die, and he would continue to amuse himself with Giolona; he would be gay, as she wanted all men to be, indifferent and cynical like Balli.

5

I T was true what Balli had said. It was because of Angiolina that the relations of the two friends had become so cold. Up to the evening of their dinner together Emilio had hardly ever been to see his friend, but was not conscious that he had neglected him till Balli had ended by taking offence and had stopped running after him, though he still cherished their friendship, like all his other habits. The dinner broke down Stefano's obstinacy and also made him fear that he might have offended his friend. Emilio's unhappy state of mind had not escaped him and so soon as the intense pleasure he took in knowing himself to be loved by both the women at once had died down – and it lasted only a fraction of an hour – his conscience smote him. In order to silence it he hastened to Emilio's house at noon the following day, under the pretence of giving him some good advice. A little sound argument would probably be more efficacious than example in curing Emilio, and even if it did not altogether work, it would at least enable him to appear again in the guise of a friend and to give up the role of rival which he had only assumed from weakness and for the sake of a moment's distraction.

Amalia came to open the door. The poor girl inspired in Balli a rather uncomfortable feeling of pity. He held that it was permissible to live in order to enjoy fame or beauty or physical strength, but that otherwise there was no justification for one's being alive; one simply became an odious encumbrance to other people. Why then was this poor creature alive? It was evidently a mistake on the part of Nature. Sometimes, if he did not find his friend at home when he came to the house, he would make an excuse for going away on the spot, for her pale face and hoarse voice produced in him a feeling of profound depression. She, on the other hand, who liked to feel she was sharing Emilio's life, had looked upon herself as a friend of Balli.

'Is Emilio at home?' he asked, full of the purpose for which he had come.

'Come in, Signor Stefano,' said Amalia joyfully. 'Emilio!' she cried, 'here is Signor Stefano.' Then she administered a slight rebuke to Balli. 'It is such a long time since we had the pleasure of seeing you. I was afraid you had forgotten us like everyone else.'

Stefano burst out laughing. 'It is not I who have given up Emilio. It is he who never comes to see me now.'

While she led him towards the dining-room door, she smiled at him and whispered: 'Yes, yes, I understand.' She felt as if they had already talked about Angiolina.

Their small apartment consisted only of three rooms, which did not open directly on to the passage, but had to be reached by this one door. So that if Emilio had a visitor in his room his sister was kept a prisoner in hers, which was the last room of the three. She would not have dreamt of appearing without introduction, for she was even shyer with men than Emilio was with women. But from the first day on which Balli set foot in the house she had made him an exception to the rule. After constantly hearing him spoken of as rather a bear, she had seen him for the first time on the occasion of her father's death. She had at once made friends with him, and was astonished by his gentleness. He had proved the most exquisite of comforters. He had known just when to keep silence and when to speak. By putting in a discreet word here and there he had succeeded in stemming and even in reasoning about the girl's violent and uncontrollable grief; sometimes he had helped her to analyse her feelings, and to find the words which should give a saner outlet to her sorrow. She had become accustomed to him and could weep freely in his presence; and he used to come very often, taking a certain pleasure in the role of comforter which he. so well understood. When that incentive to his visits was over he had retired from the scene. Family life was not at all what he was suited for; he only loved a beauty which was shameless, and the sisterly affection offered him by that plain girl could not but bore him. This was indeed the first time that she had ever reproached him for his desertion, for she thought it quite natural that he should find it more amusing to spend his time elsewhere.

The small dining-room contained only one piece of furniture which bore witness to the fact that the family had once been well-to-do, a magnificent table of dark inlaid wood. The remaining furniture was a rather shabby sofa, four chairs somewhat similar but not identical in shape, a large armchair and an old cupboard. The poverty-stricken impression which the room made on one was increased by the extreme care obviously lavished on the few articles of furniture it contained.

On entering the room Balli was reminded of the consoling function which he had once so faithfully fulfilled there; he felt as if he were returning to a place in which he had suffered himself, though his sufferings had been sweet. He remembered with satisfaction his own kindness of heart and felt he had made a mistake in avoiding for so long a place which gave him more than ever the sensation of being a superior person.

Emilio welcomed him with studied politeness, just because he was anxious to hide the resentment he was secretly nursing; he did not want Balli to see how much he had been wounded; he intended, it is true, to upbraid him severely for his conduct, but hoped at the same time to keep his own wound hidden. He treated him almost as if he had been an enemy. 'What good wind blows you here?'

'I was passing this way and I thought I should like to call on your sister whom I have not seen for a long time.

I think she is looking much better,' said Balli, observing Amalia's pink cheeks and dancing grey eyes.

Emilio looked at her but noticed nothing. His resentment knew no bounds when he thought he perceived that Stefano was absolutely oblivious of the events of the previous evening, and could continue to behave before him as if nothing had happened. He said sarcastically: 'You enjoyed yourself thoroughly last night, and a good deal at my expense.'

Balli was startled by his friend's tone. The fact that he could say such a thing in Amalia's presence, where such words were quite out of place, brought home to him how deeply he was offended. He had really done nothing to offend Emilio; at least, his intentions had been such as rather to deserve a hymn of gratitude. The better to arm himself against such an attack, he lost on the spot all consciousness of his own misdeeds and felt himself pure from every stain.

'We will talk about that later on,' he said, out of regard for Amalia. She, however, at once left the room, though Balli, who was in no hurry for an explanation with Emilio, did his best to detain her.

'I don't understand what you can reproach me with.'

'Oh no, nothing at all,' replied Emilio, who, in face of a frontal attack, could think of nothing better than an ironical reply.

Balli, now that he had recovered the conviction of his own innocence, consented to be more explicit. He said that he had behaved exactly as he had proposed to behave when he offered to give Emilio an object-lesson. He supposed that if he had begun to bleat love-lyrics too, the cure would have worked all right. No, Giolona had got to be treated exactly as he had treated her, and he hoped that in time Emilio would come to imitate him. He did not believe, he could not possibly believe, that a woman of her sort should be taken seriously, and he proceeded to describe her in exactly the same terms as Emilio had used several days ago in talking of her. He had found her so exactly like the picture which had then been drawn of her that it had been easy for him to see through her completely, at once.

But Emilio was by no means impressed when he heard his own words repeated in this way. He replied that this was his way of making love, and he was incapable of behaving in any other way, for tenderness seemed to him an essential factor in his enjoyment. This did not at all mean that he wanted to take the woman too seriously. For instance, he had not promised to marry her, had he?

Stefano laughed heartily. Emilio had undergone an extraordinary change during the last few hours. It was only a few days ago – surely he must remember? – that he had been so overwhelmed by his own state of mind as to call on all and sundry for their assistance. 'I have nothing against your amusing yourself, but you don't look to me as if you were amusing yourself very much.'

Emilio did indeed look very tired. His life had never been a very gay one, but since his father's death he had enjoyed complete peace of mind, and he was suffering physically from the change of regime.

Amalia, unobtrusive as a shadow, was wanting to pass through the room without being noticed, but Emilio made her stay, hoping to silence Stefano. The two men, however, could not at once give up the subject of their conversation, and Balli jokingly said that he should call on her to act as judge in a matter of which she could not have any experience. A dispute had arisen, he said, between them, old friends though they were. The only course open to them was to get Amalia to decide the issue with her eyes shut, relying on the divine providence, which had evidently been invented for just such a case as theirs, to guide her aright.

But there could be no question of a blind decision, for Amalia had already grasped what it was all about. She gave Balli a look of gratitude in which there was an intensity of expression such as one would have thought impossible in those small grey eyes. She had at last found an ally, and the bitterness of spirit which had so long oppressed her was lifted, and its place taken by a feeling of great hopefulness. She said simply: 'I know quite well what it is all about. You are so right; you should see how absent-minded and sad he always is; his eagerness to get away from this house in which he leaves me so much alone, is written all over his face.' There was a tone in her voice which sounded more like a cry for help than a justification of Balli.

Emilio listened to her anxiously, afraid every moment that her complaint would degenerate, as it generally did, into tears and sobs. But now that she was actually telling Balli of her great sorrow she remained calm and smiling.

Balli, who only looked on Amalia as an ally in his quarrel with Emilio, accompanied her words with deprecatory gestures towards his friend. But Amalia's words no longer matched the gestures. Laughing merrily she went on to relate that some days ago she had been out walking with Emilio and had noticed that he became uneasy whenever he saw in the distance women of a certain height and colouring; very tall they had to be and very fair. 'Was I right?' and she laughed with satisfaction when Balli nodded. 'Really as tall and fair as that?' There was nothing for Emilio to be offended at in her gentle mockery. She had gone over to him and stood leaning against him, her white hand resting affectionately on his head.

Balli confirmed what she had said. 'As tall as one of the King of Prussia's guards and so fair that you might say she is almost colourless.'

Emilio laughed, but he had not forgotten his jealousy. 'It would be all right if I could be sure she does not please you.'

'Just imagine, he is jealous of me, who am his best friend,' shouted Balli indignantly.

'I quite understand it,' said Amalia gently, almost as if she were begging Balli to be indulgent to his friend.

'You ought not to say that!' protested Stefano. 'How can you say that you understand anything so monstrous?'

She did not reply, but remained of the same opinion as before, and wore the confident air of someone who is sure of what he is saying. She believed herself to have been thinking intensely, and to have thereby divined intuitively the state of mind of her unfortunate brother; but she had really only divined it in her own feelings. A rosy glow overspread her face. Certain tones of that conversation echoed in her heart like the sound of bells in the desert; they went on for a long time traversing huge empty spaces, searching them from end to end, unexpectedly measuring their emptiness, waking them suddenly to life and feeling, enriching them abundantly with joy and pain. She remained silent for a long while. She forgot they had been talking about her brother, she was thinking of herself. A strange, a miraculous thing had happened to her. She had talked of love before now, but how differently; with intolerance, as of something outside the pale. How seriously she had always taken the injunction which had been dinned into her ears since infancy! She had hated and despised all those who had not obeyed it, and had stifled the least tendency towards rebellion within herself. She had been deceived! It was Balli who stood for virtue and strength, Balli who spoke so serenely about love which for him had never been a sin. How many human beings he must have loved! With that sweet voice and those blue eyes of his he must always love everything in the world, all living beings, including herself.

Stefano stayed to dinner. Amalia had announced rather anxiously that there was very little to eat, so Balli was all the more surprised to discover that they fed extremely well in that house. For years past Amalia had spent a great part of her day in the kitchen, and she had made herself into a very good cook, able to cater for Emilio's delicate palate.

Stefano was very glad to stay. He felt he had had rather the worst of it in the discussion with Emilio, and he was looking forward to getting his own back, confident that Amalia would always agree with him, excuse him and back him up, for he felt her to be entirely under his sway.

He and Amalia were extremely gay during the whole meal. He talked a great deal. He related his early youth with its surprising adventures. He was continually being forced by poverty to resort to more or less doubtful but always amusing expedients, and just as it seemed that there was nothing for it but to starve, help would always come. He told in great detail how he had once been saved from hunger by winning a reward offered for a lost dog.

And so it had gone on. When he had finished his studies he migrated to Milan with the intention of accepting a post he had been offered as inspector in some commercial undertaking. It was too difficult to begin his career as a sculptor; he would have died of hunger before he even started. One day he was passing a palace in which were exhibited the works of an artist recently dead, and he went in to say a last farewell to sculpture. He met a friend there, and together they began mercilessly to criticize the works on exhibition. With a bitterness derived from his desperate position Balli declared that everything was mediocre, of no importance whatever. He was talking at the top of his voice, heated by argument; that criticism was to be his final artistic activity. When they reached the last room, which contained the work which the dead sculptor had left unfinished when the illness which was to prove fatal overtook him, Balli stood still in amazement at finding himself unable to continue his criticism on the same note as heretofore. The plaster cast of a woman's head was there – a strong profile roughly sketched, but every line significant in the portrayal of an intense and tragic nature. Balli loudly proclaimed his admiration. He declared that the dead sculptor had remained an artist till his rough cast was finished, but at that point his academic training had always intervened to destroy all that was personal in his art, all his first impressions and feelings, so that only impersonal dogmas and old prejudices remained. 'Yes, it is quite true!' said a little old man in glasses who was standing by him, with the point of his nose almost resting on the cast. Balli grew more and more eloquent in his admiration, and made a moving speech about the artist who had died in old age and would have carried his secret with him to the grave if death had not this one time prevented its concealment.

The old man stopped looking at the plaster cast and turned to consider the critic. It was a mere chance that Stefano introduced himself as a sculptor and not as a business man. The old man, who was a fabulously rich eccentric, gave him first an order for his own bust and then for a memorial sculpture, and finally left him a legacy. So that Balli had work for two years and enough money to support him for ten.

Amalia said: 'How lovely it must be to know people who are as good and intelligent as that!'

At this Balli protested. He described the old man in terms of vivid dislike. He was a pretentious Maecenas who had never left him a moment's peace, and had compelled him each day to accomplish a given amount of work. He was a true bourgeois, without any taste of his own, and had only been able to love a work of art when it was explained to him and its virtues demonstrated. Balli had been worn out every evening by so much work and conversation and he sometimes felt as if he had really landed in the business post from which chance seemed to have freed him. He went into mourning when the old man died, but to keep up his spirits while mourning he did not touch modelling clay for several months.

What a splendid destiny Balli's seemed; he did not even need to feel gratitude for the benefits which rained on him from heaven. Riches and happiness were his by the decree of providence; why should he be surprised when they fell to him by lot? Why should he be grateful to the individual appointed by providence to distribute its gifts. Amalia listened spellbound to his recital, which confirmed her in the belief that there was a life very different from that which she had known. It was natural that she and her brother should find it so hard, equally natural that to Balli it should be like a triumphal pageant. She admired Balli's happiness and loved the strength and serenity which were the two best gifts of fortune to him.

Brentani, on the contrary, was full of bitterness and envy as he sat listening. To him Balli seemed to be boasting of his good luck as if it had come to him by some virtue of his own. Emilio had never had anything delightful happen to him, nor even anything unexpected. His evil fortune had announced itself long before it actually came, and as it drew nearer it had taken more and more definite shape. When it actually arrived – poverty and the death of his parents – he was already prepared for it. So though he had suffered for a longer period he had suffered less acutely, and all the many minor misfortunes which had befallen him had never shaken him from the dull apathy which he attributed to a monotonous, colourless destiny. He had himself never inspired any strong emotion, be it love or hatred; the old man so unjustly loathed by Balli had never intervened in his life. The jealous feelings in his heart acquired such sway over him that he even envied the admiration which Amalia obviously felt for Balli. The dinner became very animated because he also took part in the discussion, striving to divert Amalia's attention to himself.

But he was unsuccessful. What could he possibly say that could worthily compete with Balli's bizarre auto-biography? There was nothing but his present passionate adventure and as he could not speak about that he was at once doomed to play the secondary part to which fate had condemned him. All Emilio's efforts only served to produce some idea which might be used by Balli to adorn his tale. And Balli, without being conscious of it, felt the conflict that was going on, and embroidered his theme with increasing fantasy, invention and lively colouring. Never had Amalia been the object of so much attention. She listened enchanted to the sculptor's con-fidences and she did not deceive herself in thinking that they were made on purpose to win her. She felt herself wholly his, but the poor girl's humble mind harboured no hopes for the future. She was living solely in the present, rejoicing in the one hour in which she felt herself important and an object of desire.

They all went out together. Emilio would have preferred to go alone with Balli, but she reminded him of the fatal promise of the day before to take her with him. She was determined her happy day should not end so soon. Stefano supported her. He thought that Amalia's company would do something to combat the influence of Angiolina on Emilio, quite forgetting that only a few minutes before he had himself been trying to come between brother and sister.

She was ready in the twinkling of an eye, but had found time nevertheless to arrange on her forehead the curls of her fine but curiously shaded hair, of which it would have been hard to name the actual colour. The smile she gave Balli when, having drawn on her gloves, she invited him to start, was almost like a prayer that she might find favour in his sight.

In the street she seemed more insignificant than ever, dressed entirely in black with a little white feather in her hat. Balli teased her about the feather. He said, however, that he liked it, and managed to conceal his ill-humour at having to cross the whole town in the company of this strange little woman, whose taste was so perverse that she must needs display a white flag at so short a distance from the ground.

The air was warm but the sky, behind its dense covering of white mist, seemed quite wintry, and Sant' Andrea looked like a snow landscape, with all those trees with their long bare, dry boughs not yet cut, and the white light that was diffused over everything. A painter who tried to render the scene, without of course being able to suggest the mildness of the air, would certainly have conveyed an illusion of snow.

'We three seem to know the whole town,' said Balli. They were continually obliged to slacken their pace on their walk. A gay and noisy crowd of officials filled the vast melancholy landscape beside the limitless sea, like a swarm of ants suddenly disturbed.

'It is you who know them, not we,' said Amalia, who remembered often having been that walk before without finding at all too many people to bow to. Everyone they passed had a friendly or respectful greeting for Balli, even the people in carriages were bowing to him. She felt so happy beside him, and enjoyed his triumphal progress as much as if part of the respect shown to the sculptor had been intended for her.

'What a tragedy it would have been if I had not come!' said Balli, returning with great dignity the greeting of an old lady who was leaning half out of her carriage in order to see him better. 'Everyone would have had to go home disappointed.' They were always sure to find him, he said, on the Sunday promenade where he, like any other labourer, might always be seen disporting himself with Brentani, who was shut up in his office on weekdays.

'*Ange!*' whispered Amalia suddenly, concealing her laughter. She had recognized her by the description she had been given of her and by Emilio's obvious agitation.

'Don't laugh,' said Emilio earnestly, thereby confirming her discovery. For him also there was a novelty to be seen: the tailor Volpini, a ridiculous little figure of a man, who seemed more insignificant still because of the splendid carriage of the young woman at whose side he walked and whose graceful and easy steps he rather absurdly strove to emulate. Balli and Emilio greeted them and Volpini replied with exaggerated politeness. 'He has the same coloured hair as Angiolina,' Balli said laughing. Emilio protested indignantly: how could anyone compare Volpini's straw-colour with Angiolina's gold? He turned and saw Angiolina bending down to speak to her companion, who was straightening his bent little back in order to catch what she said. They were obviously talking about the other three.

It was not till later in the afternoon, when they were back in the town and about to separate, that Amalia broke the silence which had suddenly descended on her as she felt herself drawing near to the scene of her usual solitude, and its influence coming out to swallow her up, by asking who the man was who was walking with Angiolina. 'Her uncle,' said Brentani gravely, after a moment's hesitation, while Stefano watched him ironically; his blush naturally did not escape notice. His sister's innocent eye made him ashamed of his deception. How surprised Amalia would have been if she had known that her brother could stoop so low to enjoy his love, the love for which she had already suffered so much!

'Thank you!' said Amalia, taking leave of Stefano. Oh, what a sweet memory those hours would have left with her, had she not noticed that at the moment of farewell Balli was struggling to suppress a yawn which paralysed his mouth and prevented him from replying.

'You were bored I am afraid. Thank you all the more.' She was so humble and so kind that Stefano was deeply touched, and he suddenly felt that he almost loved her. He explained that yawning with him was a nervous affection. He hoped to prove to her that he was far from being bored in their company; in fact it was they, he said, who would complain of his coming too often.

And he kept his word. It would have been hard to say why he took to mounting their stairs every day in order to take coffee with the Brentanis. Probably it was jealousy; he was fighting to keep Emilio's friendship. But Amalia was incapable of guessing that. For her it was sufficient that he came more often to see them simply out of affection for her brother, and that she herself profited by their affection because she could sit in its warmth and sun herself.

There were no further discussions between the brother and sister. Emilio was too unobservant to be surprised at this, and simply felt that his sister had come to understand him better, and put up with him. He even felt that the new atmosphere of benevolence extended to his love. Now, whenever he spoke of it, Amalia's face would light up and become quite radiant. She even tried to make him talk about love, and never told him to be on his guard or that it was his duty to give up Angiolina. Why should he give up Angiolina, seeing that she stood for happiness? One day she said she should like to know her, and several times afterwards expressed the same desire; but Emilio took care not to comply with her wish. All she knew about the young woman was that she was a very different being from herself, stronger and more full of life, and Emilio congratulated himself on having created in her mind an Angiolina so very different from the real one. When he was alone with his sister that image pleased him, he began to embellish it, to endow it with all the qualities which he would have liked to find in Angiolina, and his heart leapt for joy when he realized that Amalia was collaborating in that artificial creation.

When she heard them talking about a woman who had overcome all prejudices of birth and money in order to belong to the man she loved, she whispered in Emilio's ear: 'She is like Angiolina.'

'Oh, if only she were!' thought Emilio within himself while forcing his features to express agreement. Then he persuaded himself that she really was rather like her, or at least would have been if she had grown up in other surroundings, and he smiled with genuine pleasure at the thought. What reason had he for supposing that Angiolina would have let prejudices stand in her way? Seen through the veil of Amalia's idealism his love for Angiolina was adorned at that moment with every illusion.

But in reality the woman who broke down every obstacle had more resemblance to Amalia herself. She felt an enormous force in her long white hands, sufficient to tear asunder the strongest chains. She felt that all the chains had fallen from her life and that she was as free as air; yet nobody asked of her resolution or strength or love. How would the great force she felt imprisoned in her weak body find a means of expression, a way of escape?

Balli meanwhile, stretched at his length in the old arm-chair, sipped his coffee with infinite satisfaction, and looked back with disapproval on the days when he used at that very hour to sit discussing art at the café: a bad habit! He was so much better off here, with these two dear creatures who loved and admired him.

His intervention between the two lovers was, however, extremely unfortunate. During his brief acquaintance with Angiolina he had assumed the right of saying any impertinence that came into his head, and she always listened smiling, not in the least offended. At first he used to come out with them in Tuscan, in such softly breathed accents that they seemed to her a caress; but even when they came pouring forth in the Triestine dialect, in all their harsh obscenity, she showed no sign of taking offence. She felt, and even Emilio could not help feeling, that they were uttered without a grain of malice, that it was something to do with the way he held his mouth, a quite innocent trick of the tongue. That was the worst part of it. One evening when Emilio could endure it no longer he ended by asking Balli to leave them alone. 'I really cannot bear to hear you insulting her like that.'

'Really?' asked Balli, opening his eyes very wide.

Forgetful as ever, he had quite persuaded himself that he was obliged to behave like that in order to cure Emilio. He let himself be persuaded that he was wrong and for a certain time he left them in peace. 'I don't know any other way of behaving with women like that.' But then Emilio felt ashamed of showing himself so weak and rather than confess his real feelings resigned himself to putting up with Balli's behaviour.

'Come sometimes with Margherita.'

The so-called 'veal dinner' was frequently repeated under conditions very similar to the first one, Emilio condemned to silence, Margherita and Angiolina prostrate at the feet of Balli.

One evening, however, Balli was very quiet; he neither shouted nor ordered people about, and for the first time Emilio felt him to be a companion after his own heart. 'How happy you must be to feel that Margherita loves

you so much!' he said on the way back, in order to say
something friendly. The two women were walking together a little way in front.

'Unfortunately,' said Balli in a tone of resignation, 'I
have reason to think she loves a good many other men
just as much. She is the kindest of souls.' Emilio fell to
earth with a crash.

'Don't say any more now,' Balli adjured him, seeing
that the two women had stopped and were waiting for
them.

Next day, when Amalia had gone into the kitchen for
a few minutes, Balli told him that owing to a mistake of
the postman he had discovered that Margherita had
appointments with someone else as well – an artist too,
he added desperately. 'I am very sad indeed about it. It is
shameful to be treated like that. I began making some
inquiries and just as I thought I had discovered who my
rival was I found that in the interval he had become two.
That gave a much more innocent aspect to the affair. It
was only then that I deigned to make some inquiries
about Margherita's family and found that it consisted of
a mother and a brood of sisters, all quite young. Do you
understand? She has to provide for the bringing up of all
those children.' And Balli concluded, in a voice of deep
emotion: 'Just think, she has never consented to receive
a single penny from me. I want her to confess, I want her
to tell me everything. I shall give her one last kiss and tell
her that I bear her no grudge, and then I shall leave her,
but always preserve the sweetest memory of her.' Then
he suddenly recovered himself and went on smoking, and
when Amalia came in he was humming in an undertone: *'Prima confessi il delitto e poscia muoia!'*

That same evening Emilio told Angiolina the story.
She gave a joyful start which it was impossible for her to
conceal. Then she realized herself that she must win
Emilio's forgiveness for such an infamy. Her task was not
easy. It was terribly painful for him to see how lightly
and easily the sculptor carried off the prize which he
could not win even at the cost of so much suffering.

But at that moment he was going through a period of strange illusion with Angiolina. One of those dreams, to which he was often subject, even in his waking hours, persuaded him that it was he who had first corrupted the girl. As a matter of fact, during the very first evenings he had known her, he had preached her those magnificent sermons about honest women and about making the best of one's opportunities. He could not know what she had been like before going to school with him. How was it he had not understood that a virtuous Angiolina meant his own Angiolina? He began his interrupted sermons again, but in quite a different key. He very soon perceived that cold and complex theories did not do for Angiolina. He spent a long time thinking out the best method to follow in re-educating her. In his dream he caressed her as if he had already made her worthy of him. He tried to do the same in reality. Surely the best method must be to make her feel how sweet it was to be respected, in order to give her the desire to win such respect for herself. It was for this reason that he was continually on his knees before her, exactly in the position in which it would have been most easy to humble him, if Angiolina should have thought fit one day to give him a kick.

6

ONE evening at the beginning of January, Balli, in the worst of humours, was walking alone along the Aqueduct. He missed Emilio, who had gone somewhere with his sister to pay a call, and Margherita had not yet been replaced.

The sky was clear in spite of the sirocco which had been hanging over the town since morning. The carnival was to open that evening with the first fancy-dress ball of the season, a paltry affair which would surely not survive in that cold, damp atmosphere. 'Oh, if only I had a dog here to take a piece out of their calves!' thought Balli to himself, as two pierrettes with naked legs went by. That carnival with its shoddy magnificence aroused his moral indignation; later on, no doubt, much later, he would be taking part in it himself, revelling in the finery and bright colours, and altogether forgetting his indignation. But for the moment he was conscious of assisting at the prelude to a tragi-comedy. The whirlpool was beginning to form which would swallow up the factory-hand, the sempstress, the poor bourgeois, and withdraw them for a moment from the dreary round of common life only to fling them out again into greater suffering. Some would return bruised and ruined to take up their old burden and find it heavier than before; there were some who would never find their way out at all.

He yawned again; even his own thoughts bored him. 'There is sirocco about still,' he thought, and looked up again at the bright moon which seemed to rest on the mountain as on a pedestal. Suddenly his eye was arrested by three figures coming towards him along the Aqueduct. He was struck by them because he noticed at once that they were all holding each other by the hand. There was a short, thick little man in the middle and a tall, graceful woman on each side of him; he was struck by the irony of the group and decided to sculpture it. He would dress the two women, he thought, in Greek dress and the man in modern costume; he would show the women laughing loudly like bacchanti and make the man's face express weariness and boredom.

But when the three figures drew near, he entirely forgot his dream. One of the women was Angiolina, the other was a rather plain girl called Giulia whom Angiolina had introduced to him and Emilio. He did not know the man, who passed quite close to him smiling and holding his head high; a brown beard gave him an imposing appearance. It was certainly not Volpini, for he was fair.

Giolina was laughing; it was her familiar, sweet ringing laugh. The man was clearly there on her account and he only pressed Giulia's hand from time to time as a concession. Balli was certain of this though he could not exactly have said why. He found his own powers of observation so entertaining that he quite forgot how bored he had been all the evening. 'Quite a novel occupation for me, acting as spy!' He followed them, keeping in the shade under the trees. Giolina was laughing a great deal, almost without interruption, and the two were so absorbed in each other as often to forget that Giulia was there, so that she was obliged to lean forward in order to take part in the conversation.

Very soon, however, it was no longer necessary to have unusual powers of observation. They had halted a few steps away from the *caffé all'Acquedotto*. The man let fall Giulia's hand altogether, and took Angiolina's in both of his, while Giulia stood tactfully aside. He was trying to get her to promise something and was continually putting his bushy beard right up into Angiolina's face. Then they all went together into the café.

They sat down in the outer room close to the entrance, but Balli could only see the man's head. This, however, was in full light. His face was so dark as to be almost black, and was framed by a thick beard which reached right up to his eyes; but his head was bald and shining and yellow. 'The man from the umbrella-shop in Via Barriera!' laughed Balli to himself. So now Emilio had an umbrella-maker as a rival! So much the better, that trade would surely cure him. Balli thought that he would be able to make the adventure sound so ridiculous that Emilio would be obliged to laugh at it and would forget his suffering. Balli had complete confidence in his own wit.

All the umbrella-man's attention was directed towards someone sitting beside him, and Balli was anxious to ascertain whether that someone was Angiolina. So he went in. Yes, it certainly was Angiolina. She was sitting with her back to the wall, while Giulia sat opposite quite apart from them both, and was sipping a small glass of some semi-transparent liqueur. But though this occupied a good deal of her attention she had still some time to spare for looking about her, and it was not long before she caught sight of Balli and gave the alarm. Too late! He had had time to see that two hands had joined again under the table, and to be struck by the affectionate expression in Angiolina's face when she looked at the umbrella-maker. Emilio was right; her eyes sparkled as if something were actually burning in their flame. How Balli envied the umbrella-maker! How much he would have preferred that man's place to his own at that moment!

Giulia nodded to him, and said, 'Good evening.' He was irritated to see that she evidently expected him to go up and speak to her. He had just been able to put up with her for one evening, in order to be with Emilio and Angiolina. He went slowly out, giving a slight nod to Angiolina. She had retired into her corner so as to seem further off from her companion, and she looked at Balli with great expressive eyes, ready to smile at him if he set her the example. But he did not smile, and left the café without returning the umbrella-maker's greeting.

How expressive we were! he thought. She begged me not to say anything to Emilio about this meeting, and I replied that I should tell him everything as soon as I saw him.

From outside he cast one more glance at Angiolina's companion, at his radiant face in the midst of its forest of hair and crowned by his bald head. If only Emilio could have seen him.

'Good evening, Signor Balli,' he heard someone saying respectfully behind him. He turned, and saw his servant Michele. He had arrived in the nick of time.

Balli made up his mind rapidly, and asked him to go at once to Emilio Brentani; if he found him at home he was to bring him back with him immediately; if he were not in, he was to wait till he came back. Michele hardly gave himself time to hear the order before he set off at full speed.

Balli leaned against a tree opposite the café and stood waiting impatiently. He thought he would be able to prevent a collision between Emilio and the other two. He felt confident of his own power to calm him and set him free for ever from the bondage of Angiolina.

Giulia had meanwhile come to the door and stood looking intently around her; but as she was in the light and Balli in shadow she did not notice him. Balli stood motionless, he had no particular reason any longer for wishing to hide himself. Giulia went in again and soon came out accompanied by Angiolina and the umbrella-maker, who no longer dared hold his mistress's hand. They set off at a rapid pace, in the direction of *caffè Chiozza*. They were running away! As far as the Chiozza, Balli's task was easy enough, for Emilio would have to come that way; but when they turned off to the right, towards the station, he found himself in a very awkward position. In his impatience he lost his temper.

'If Emilio does not arrive in time I shall give Michele notice.'

His excellent sight enabled him to keep them under observation from a long way off. 'Oh, the cad!' he muttered angrily, seeing the umbrella-maker again seize Angiolina's hand when he felt himself to be at a safe distance. Soon afterwards he lost them from sight under the shadow of some old houses with projecting roofs; and by the time Emilio came there was no hope of catching them up. Balli's annoyance at this made him receive his friend with the words: 'What a pity to have missed such a salutary spectacle!' Then he began humming '*Si, vendetta tremenda vendetta*', and possibly in the hope that they might have stopped to wait for them, he began dragging Emilio with him towards the station.

Emilio had realized that it was something to do with Angiolina, but as he walked beside Balli he continued to put questions to him which purposely did not betray that he had an inkling of the real truth. It was slowly dawning upon him, and the lump he felt in his throat came, he knew, from the horrible blow his vanity had received. First of all he must free himself from that. He stood still in the middle of the road and refused to move. He would not go a step further, he said, unless Balli told him exactly what it was all about. Let him say everything quite openly; there was no need for all this mystery. It concerned Angiolina, he supposed. 'Nothing you can have to tell me about her comes up to what I know already,' he laughed. 'So stop all this play-acting.'

He felt pleased with himself, especially when he perceived that he had at once obtained what he wanted from Balli. The latter immediately became serious and told him how he had met Angiolina and had caught her *in flagrante.* 'If they had been in bed together it could not have been plainer. That man was there for Angiolina, not for Giulia, and Angiolina was there for him. You should have seen the way she squeezed his hand, and the way she looked at him! No, it was not Volpini, my dear.' He broke off to look at Emilio and see whether his perfectly calm demeanour was due to the fact that he believed the man she had betrayed him with to be Volpini.

Emilio continued to listen, pretending to be surprised by this news. 'Are you quite sure of it?' he asked conscientiously. As a matter of fact he knew that Volpini was not in Trieste just then, so he had not even given him a thought.

'Oh, rather! I know Volpini and I know the other one quite well too. It is the umbrella-maker at Barriera Vecchia. You know, the one who sells those common coloured umbrellas.' Then followed a detailed description of the umbrella-maker lit up by the yellow gaslight and by Angiolina's eyes. 'Bald, and as dark as you make them! He is a freak of nature, for he stays black whatever light you see him in.' Balli finished up his story by saying: 'As there is no need for me to pity you I reserve all my sympathy for that poor Giulia. The umbrella-maker hasn't got someone like me for a friend, with whom to saddle the heavier part of his baggage when he is out on the spree. She was very badly treated, poor thing. She was obliged to content herself with a little glass of rosolis, while Angiolina was giving herself great airs over some chocolate and lots of cakes.'

Emilio appeared to be very interested in all his friend's witty observations. Nor did it need any particular effort for him to simulate indifference; his expression had become, as it were, crystallized by his initial effort and he felt as if he could almost have fallen asleep with that stereotyped, calm smile still on his face. His simulation was so intense that it penetrated far beneath the skin. He sought in vain in himself for any other reaction, and found nothing but an immense weariness. Nothing! Perhaps it was that he was bored with himself, with Balli and Angiolina. And he thought: 'I shall be much better when I am alone.'

Balli said, 'Now let us go to bed. You know now where you will find Angiolina tomorrow. You can say a few words of farewell to her, and then it will be all over between you, as between me and Margherita.'

The suggestion was a good one; only perhaps it would have been better not to express it. 'Yes, that is what I will do,' said Emilio. He added quite sincerely: 'Only perhaps not tomorrow.' He felt as if he should like to sleep very late the next day.

'Ah, now you are really worthy of being my friend,' said Balli with profound admiration. 'You have won again in a single evening all the respect you had lost by the follies you have committed during all these past months. Will you come a little way home with me?'

'Only a little way,' said Emilio yawning. 'It is very late, and I was just going to bed when I was called by Michele.' He evidently regretted having been suddenly disturbed like that.

He did not really come to himself even when he was alone. What else was there for him to do that evening? He set off towards home, intending to go to bed.

But when he reached the Chiozza, he stood still and looked towards the station, towards that part of the town where Angiolina was making love with the umbrella-maker. And yet, he thought, uttering the words aloud, it would be a good thing if she were to pass this way so that I could tell her at once that everything is over between us. For then everything would really be over and I could go to bed and sleep peacefully. She will have to come this way!

He stood leaning against a road shelter and the longer he waited the more passionately he hoped to see her that very night.

He turned over in his mind what he wanted to say to her, so as to be ready when she came. Should he speak gently? Why not? 'Farewell, Angiolina. I tried to save you and you have made a laughing-stock of me.' Mocked at by her, mocked at by Balli! He was suddenly full of impotent rage. This roused him from his lethargy, but it seemed to him that he suffered less from the agitation and fury that now possessed him than at the thought of his indifference of a few moments ago, a state of captivity within himself which had been forced on him by Balli. Soft words to Angiolina? No, no. Short and sharp and cold. 'I knew all the time what you were like. I am not the least surprised. Ask Balli. Good-bye.'

He started walking in order to calm himself, for the thought of those cold words seemed to burn him. They were not insulting enough! Words like that were only insulting to himself; he felt himself grow giddy. In a case like this one must kill, he thought, not talk. A great fear of himself helped to calm him. He would be just as ridiculous if he killed her, he said to himself, as if he had really thought of murdering her. He had not, of course; but once he had reassured himself about this, it amused him to picture himself avenged by Angiolina's death. Such a vengeance as that would make him forget all the wrong she had done him. He would be able to weep for her sincerely afterwards, and he was so overcome by emotion at the thought that tears actually came into his eyes.

It occurred to him that he ought to adopt the same system with Angiolina as he had with Balli. These two enemies of his ought to be treated in the same way. He should tell her that he was not giving her up because she had betrayed him – he expected that – but because she had chosen such a disgusting individual as his rival. He could not kiss her again where the umbrella-maker had kissed her. So long as it was a question of Balli, of Leardi, or even of Sorniani he had kept one eye shut, but the umbrella-maker! In the dark he practised the scornful smile with which he would utter that word.

Whatever words he pictured himself as addressing to her he was always seized by convulsive laughter. Was he going on talking to her like that all night? In that case it was necessary for him to see her at once. He remembered that Angiolina would probably be returning home along the Via Romagna. If he walked fast he should still be able to catch her up. He had hardly finished thinking this before he set off running, glad to be able to come to a decision which solved his doubts and numbed his thoughts. The rapid movement gave him some relief at first. Then he slowed down again as a new idea struck him. If they were going home that way, wouldn't he be more sure of finding them if he went as far as Via Fabio Severo by way of the Giardino Pubblico, and then went all down the Via Romagna to meet them? He was not afraid of a long walk and would readily have set off on that immense detour; but at that moment he thought he saw Angiolina passing the *caffé Fabris* accompanied by Giulia and a man who must be the umbrella-maker. Even at that distance he recognized the girl by those playful little bounds of hers he liked so much. He stopped running, for he had plenty of time now to catch them up. He could think over quietly, and without agitation, what he wanted to say to her, so as to be ready with it at once. Why must he adorn that adventure with so many strange details and fancies? It was quite an ordinary adventure and a few minutes hence it would be put an end to in the simplest way possible.

When he reached the bottom of the hill in Via Romagna he could no longer see the three individuals he was looking for. They must have passed already. He walked faster, suddenly assailed by a doubt which tired him more than the actual ascent. Supposing it had not been Angiolina? How could he live through the night continually fighting against his own agitation, which as fast as he allayed it began again to torment him?

Although they were now only a few steps away from him he persisted in thinking that those three people were the three he was looking for. A broad, powerfully built man was walking between two women, and was arm in arm with the one he had taken for Angiolina, who now that he saw her closer had nothing characteristic about her way of walking. He looked her full in the face with the calm, ironic expression which he had taken so much trouble to prepare. He was startled to see the unknown face of an old woman, all dried up and wrinkled.

It was a painful awakening. Feeling that he could not at once leave that group to which he had clung with so much hope, it occurred to him to ask them if they had by chance seen Angiolina, and he was already thinking out how he could best describe her to them. He was ashamed to speak! At the first word he said they would at once guess everything. He went on walking at so rapid a pace that it soon developed into a run. He saw stretching out before him a long vista of white road, and remembered that when he had turned the corner he would see another and then another. Interminable! But he must set his doubts at rest, and for the moment the question was whether Angiolina was on that road or elsewhere.

He again thought over the things he had planned to say to her that night or the following morning. Speaking with great dignity – the more his agitation increased the calmer he imagined himself to be – with great dignity he would tell her that if she had wanted to get rid of him she had only to say one word, one single word. There was no need to make a mock of him. 'I should have withdrawn at once. There was no need to chase me from my post by an umbrella-maker.' He repeated this short sentence several times, altering a word here and there, and trying to perfect the tone of his voice, which became each time more bitingly ironical. He stopped when he perceived that by dint of trying to find the exact expression he was beginning to shout.

In order to avoid the thick mud in the middle of the road he crossed over to the gravel at the side, but he took a false step on the uneven surface and in trying to save himself from falling bruised his hands against the rough wall. The physical pain excited him, and stimulated his desire for vengeance. He felt himself more mocked at than ever, as if his fall had been a fresh blow struck at him by Angiolina. He again thought he saw her walking along some way in front of him. A reflection, a shadow, a movement, everything assumed the form and expression of the phantom he was pursuing. He began running to catch her up, no longer calmly ironical as when climbing the hill of Via Romagna, but with the firm intention of treating her brutally. Fortunately it was not she, and his tortured soul felt that all the violence to which he had been on the point of abandoning himself was now directed against himself; it took his breath away and deprived him of every possibility of calm, temperate thought. He bit one of his hands like a madman.

He had reached the middle of the long road. Angiolina's house stood huge and solitary, a great barracks with its white face lit up by the moon. It was shut up and wrapped in silence; it seemed deserted.

He sat down on a low wall and forced himself to think out some arguments which should calm him. To see him in that state one might have thought he had learned that evening that he was betrayed by a woman whom he had till then believed faithful to him. He looked at his wounded hands: these wounds were not there before, he thought. She had never treated him like that before. Perhaps all the pain and agony he was suffering now were a prelude to his recovery. But he said to himself sorrowfully: If I had once possessed her I should not suffer so much. If he had desired her, actively desired her, she would have been his. Instead he had tried to put into the relationship an idealism which had ended by making it ridiculous even in his own eyes.

He got up from the wall quieter but more depressed than when he had sat down. The whole fault was his. It was he who was an abnormal, unhealthy creature, not Angiolina. And this depressing conclusion accompanied him all the way home.

After he had stopped once more to inspect a woman who had a figure like Angiolina, he had sufficient strength of mind to shut the door behind him. It was all over for that evening. The circumstance he had hoped for up to that moment could no longer happen to him there.

He lit a candle and went with slow steps towards his room, so as to put off as long as possible the moment when he would be lying stretched out on his bed with nothing further to do, and no hope of being able to sleep.

He seemed to hear someone talking in Amalia's room. At first he thought it was an hallucination. There were no excited cries; it sounded like two people engaged in quiet conversation. He opened a crack of the door very cautiously and could no longer have any doubt about it. Amalia was talking to someone: 'Yes, yes, that is exactly what I want too.' She had spoken the words in a calm clear voice.

He seized his candle and hurried back. Amalia was alone. She was dreaming. She was lying on her back with one of her thin arms crossed behind her head, the other lying on the grey coverlet beside her. Her waxen hand looked charming on the grey. Directly the light fell on her face she became silent, and her breathing grew less quiet; she several times made an effort to get out of the position she was in, as if it were an uncomfortable one.

He took the light back to his own room and began to undress. At last his thoughts had taken a new direction. Poor Amalia! Life could not be very happy for her either. Her dream which, as far as he could judge from her voice, had been a happy one, was only her natural reaction to the melancholy reality.

Soon afterwards the same words, pronounced very distinctly and calmly, so that one could hear each syllable of them, reached him again from the next room. There was no apparent connexion between the separate words, but there could be no doubt that she was talking to someone she loved very much. There was a great sweetness both in the sound and the sense, a great condescension. For the second time she was saying that the other person – the one she imagined she was talking to – had guessed her wishes: 'Is that what we shall do? I could never have hoped it!' Then there was an interval, broken by indistinct sounds which showed that the dream was still going on, and again some words expressing the same idea. He stood there a long while listening. Just as he was going away again a complete sentence arrested him: 'Everything can be allowed on a honeymoon.'

Poor girl! She was dreaming of getting married. He felt ashamed of spying on his sister's secrets like that, and closed the door. He would try and forget having heard those words. But his sister must surely suspect him of knowing something about those dreams of hers.

When he was in bed his thoughts did not turn again to Angiolina. For a long time he lay listening to the words which reached him from the other room, muffled and calm and gentle. He was so tired that his mind was incapable of holding any emotion, and he felt almost happy. Once his relation with Angiolina was broken off he would be able to devote himself wholly to his sister. He would live for duty alone.

7

HE woke a few hours later in full daylight, and was immediately aware of what had taken place the evening before. But he was not at once acutely conscious of his sufferings, and he flattered himself that what had so distressed him was the impossibility of taking an immediate vengeance on his betrayer, rather than the fact of his having been betrayed. In a very short time now she would experience his anger and find herself abandoned. Once he had given vent to his indignation, what was now the chief bond between them would be dissolved.

He went out without saying a word to his sister. He would very soon be back again to cure her of the dreams he had spied upon unawares.

A light wind was blowing and as he went along the Giardino Pubblico he was conscious of a certain fatigue in walking uphill against the wind, but it was a different kind of fatigue from the agonizing weariness of the night before. It was a lovely fresh morning and he was glad to be obliged to take some muscular exercise in the open air.

He never gave a thought to what he was going to say to Angiolina. He was too sure of himself to need any preparation, too sure that he was at last going to strike her down and then abandon her.

Angiolina's mother came to open the door. She led him along to her daughter's room, and as Angiolina was still dressing in the next room she offered as usual to keep him company.

This fresh delay even of a few minutes made him suffer again. 'Was Angiolina very late in coming home last night?' he asked, with a vague idea of making a few inquiries.

'She was at a café with Volpini till about midnight,' the old woman answered all in one breath, and her nasal voice made all the words sound as if they were glued together.

'But Volpini surely went away yesterday?' said Emilio, surprised to find mother and daughter in agreement.

'He ought to have gone, but he lost his train and he must be just starting now.'

He did not want to let the old woman see that he did not believe her, and remained silent. Everything was perfectly clear, and there was no possibility of deceiving him or making him doubt the facts. Balli had foreseen the lie they would be certain to invent.

He found no difficulty in greeting Angiolina in front of her mother with the placid face of a contented lover. It even gave him genuine satisfaction. He had caught her at last and this time he was not going to yield to his usual impulse to clear things up at once. He would let her speak first. He would let her run through her whole repertory of lies so that he could show her up in all her baseness.

When they were left alone she placed herself in front of the looking-glass arranging her curls and, without ever turning round to look at him, told him all about the evening before in the café and how Balli had spied on them. She was laughing merrily all the time, and looked so fresh and rosy that Emilio was almost more indignant at that than at her lies.

She told him that Volpini's unexpected return had annoyed her very much. According to her she had received him with the following remark:

'Aren't you tired yet of worrying me like this?'

She went on talking, apparently in the hope of giving him pleasure. He, on the contrary, was thinking that of the two it was not Volpini who cut the most ridiculous figure. She had to take more trouble when it came to deceiving him, all kinds of ingenious devices and deceptions of which he probably only suspected a very small part. The other had fallen obligingly into the first trap they laid for him; it did not take much to deceive Volpini. If, as seemed likely, Angiolina's intrigues were almost as amusing to her mother as to her, it was probably he whom they laughed at most, while they felt Volpini was still somewhat to be feared.

He was seized by one of those intense fits of anger which sometimes made him tremble and turn pale.

But she went on talking and talking, almost as if it had been her aim to stupefy him and as if she were now giving him time to recover himself.

Why be so miserable? Why revolt against the laws of

nature? Angiolina was a lost woman even in her mother's womb. This complicity between her and her mother was what revolted him most.

It was useless to punish her: she did not even deserve it; she was only the victim of a universal law. The naturalist who somewhere lay hidden in him revived, but he could not at once give up his desire for vengeance.

Angiolina must at last have become conscious that his demeanour was odd. She turned to him and said with a reproachful air: 'You haven't given me a kiss yet.'

'I shall never kiss you again,' he replied quietly, his eyes fixed on those red lips which he was renouncing for ever. He could think of nothing else to say, and stood up. It had not even entered his head that he could go away at once, for that short sentence could surely not be all, it was not at all a sufficient recompense for suffering such as his. But he wished to make her think that he was going to leave her for ever with those words. It would indeed have been a very dignified way of putting an end to that vile connexion.

She at once guessed everything, and thinking that he did not want to give her time to defend herself she added in an expressionless voice: 'It was wrong of me to tell you that man was Volpini. He wasn't! It was Giulia who begged me to say so. It was for her that he was there with us. She has several times come with us and it was only fair that I should go with her just for once. It seems funny, but he is head over heels in love with her; even more than you are with me.'

She stopped short. She saw by the look on his face that he did not for a moment believe her, and it was mortifying to her vanity to have told him two such patent lies. She rested both her hands on the back of the nearest chair and was evidently exerting a great muscular effort to keep hold of it. Her face was entirely devoid of all expression, and she kept on staring obstinately at a grey stain on the wall. That must be what she looked like when she was suffering.

Then he experienced a strange pleasure in showing

her that he knew absolutely everything, and that in his eyes she was utterly ruined. A short while before a few words would have been almost enough to satisfy him, but now Angiolina's sad embarrassment made him talkative. He was conscious of experiencing an enormous sensation of pleasure. On the sentimental side it was the first time that Angiolina had given him complete satisfaction. Standing there in silence she was the perfect embodiment of a false but loving mistress convicted of infidelity.

Soon afterwards, however, there was a moment when the conversation threatened to become almost comic. In order to wound her, he enumerated the things she had taken at the café at the expense of the umbrella-maker. 'Giulia had quite a small glass of a transparent liqueur, you had a cup of chocolate with any amount of cakes.'

Thereupon she, alas! began to defend herself energetically, and her face flushed with what was no doubt intended to resemble offended virtue. At last she had been accused of something of which she was innocent, and Emilio saw that Balli must have been mistaken on that point.

'Chocolate! I who simply can't endure it! The idea of my drinking chocolate! I took a tiny glass of something, I really don't remember what, and I didn't even drink it.' She put so much energy into this assertion that she could not possibly have put more if she had been trying to prove her own perfect innocence. But there was present in the tone of her voice a certain note of vexation, almost as if she deplored not having eaten more, since her abstinence had not sufficed to save her in Emilio's eyes. It really was to him that she had made that sacrifice.

He made a violent effort to obliterate that false note, which bade fair to spoil his last farewell.

'Enough, enough,' he said contemptuously. 'I have only one thing more to say to you. I loved you very much and that alone ought to have given me the right to be treated differently. When a girl allows a young man to tell her he loves her she belongs to him and is not free to do as she likes.' This phrase was rather feeble, but it expressed exactly what he wanted to say, which is a great deal to expect of a lover's reproach. He had in fact no other claim to plead save the fact that he had told her he loved her.

Feeling that speech would betray him in a situation like the present, because of his tendency to analyse everything, he immediately had recourse to what he knew to be a more forcible argument: abandoning her. A little earlier, when he was revelling in Angiolina's distress, he had thought that he might stay with her till much later. He had hoped that the scene would develop very differently. Now he felt a danger hanging over him. He had himself alluded to his own lack of rights, and it was only too likely that she, when she ran short of arguments, might accept his own suggestion and ask him: 'What have you done for me, that you dare exact of me that I should conform to your wishes?' He decided to fly from this danger: 'I will wish you good-bye,' he said gravely. 'When I have recovered my peace of mind it will be possible for us to meet again. But it will be better that we should not see each other for a long time to come.'

He went away, but not without having admired her one last time as she stood there all pale, her eyes wide open, half from fear and half, perhaps, from doubt as to whether she should tell him another lie and try to make him stop with her. He left the house with such intensity of purpose that his impetus carried him far on his way. But as he walked on with the same air of unalterable resolution he bitterly lamented not being able to go on watching her in her grief. The cry of agony which had burst from her when she saw him going away still rang in his ears, and he went on listening to it so that he might imprint it still better on his mind. He felt he must always preserve it. It was the most precious gift she had ever made him.

Ridicule could not touch him any more, at least not in regard to Angiolina. Whatever her life was to be in future, it would be many years before she could forget the man who had loved her not simply as an object of his lust, but with his whole soul, so that the first wrong she had done him had wounded him so much that he had renounced her altogether. Who knows whether such a memory as that might not suffice to save her? The anguish in Angiolina's voice had entirely banished from his mind any scientific conclusion he had been intending to draw from the case.

Oh no! he felt it impossible to go and shut up his agitation in an office. He returned home, intending to go straight to bed. In the quiet of his own room, with his body at rest, he would be able to prolong his enjoyment of the scene with Angiolina, as if it were still actually going on. The excitement of mind he felt that day would probably have led him to confide in his sister, but he remembered the discovery he had made the previous night and decided to say nothing to her, feeling her a long way removed from him and entirely occupied with her own desires. The time would certainly come when he would again surround his sister with every care, but he felt that he wanted first to devote a few days to himself and to his own passion. To shut himself up indoors and expose himself to Amalia's questions seemed to him intolerable; he altered his plan. He told his sister he was not very well, but that he was going out because he thought the open air would do him good.

She did not in the least believe him when he said he was unwell. Hitherto she had always guessed aright the phase through which Emilio's love-affair was passing at the moment; today for the first time she made a mistake and believed that he was staying away from the office in order to spend the whole day with Angiolina, because his face wore a look of satisfaction, which she had not seen on it for a long time. She asked no questions: she had often tried to get him to confide in her and the only grudge she bore him now was that he had always refused.

When Emilio found himself out in the road again, alone, with Angiolina's cry of anguish still in his ears, it was all he could do not to return to her on the spot.

What could he possibly do idle all day by himself in his present state of agitation, which was in fact only a state of acute desire, of impatient expectation of something unforeseen which might come to him any moment, a hope of something new such as he had never had from Angiolina before?

He could not possibly go to look for Balli, and he hoped very much that he would not meet him. He was afraid of him; in fact this fear was the only painful sensation of which he was conscious.

He said to himself that his fear sprang from the knowledge that he could not have imitated Balli's calm when he had been obliged to leave Margherita.

He turned his steps towards the Corso. It was possible that Angiolina might take that route on the way to her work at the Deluigis. He had not had the time to ask her where she was going, but he was certain she would not be staying at home. If he met her he would bow to her distantly but politely. Had he not told her that when he had recovered from his indignation he should be glad to be friends with her again? Oh, how he longed for that moment to come quickly, quickly, so that he might be with her again. He looked round him so as to be sure of seeing her in good time supposing he were to meet her.

'Hullo, Brentani! How are you? So you are still alive, though one never sees you now.' It was Sorniani, prosperous as ever, though with the same yellow complexion. His face was always unhealthy-looking, and his eyes were by contrast unusually lively, whether from vivacity or restlessness it would have been hard to say.

When Brentani turned towards him, Sorniani stared at him with some surprise. 'Aren't you well? You are looking so odd.'

It was not the first time that Sorniani had told him he looked ill; no doubt he projected something of his own jaundiced complexion on to the faces of those he was talking to.

Emilio was glad to be told he looked ill; it gave him an excuse for complaining of something other than his own unfortunate love-affair, since he was unable to talk about that. 'I seem to have something wrong with my stomach,' he said dismally. 'It isn't that which bothers me so much, but that I feel so dreadfully low-spirited in consequence.' He remembered having heard it said that stomach-ache produced depression. Then he proceeded to dilate on his low spirits, for he found it easier to analyse aloud.

'It is very curious. I should never have believed it was possible for a bodily disorder to become unconsciously transformed into a moral sensation without one being conscious of it. What depresses me is that I feel completely indifferent about everything. I believe that if all the houses in the Corso were suddenly to begin dancing, I should not even look at them. And if they threatened to fall on me and crush me I should take no steps to prevent it.' He stopped suddenly on seeing a young woman approach who bore a slight resemblance to Angiolina. 'It is a lovely day today, isn't it? I imagine that the sky is blue, and that the air is warm and sunny. I can grasp it with my mind but I cannot feel it. To me everything looks and feels grey.'

'I have never been as ill as all that,' said Sorniani, in a tone of satisfaction which it was impossible for him to disguise, 'and now I believe I am completely cured.' He went on to talk of various drugs from which he expected marvels.

Emilio suddenly felt a great longing to escape from this tiresome fellow, who could not even listen to what was said to him. He put out his hand without a word and made as though he were about to leave him. Sorniani took his hand but did not let it go at once. He asked instead:

'How is your love-affair getting on?'

Emilio pretended not to understand. 'Which love-affair?'

'Why, that blonde, Angiolina.'

'Ah, yes,' said Emilio casually. 'I broke with her long ago.'

'I'm very glad to hear that,' cried Sorniani with great warmth, and coming still nearer. 'She wasn't the sort of woman for a young man like you, especially if you're so delicate. She sent poor Merighi quite off his head, and since then half the town have amused themselves with her.'

The expression wounded Brentani. If that horrid little yellow man had not hit the mark in alluding to Angiolina's amorous propensities he would have paid no attention to his chatter, but now everything suddenly wore an air of startling veracity. He protested, however, saying that judging by the little he knew of her he should say she was quite a serious young woman, and he succeeded in spurring on Sorniani to tell his tale. Looking more bilious than ever – his stomach too, no doubt, had something to do with it – he proceeded to pour his supply of gossip into the ears of the rash young man who had provoked him.

Serious? Angiolina? Why, even before Merighi came upon the scene she must already have begun to make experiments with the other sex. When she was quite a child you would see her trotting about the streets of the Old Town always with some boys at her heels – she preferred them without moustaches – long after she ought to have been at home. Merighi fortunately saw how things were going, and carried her off to the New Town which remained in future the scene of her activities. She let herself be seen about everywhere, always on the arm of one of the richest young men of the place, and always with the same trustful, confiding air of a newly married bride. He ran through the list of names which Brentani knew already, from Giustini to Leardi, all of whose photographs he had seen displayed to so much advantage on the wall of Angiolina's bedroom.

There was not a new name amongst them. It seemed unlikely that Sorniani should invent with such accuracy. An agonizing doubt drove the colour to Emilio's cheeks; surely in the end Sorniani would name himself among Angiolina's lovers. He continued to listen to him with great anxiety, while he kept his right fist clenched ready to knock him down if he heard the dreaded name.

But Sorniani broke off with the question: 'Are you feeling unwell?'

'No,' said Emilio, 'I am quite all right.' He stopped, wondering whether it was worth while to let him go on chattering any more.

'But I am sure you are not feeling well. You have changed colour two or three times.'

Emilio opened his clenched hands. This was not a case for blows. 'I assure you I am quite well.' Hit Sorniani? That would be a fine vengeance! He had better begin by hitting himself. Oh, how he loved her! He confessed it to himself, with a degree of anguish which he had never known before. In a fit of cowardice he said to himself that he would go back to her, and at once. That morning he had gone full of resolution to avenge himself. He had upbraided her and then left her. What an intelligent thing to do! He had only punished himself. They had all possessed her except himself. So he was the only one of them all who was really ridiculous. He remembered that in a few days time Volpini would be coming to enjoy her in anticipation of his marriage, as they had agreed; and he himself must just choose that moment to get angry about things which he had always suspected. What would Angiolina do after having given herself to the tailor? It was only too obvious that having given herself to him in order to betray him more easily, she would betray him with others, seeing that Emilio had just that moment deserted her. She was lost to him. He saw her whole future spread out before his eyes exactly as if it were all happening a few steps away from him on the Corso. He saw her leaving Volpini's arms in disgust and flying at once in search of a refuge from such an infamous embrace. She would certainly be faithless to him then, and this time the right would be on her side.

But it was not only the fact that he had never possessed her which tormented him. Up to that moment he had found comfort in the cry of anguish which he had caused her to utter. But what could a cry like that signify in the life of a woman who had experienced far greater delight as well as far greater pain in the arms of others? No, it was impossible for him to go back on what he had done. He had only to conjure up what Balli would say about it, to reject any temptation of that sort.

He thought that but for the presence of that stern judge at his side he should not care what became of his dignity now that he realized that in the effort to sustain it he had only bound all his thoughts and all his desires more abjectly to Angiolina.

A certain time had already elapsed since his conversation with Sorniani and the tumult which the latter's words had aroused in his breast had not yet subsided.

Perhaps she would make some attempt to get into touch with him again. In that case his dignity would not prevent him from receiving her with open arms. But it would not be the same as before. He should want to get at once to the reality – that is to say, to possessing her. Down with all pretence! 'I know you have been the mistress of all these –' he would shout the names at her – 'but I love you all the same. Be mine too, and tell me the truth so that I may no longer have any doubts.' The truth? Even when he was picturing the most brutal frankness he still idealized Angiolina. The truth? Could she tell it? Did she know how to? Supposing that Sorniani had only told part of the truth, lying must be so much a part of her nature that she could never escape from it. He forgot what at certain moments he had perceived so clearly, namely, that he had worked hard to see in Angiolina exactly what she was not, that it was he who had invented the lie.

Because I did not recognize, he continued to himself that that lie was the only thing which made me ridiculous. Now that he knew everything and could confront her with it point by point there was no further fear of his making himself ridiculous. Everyone is free to love what takes his fancy. He pictured himself repeating all this to Balli.

The wind had gone down and the day had assumed

quite a spring-like character. If he had been in any other state of mind, to be free on such a day as this would have filled him with joy, but what was the good of his liberty if he could not go and see Angiolina?

Yet he could have found various excuses for going to her immediately. If for nothing else, he could have gone to administer a fresh rebuke. For up to that moment he had never suspected the existence of those soft-cheeked boys who had preceded Merighi; he had heard of them for the first time today from Sorniani. 'No!' he said aloud. 'Such weakness as that would put me completely in her power. I must have patience for ten days or a fortnight. She will not wait for me to come to her!' Patience! But meanwhile how was he going to spend that first morning?

Leardi! The tall, strong, handsome youth, so fair and boyish in complexion, so virile in body, was walking along the Corso with his usual serious air, dressed in an overcoat of some light material exactly suitable to the mild winter's day. As a rule Brentani and Leardi scarcely bowed to each other, both of them being very proud though for totally different reasons. Emilio, face to face with that elegant youth, could not forget that he was a writer of a certain reputation; while the other thought that he could treat him *de haut en bas* because he was less correctly dressed and because he had never met him at any of the fashionable houses in the town, where he on the contrary was received with open arms. He wished, however, that his superiority should be recognized by Brentani as well, and responded graciously to his salute. He was on the whole more gratified than surprised when he saw Brentani advancing towards him with out-stretched hand, and received him warmly.

Brentani had yielded to an irresistible impulse. As he could not go to Angiolina the only thing that remained for him to do was to tack himself on to somebody who in his thoughts was continually associated with her. 'So you have taken advantage of the fine weather too, I see, to go for a walk.'

'I'm just taking a stroll before luncheon,' said Leardi, accepting Brentani's company.

Emilio spoke of the fine weather, of his own slight indisposition and of Sorniani's illness. He went on to say that he did not much like the latter because he was always boasting about his successes with women. He spoke with great fluency, for he had a strange presentiment of being near to someone who was of vital importance in his life and he would have liked every word he uttered to contribute towards winning his friendship. He watched him anxiously when he got on to the theme of Sorniani's success with women. Leardi did not move a muscle, though Emilio had expected to see him smile a superior smile. If he had smiled in that connexion Emilio would at once have regarded it as a confession that he was one of Angiolina's lovers.

But Leardi was talkative as well. He was evidently anxious to display his gifts to Brentani. He complained that one always met the same faces on the Corso, and said in this connexion that he thought it deplorable how little life and artistic activity there was in Trieste. The town did not suit him at all, he said.

Brentani, meanwhile, was seized with a violent desire to make him talk about Angiolina. He hardly listened to the other's conversation, only picking out a word here and there, almost mechanically, which had a sound that might remind him of Angiolina's name, so that he could invent an excuse for introducing her into the conversation. Unluckily he could not find any, but suddenly irritated beyond endurance at having to listen to all that pretentious twaddle, produced with so much nasal emphasis, he interrupted him without ceremony, pointing out with feigned surprise an elegant woman who bore, in fact, no resemblance whatever to Angiolina. 'Look, look,' he said; 'there is Signorina Angiolina Zarri.'

'Nonsense,' replied Leardi, annoyed at the interruption; 'I saw her face, it is not the least like her.'

He again began talking about theatres which hardly anyone went to, and society women who were too dull for words, but Brentani had made up his mind not to submit any longer to this lecture, and asked abruptly: 'Do you know Signorina Zarri?'

'Why, do you know her too?' asked the other in a tone of unfeigned surprise.

It was a moment of agonizing doubt for Brentani. He saw clearly that he could not make a man like Leardi talk against his will, however cunning he might be. Since it was so important to him to dissipate every lie which might prevent him seeing Angiolina as she really was, wouldn't it be better if he opened his heart to Leardi and implored him to tell the truth? It was only the instinctive antipathy he felt for Leardi which prevented him from doing so. 'Yes, a friend introduced her to me a few days ago.'

'I was a friend of Merighi's. Years ago I used to know her intimately.'

'Very intimately, eh?' Brentani insinuated, in a perfectly calm voice, and keeping his face under complete control.

'Oh, no,' said Leardi, very gravely. 'How could you imagine such a thing!' He played his part very well, only allowing himself this expression of surprise.

Brentani understood at once the rôle which Leardi had chosen, and did not insist. He behaved as though he had forgotten his indiscreet question of a few minutes earlier, and said with the utmost gravity: 'Tell me something about what happened with Merighi. Why did he give her up?'

'In consequence of his financial embarrassment. He wrote and told me that he had been obliged to give Angiolina her freedom. Which reminds me that I heard only a few days ago that she had got engaged again, to a tailor, I believe.'

He *believed*, did he? Oh, nobody could have acted better. But to act like that, to force himself to play a part so carefully thought out and studied with such pains, and evidently *à contre-coeur*, – for otherwise why should it be so difficult to get him to speak about Angiolina? –

he must have a very good reason for wishing to keep his knowledge secret; evidently he had renewed his connexion with her quite recently.

Leardi had already passed on to something else, and soon afterwards Emilio left him. In order to escape he was again obliged to plead a slight indisposition, and Leardi saw him looking so haggard that he believed in it, and expressed a sympathetic interest for which Brentani felt compelled to thank him. But in reality how he hated him! He longed to be able to spend that whole day, at least, in spying on him; he felt sure that he would track him down at last to Angiolina's house. He ground his teeth in his insane rage, and almost immediately afterwards reproached himself with bitter irony for the very anger he had felt. Angiolina was certainly betraying him today, of that he could be certain; perhaps with people he had never heard of. How superior that empty-headed idiot Leardi was to himself! To keep calm! That was the true art of living. 'Yes,' thought Brentani, and he felt he was saying something which ought to strike shame not only into his own heart, but into the hearts of all the elect among the human race – 'it is the wealth of images in my brain which makes me inferior.' If, for instance, Leardi had thought that Angiolina was betraying him, he would have been incapable of representing her to himself in an image as full of colour and life and movement as he himself did when picturing her with Leardi. Why, directly the naked body was uncovered which he had only dreamed of, the commonest porter would find immediate satiety and peace of mind. It was a short, brutal act; a mockery of all his dreams, of all his desires. But when wrath darkened the dreamer's sight the vision disappeared, leaving in his ears a mocking echo of loud laughter.

At dinner Amalia could not help noticing that whatever it was which agitated Emilio, it was by no means something joyous. He shouted at her because the dinner was not ready; he was hungry and had to go out directly after dinner. It was a torture to him to eat after making such a compromising statement; and when he had finished he went on sitting there before his empty plate, undecided what to do. At last he made up his mind; he was not going to see Angiolina that day; in fact, he would never go near her again. The strongest emotion he felt at that moment was his sorrow at having hurt his sister's feelings. She went about looking sad and pale. He wanted to ask her pardon, but he did not dare. He felt that if he were to say a single word to her he should break down and cry like a child. At last he said abruptly, but evidently wanting to make it up: 'You ought to go out; it is such a lovely day.' She made no reply but left the room. Then he got angry again. 'Surely I am wretched enough? She ought to have understood the state of mind I am in. My kind suggestion that she should go out ought to have been enough to make her nice to me and not go on distressing me with her resentment.'

He felt tired. He lay down in his clothes and fell at once into a state of torpor which did not, however, deaden his misery or bring forgetfulness. Once he raised his head to wipe the tears from his eyes, and thought bitterly that it was Amalia who was responsible for those tears. Then he forgot everything.

When he awoke he found that night was falling, one of those melancholy sunsets at the close of a lovely winter's day. He sat up on his bed, still undecided as to what he should do. Often he used to study at that hour, but now his books looked down from their shelves in vain. All those titles spoke of something dead and gone and quite incapable of making him forget for a single instant the painful life-struggle which was still being waged in his breast.

He looked into the dining-room next door to his own room and saw Amalia sitting by the window bending over her embroidery frame. With forced gaiety he asked her affectionately: 'Have you forgiven me for flaring up like that today?'

She only raised her eyes for a moment. 'Don't let us

talk about it any more,' she said sweetly, and went on with her work.

He had expected her to reproach him, and was disappointed to find her so calm. So everyone around him was calm except himself? He sat down beside her and remained there for a long time admiring the deft way in which her needle drove the silk in and out over the design. He tried to find something else to say, but could not.

And she asked no questions. His love, which had caused such an upheaval in her life, his love which at first she had rebelled against so much, no longer made her suffer at all. Once more Emilio put the question to himself:

'Why did I, in fact, abandon Angiolina?'

8

BALLI had proposed to himself to complete his friend's cure. That same evening he came to supper with Emilio. At first he did not betray any anxiety to discover what had taken place and it was only once when Amalia had left the room that he asked casually, while continuing to smoke and look up at the ceiling: 'Did you teach her whom she had to deal with?'

Emilio said yes in a rather boastful tone of voice, but would have been hard put to it to utter a single other word in the same tone.

Amalia came back almost immediately. She told of the slight dispute she had had with her brother at mid-day. She said it was very unjust to blame a woman because the dinner was not ready. It depended on the heat of the oven and the thermometer had not been introduced yet into the kitchen. 'But,' she added, smiling affectionately at her brother, 'he was not responsible for what he said. He came home in such a bad temper that if he had not found an outlet somehow he would have made himself quite ill.'

Balli gave no sign of wishing to connect Emilio's ill humour with the events of the previous evening. 'I was in a shocking temper today myself,' he said, in order to keep the conversation on a light level.

Emilio protested that he had been in the best of humours. 'Don't you remember how jolly I was this morning?'

Amalia had told the story of their quarrel as if it were a subject for mirth; it was evident that she had mentioned it only in order to amuse Balli. She had forgotten that she had been in any way wounded by it, and did not even remember that Emilio had begged her pardon. He felt very much offended by this forgetfulness on her part.

When the two men were alone together in the street, Balli said: 'See how free we both of us are now; isn't it much nicer like this?' and he put his arm through his friend's and pressed it affectionately.

But Emilio could not feel like that about it. He realized that an unusual show of affection was expected of him, and said: 'Of course it is better like this, but it will be some time before I am able properly to appreciate the new state of things. At the moment I feel very desolate even when I am with you.' Without being asked he then proceeded to relate his visit that morning to Via Fabio Severo. He did not say that he had been there the night before too. He spoke of the tone of anguish in Angiolina's voice. 'That was the one thing which moved me. It was hard to leave her just at the very moment when I felt she loved me.'

Balli became unusually serious: 'Preserve that memory,' he said, 'and never see her again. But remember as well the state of jealousy into which she threw you, and you will no longer feel any desire to see her again.'

Emilio was sincerely moved by the affection which Balli showed him. 'All the same,' he said, 'I have never suffered so much from jealousy as now.' Planting himself in front of Stefano he said in a deep voice: 'Promise always to tell me anything that you ever hear about her. But don't ever try and see her – never, never – and if you should ever meet her out of doors I want you to tell me at once. Promise me that faithfully.'

Balli hesitated a moment; it seemed to him so strange to be expected to make a promise like that.

'I am sick with jealousy, nothing else but jealousy. I am jealous of the others too, but most of all of you. I have got accustomed to the umbrella-maker, but I shall never get accustomed to you.' There was not the faintest touch of humour in his voice; he was trying to arouse pity so that he might the more easily get Balli to promise what he wanted. If he had refused, Emilio had made up his mind to rush round to Angiolina at once. He did not want his friend to be able to profit by a state of affairs for which he himself had been largely responsible. There was a threatening look in his eyes, which he kept fixed on Stefano.

Balli was not slow to guess what was passing in Emilio's mind, and he felt a profound pity for him. He promised him solemnly to do as he wanted. Then, in the hope of distracting Brentani's thoughts a little, he said that he regretted all the same not being allowed to see Angiolina. 'I have long wanted to make a sketch of her, because I thought you would like to have it.' For a moment his eyes took on a dreamy look, as if he were mentally drawing the outlines of her figure.

Emilio at once took alarm. In childish anxiety he reminded Balli of his promise of a few moments ago. 'You have promised me now, you can't go back on it. Try to find your inspiration elsewhere.'

Balli laughed heartily. But he was startled by this fresh proof of the violence of Emilio's passion and said: 'Who could have foreseen that an adventure like that would ever take such an important place in your life? If it were not so painful for you, it would really be rather ridiculous.'

Then Emilio began lamenting his sad fate with an irony of self-analysis which removed from it every trace of the ridiculous. He said that he wanted all his friends to know how he looked at life. In theory he considered it to be without any serious content, and he had in fact never believed in any of the forms of happiness which had been offered him; he had never believed in them, and he could truly say that he had never pursued happiness. But how much less easy it was to escape suffering! In a life deprived of all serious content even Angiolina became serious and important.

That first evening Balli's friendship was of great service to Emilio. The sympathy which Balli felt for him helped to calm him considerably. In the first place he could be sure that for that moment at least Stefano and Angiolina were not together; and then he had a gentle nature which was always in need of tender treatment. Since the previous evening he had been seeking in vain for someone to lean on. It was perhaps this lack of support which had allowed him to fall so hopelessly under the power of his own feelings. He would have been able to make a stand against them if he had had an opportunity of explaining himself and of reasoning about his feelings, and the necessity of listening to someone else would have forced him to master his agitation.

He returned home in a much quieter frame of mind than he had gone out. His obstinacy, which he was sometimes inclined to boast of as a source of strength, had been exorcized. He would not go and see Angiolina unless she asked him to do so. He could wait, and their relationship could not and must not be resumed on his side by an act of submission.

But sleep would not come. In his vain efforts to woo it, his agitation increased again as it had done during the previous evening. His excited fancy built up the whole fabric of a dream in which he was betrayed by Balli. Yes, Balli had betrayed him. Only a short while ago he had confessed to having wanted to get Angiolina to sit for a sketch. Now, surprised in his studio by Emilio, while he was copying her half-naked, he remembered his former confession and begged Emilio to forgive him. And

Emilio had found words full of burning hatred and contempt to punish him with. They were very different from those he had addressed to Angiolina, for here he had every right on his side: first of all their long friendship and then the solemn promise Balli had made him. And how subtly his words were interwoven! for here at last they were addressed to someone who would understand them as they were spoken.

He was snatched from these dreams by the voice of Amalia, sounding very clear and calm from the next room. He was relieved to have his nightmare phantasy broken and sprang out of bed. He put his ear to the keyhole and listened. For a long time he could make no sense of the words; he could only hear that they were spoken with great tenderness. The dreamer again seemed to be desiring something which the other person desired too; it seemed to Emilio as if she wanted to give even more than was asked of her: she wanted the other person to insist. It was obviously a dream of submission. Was it perhaps the same as on the previous night? The poor woman had built up a second life for herself; night bestowed on her the small degree of happiness which day denied.

Stefano! She had pronounced Balli's Christian name. 'She too!' thought Emilio bitterly. How was it that he had never noticed before? Amalia only became animated when Balli was there. And suddenly he realized that she had always offered the sculptor the same submission that she now offered him in her dreams. Her grey eyes shone with a new light when they rested on Balli. There was no longer any possible doubt; Amalia was in love too, and in love with Balli.

Unfortunately, when Emilio went back to bed he could not get to sleep. He remembered bitterly how Balli had boasted of the love he always aroused in women and how he had said with a self-satisfied smile that the only success he lacked in life was an artistic one. He fell at last into a troubled state between sleeping and waking in which he had the most absurd dreams. Balli took advantage of Amalia's abject submission and refused to make any honourable amends. When the dreamer became fully conscious he did not laugh at himself for those dreams. Between a man so corrupt as Balli and a woman so innocent as Amalia anything was possible. He resolved to undertake to cure Amalia. He would begin by banishing the sculptor from the house; for some time past, through no fault of his own, Balli had been a harbinger of misfortune. If it had not been for him, Emilio's relations with Angiolina would have been tenderer, and not complicated by such bitter jealousy. And the separation would also have been easier for him now.

Emilio's life in the office had become more and more trying. It cost him a great effort to devote sufficient attention to his work. He took advantage of every pretext for leaving his table and spending a few more moments in nurturing and caressing his grief. His mind seemed made for this, and when it was possible for him to cease for a moment from the effort of attending to other things he automatically returned to his pet ideas and filled himself to the brim with them like an empty vessel. It gave him the feeling of an intolerable weight having been lifted from his shoulders. The muscles relaxed and expanded and returned to their natural position. When at last the hour struck for him to leave the office he felt definitely happy, though it lasted for a very short time. At first he would plunge with rapture into his sorrows and desires, which became ever more reasoned and more obvious; he was happy till he suddenly encountered some jealous thought which caused him to tremble with pain.

Balli was waiting for him in the road. 'Well, how are you?'

'Oh, pretty well,' Emilio replied, shrugging his shoulders. 'I have had a horribly trying morning.'

Stefano noticed that he looked pale and depressed, and thought he knew very well what sort of trouble he had been suffering from. He had decided to be very gentle with his friend. He suggested coming to dinner with them, and proposed their going for a walk together in the afternoon.

Emilio's slight hesitation in accepting his offer escaped Balli's notice. He had for a moment entertained the possibility of rejecting Balli's proposal, and telling him at once what he now felt it his duty to tell him. Sooner or later it would be an act of base cowardice on his part to let the fear of losing his friend interfere with saving his sister; the deed which he meditated seemed to him no less than a trial of his own courage. If he delayed, it was only because he thought he might still be deceived as to the real nature of Amalia's feelings. 'Yes, of course, do come,' he said at last. Balli attributed the apparent warmth of his invitation to gratitude, whereas Emilio himself knew that it was due to the pleasure he felt at this opportunity of dissipating his remaining doubt.

And during the meal he was in fact able to acquire all the certainty he needed. How like Amalia was to himself. He felt as if it were actually himself he was watching having dinner with Angiolina. The desire to please produced in her a state of embarrassment which made it impossible for her to behave naturally. He even saw her open her mouth to speak and shut it again without saying a word. How she hung upon Balli's lips! Perhaps she did not even hear what he was saying. She laughed or was grave as if following an involuntary suggestion.

Emilio tried to distract her, but she paid no attention to him. Nor did Balli listen to him either; for though he was unconscious of the sentiment he inspired in the young woman it exercised over him a kind of fascination which he betrayed in the mental excitement he always fell into when he felt himself completely master of someone else. Emilio studied and analysed his friend with perfect coolness. Balli had entirely forgotten the purpose for which he had come. He told stories which Emilio knew already; it was clear that he was only talking for Amalia. They were stories of a kind he had tried already on the unhappy young woman. He was telling her of that reckless, carefree Bohemian life about which she so much loved to hear, with its mingling of violent joys and violent sorrows.

When the two men went out together, the bitter indignation which had so long slumbered in Emilio's breast against his friend suddenly surged up within him; a careless phrase of Balli's caused it to overflow. 'You see what a delightful time we spent together.'

Emilio felt he would have liked to insult him. Delightful time indeed! Certainly not for him. For him it would rank among his most unpleasant memories, like the times he had spent with Balli and Angiolina. He had in fact suffered from the same painful jealousy now as then. Above all he reproached his friend for not having noticed how silent he had been, for having had so little understanding of his feelings as to think he was enjoying himself. And then how was it possible for him not to notice that Amalia was overcome by morbid embarrassment in his presence and that she sometimes even stammered from excitement? Emilio felt at that moment so lucid as to the nature of his own feelings that he feared it might become clear to Balli too that he was speaking to him about Amalia in order to avenge himself for Balli's behaviour towards Angiolina. He must above all avoid betraying any resentment; he must try to appear in the light of a good paterfamilias moved solely by the desire to protect those dear to him.

He began by telling a lie, but as if he were relating something of no importance whatever. He said that an aged relative had stopped him that morning to inquire if it were true that Balli was engaged to Amalia. That was not all, but Emilio experienced a sense of relief at having said so much. He was now on the direct path to pointing out to Balli that he was not the superior person he believed himself to be, nor the most faithful of friends.

'No! really?' Balli exclaimed in great surprise, and laughing in all innocence.

'Yes, really,' said Emilio with a grimace which was meant to be a smile. 'People are so malicious that there is nothing to do but laugh at them.' He hoped he had implied by this that he found Balli's mirth offensive. 'But you will agree that one must be a little careful, for *we* cannot tolerate that such a thing should be said about poor Amalia.' The plural 'we' was meant to imply that Emilio wished to share with Balli the responsibility for what he was about to say. At the same time he raised his voice and spoke with considerable warmth; he could not allow Balli to take lightly a statement which it burned his own lips to make.

Stefano no longer knew what attitude he ought to take up. It could not have happened to him very often in his life to be falsely accused. But now he felt as innocent as a new-born babe. The respect he felt and had always shown for the Brentani family, not to speak of Amalia's ugliness, ought to have been enough to free him from suspicion. He knew Emilio very well and did not believe him capable of being put out by a word which some old relative had let fall; but he noticed a violence and almost a note of hatred in Emilio's voice which startled him. He at once divined the truth. He remembered how for a long time all Emilio's thoughts, his whole life, in fact, had been centred in Angiolina. Were not perhaps the violence and hatred in Emilio's voice to be traced back to his jealousy of Angiolina, though he seemed to be talking about Amalia? 'I didn't think that at our age, your sister's and mine, we should really be thought capable of such folly.' He spoke with some embarrassment. The suggestion did not leave him quite unscathed.

'Well, what can you expect? The world...'

But Balli, who was sceptical about this world of Emilio's, cried out impatiently: 'Oh, that is enough; I understand quite well what you are getting at. Let us talk about something else.'

They were silent awhile. Emilio was afraid to say anything for fear of compromising himself. What was it that Balli understood? Emilio's secret, that is to say his resentment against himself, or Amalia's secret? He looked at his friend and saw that he appeared more excited than his words might have led one to suppose. He was very flushed, and looked straight before him with a troubled expression in his blue eyes. He seemed to be finding it too hot all at once, for he had pushed his hat on to the back of his head, leaving his high forehead bare. He was evidently angry with him; Emilio's devices to wrap up his own resentment in family reasons were clearly insufficient.

Then he was seized with a childish fear of losing his friend. Cut off from Angiolina and Balli he could not have kept watch over them, and sooner or later they would have been sure to meet. He came to a rapid decision, and putting his arm affectionately inside Balli's he said: 'Listen, Stefano. You surely realize that for me to have spoken to you like that there must have been some very strong reason. It is a terrible sacrifice to give up having you in my house.' He was overcome by the fear that he might not succeed in moving his friend.

Balli was appeased at once. 'I believe you,' he said, 'but please don't talk about that old relative any more. It seems odd that you felt it necessary to lie to me, when you had such serious things to say. Tell me frankly all about it.' His agitation having subsided, he at once threw himself again with whole-hearted sympathy into the discussion of Emilio's affairs. What fresh misfortune had overtaken his poor friend?

Emilio blushed to think that he could for a moment have doubted Stefano's conception of friendship. How unjust he had been! He wanted now to remove any shadow that his words might have thrown on his friend's mind. He had given away Amalia's secret; that there could be no hope of saving. 'I am very unfortunate,' he said, hoping by his self-pity to increase the sympathy which he had already divined in Balli's words. He did not tell him that he had overheard his sister dreaming aloud about Stefano; he only spoke of the change which came over Amalia whenever Balli crossed the threshold of their house. When he was not there she seemed ill and tired and absent-minded. They must come to some decision which would cure her.

It was enough to hear this confession from Emilio's lips for Balli to believe it absolutely. He even suspected that Amalia had confided in her brother. Never had she seemed to him so ugly as at that moment. The charm which her apparent kindness had thrown over Amalia's grey face vanished completely. Now she appeared to him aggressive, regardless of her age and appearance. How dreadfully out of place love would look on a face like hers! She was another Angiolina, come to disturb his habits, but an Angiolina who made him shudder. The affectionate sympathy he always felt for Emilio increased as the latter had hoped. Poor fellow! He had to look after an hysterical sister as well.

He begged Emilio's pardon for his short outburst of anger. He was sincere as usual. 'If there hadn't been something like that, which of course I never dreamed of, this would have been the last time we should have met. Just imagine: I thought you were so mad about Angiolina that you couldn't forgive me for having been liked by her, and that you were looking for an excuse to quarrel with me.'

Emilio felt profoundly uncomfortable. Balli had been explaining to him the secret motive of his evil action. He protested energetically, so much so that Balli was obliged to beg his pardon for having suspected him, but in his own heart his protest rang false. For a moment he could think of nothing but Amalia. How strange! Angiolina had a share in his sister's fate. He tried to quiet himself by the thought that he would be able to make it all right in time, by doing all he could to make Balli realize what a fine creature Amalia was, and by devoting all his own loving care to her.

But how was he to give her a proof of his affection in the state he was in at present? That very evening he stood quite a long time in front of the table on which he had hoped to find a letter from Angiolina. He stared at the table as if he hoped to make it bring forth a letter. His longing for Angiolina had grown greater. But why? Even more than the day before he felt how vain and melancholy it was to play at staying away from her. Oh happy Angiolina! She made no one feel remorseful.

When he heard the clear, resonant voice of the dreamer coming from the next room, he was consumed by remorse. What harm would there have been in letting Amalia go on concentrating all her life force in those innocent dreams? It is true that his remorse ended by changing into profound self-pity which made him find relief in a fit of weeping. So for that night at least remorse lulled him to sleep.

9

H o w far superior Amalia was to him! She showed some surprise next day when Balli did not put in an appearance, but it would have been hard to guess from her manner that she minded his not coming. 'Isn't he well?' she asked Emilio, who remembered that she had always worn an air of indifference in talking to him about Stefano.

Nevertheless he did not doubt for a moment that he was right in his judgement about her. He replied 'No' to her question, and had not the courage to say any more. He was seized with intense compassion at the thought that suffering equal to his own was hanging over the head of that frail little creature, without her having the least premonition of it. And it was he who was about to strike her down. His hand had indeed already struck the blow, but the sword was still hanging in mid-air, to fall very soon on her defenceless head and bow it to the ground; her gentle face would soon lose the calm expression which it forced itself to wear no doubt only by an heroic effort. He would have liked to take his sister in his arms and begin to comfort her before that sorrow came upon her. But he could not. He could not, without blushing, so much as pronounce his friend's name in her presence. Henceforth there was a barrier between brother and sister: the wrong done to her by Emilio. He was not yet fully conscious of it; he still thought he would be able to approach his sister at the moment when she would, as she surely must, be looking about her for someone on whom to lean. Then he would only have to open his arms to her; of that he was sure. Amalia was made like him, in that when she suffered she leaned for support on anyone who happened to be with her at the moment. So he let her go on expecting Balli.

It was an expectation which Emilio could not have endured himself; it needed great courage to ask nothing except the usual question: 'Is not Balli coming?' There was always an extra place laid for Balli; now his glass would be slowly put away again in the cupboard which Amalia used as sideboard. The glass was followed soon after by the cup out of which Balli was to have drunk his coffee, and then Amalia would lock the cupboard door. Her movements were perfectly calm but very slow. When her back was turned he ventured to watch her attentively, and then he fancied he could read signs of suffering in each separate token of bodily weakness. Had her shoulders always drooped like that? Had not her thin neck grown much thinner during the last few days?

She came back to the table and sat down beside him, and he thought to himself: 'There! that calm look means she has decided to wait patiently for another twenty-four hours.' He could not help admiring her; he would not have been able to wait even for one night.

'Why has Signor Balli given up coming?' she asked next day as she was putting away the glass. 'I don't think he finds us amusing enough,' replied Emilio after a moment's hesitation. He was resolved to say something which would make Amalia realize Balli's state of mind. She did not seem to pay much heed to his observation, and placed the glass carefully in its usual corner.

Meanwhile he had made up his mind not to leave her with any false hopes. When he saw three cups instead of two on the tray, he said: 'You may as well spare yourself the trouble of preparing coffee for Stefano. I think he probably won't come again for a long time.'

'Why?' she asked, suddenly growing very pale, the cup still in her hand.

He lacked courage to make the speech he had already prepared. 'Because he doesn't want to,' he replied briefly. Wasn't it after all better to let her go on believing what was false, and give her time to get over her grief slowly rather than to startle her into betraying herself by a revelation which she was not yet prepared for? He said he thought Balli was unable to come any more at that hour because he was working terribly hard.

'Terribly hard?' she repeated, turning to the cupboard. The cup slipped from her hand but did not break. She picked it up, wiped it carefully and put it back in its place. Then she sat down by Emilio. 'Another twenty-four hours,' he said to himself.

Next day Emilio could not prevent Balli from coming with him as far as the door of his house. Stefano looked up absent-mindedly at the first-floor windows, but looked down again immediately. He must have caught sight of Amalia at one of the windows, and he had not waved a greeting! Soon afterwards Emilio ventured to look up himself, but if she had been there she must already have withdrawn. He had meant to scold Stefano for not having made any sign to her, but he could not be sure that he had really seen her.

He climbed the stairs with a heavy heart. She must surely have understood.

She was not to be found in the dining-room. She came in soon after, walking very fast. She stopped when she saw him and began doing something to the door which refused to shut. She had evidently been crying. Her eyelids were red and her hair was wet. It was clear that she had been bathing her face so as to remove all traces of tears. She asked no questions, though during the whole meal he felt himself continually on the point of being threatened by one. She was evidently so agitated that she could not pluck up courage to speak. She tried to explain her agitation by saying that she had slept badly. Balli's glass and coffee cup were not put out on the table. Amalia had given up waiting for him.

But Emilio was still waiting. It would have been a great relief to him to see her cry, to hear some sound of grief. But it was a long time before he had that satisfaction. He used to go home every evening divided between hope and dread of finding her in tears, ready to confess her despair, but instead he found her quiet and depressed, and always with the same slow movements of someone who is tired. She apparently did all the work of the house with the same care as usual, and she began talking about it again to Emilio as she used to do in the days after their parents died, when the brother and sister, left alone in the world, had done what they could to beautify their poor home.

It was a nightmare to have that unuttered sorrow always beside him. And her pain must be continually embittered by every kind of doubt. Emilio sometimes even wondered whether she guessed the truth, and shuddered at the thought of having to explain to her why he had done what he did, for his action now seemed to him quite incomprehensible. Sometimes he felt her grey eyes turned on him with a questioning, suspicious air. Oh – there was no sparkle in *those* eyes! They looked gravely and fixedly at things, as if trying to discover the cause for so much suffering. At last he could bear it no longer.

One evening when Balli was engaged – with some woman probably – he had made up his mind to stay with his sister. But it became painful to sit by her in the silence which so often reigned between them, since they could not talk about what filled both their thoughts. He took up his hat to go out.

'Where are you going?' she asked. With her head resting on her arm, she was amusing herself by idly tapping her plate with her fork. The question was enough to make him lose heart to leave her. She needed him. If the evening would be dreary for the two of them together, what would it not be for Amalia alone?

He threw down his hat and said: 'I was going to try and walk off my desperation.' The nightmare vanished immediately. He had had an inspiration. If he could not talk to her about her troubles, he could at least distract her by talking about his own. She had at once stopped tapping her plate and turned round facing him, in order to see what despair looked like on someone else's face.

'Poor boy!' she murmured, seeing how pale and troubled he looked, but unable to guess all the cause of his anxiety. She wanted him to confide in her, and asked: 'Haven't you seen her again since that day?'

It was a real relief to him to open his heart to her. He said he had not seen her once. Out of doors he did nothing else but look for her, though he took care not to let it be seen, and never stopped in places where he knew she was likely to pass at a certain time. But he had never seen her, never. It almost looked as if she avoided being seen in the street since he had left her.

'Yes, that is very likely,' Amalia said, whole-heartedly and devoutly bent on probing her brother's wound, in the hope of healing it.

Emilio could not help laughing at this. It was impossible, he said, for Amalia to picture to herself the stuff of which Angiolina was made. A week had passed since he left her and he could be perfectly certain that she had entirely forgotten him by now. 'Please don't laugh at me,' he said, though he saw she was very far from laughing at him. 'She is made like that.' And he began to tell Angiolina's story. He talked of her frivolity, her vanity, and all the other qualities which had proved so fatal to him, and Amalia sat listening to him in silence, without betraying the least surprise. Emilio thought she was making a study of his love-affair in order to discover in it analogies to her own.

They had passed in this way a delicious half-hour. It seemed as if all cause of division between them had disappeared, or helped now to unite them, for whereas hitherto he had never talked about Angiolina except in order to relieve himself of the burden of his love and desire, now he was doing it solely in order to give his sister pleasure. He felt very tenderly towards Amalia; he fancied that in listening to him she was solemnly assuring him of her forgiveness.

It was his very tenderness which led him to say something that made the evening end very differently. He had finished his story, and without a moment's hesitation he asked: 'And you?' He had really spoken without thinking. After resisting for so long the temptation to ask his sister to confide in him, he yielded to it in a moment of weakness. It had been such a relief to him to confide in her that it seemed only too natural to try to get Amalia to return his confidence.

But Amalia thought otherwise. She stared at him with wide-open, terror-stricken eyes. 'I? I don't understand.' If she had not understood before she must have done so when she saw the embarrassment into which he was thrown at sight of her confusion. 'I think you must be mad!' She had understood, but evidently she was still at a loss to explain to herself how Emilio had succeeded in guessing the secret she had guarded so jealously.

'I asked if you –' stammered Emilio, as disturbed as herself. He hunted round for a falsehood, but Amalia had meanwhile discovered the most obvious explanation, and she blurted it out at once. 'Signor Balli has spoken to you about me.' She positively shouted it at him. Her pain had found utterance. The blood rushed to her cheeks, her lips curled with an expression of the utmost disdain. For a moment she had become strong. In this she was exactly like Emilio. She revived the moment she could transform her pain into anger. She was no longer a weak woman given up to silent despair: she was a fury. But anger made too great demands upon her strength and could not last long. Emilio swore that Balli had never spoken to him about Amalia in such a way as to make him suppose he guessed the nature of her feelings. She did not believe him, but the faint hope which she drew from Emilio's words deprived her of all courage and she began to cry: 'Why doesn't he come and see us any more?'

'It is a mere chance,' said Emilio. 'He will certainly come in a few days' time.'

'He will never come,' cried Amalia, her violence returning with discussion. 'He pretended not to see me.' Her sobs prevented her from saying any more. Emilio ran to her and took her in his arms, but she could not endure his pity; she got up impetuously, escaped from his arms and rushed to her room to recover herself. Her sobs had become cries. Very soon they ceased altogether and she came back and went on talking as before, interrupted only by an occasional tremor which ran through her whole body. She remained standing by the door. 'I don't know why I keep on crying like this,' she said. 'The least thing throws me into such a state. I must be ill. I have done nothing which could give that man the right to behave like this. You do believe me, don't you? Well, that is all I care about. And besides, what could I have done or said to make him think it?' She went and sat down on a chair and began crying again, but more quietly.

It was clear that Emilio's first task must be to remove all blame from his friend, and he did his best, but without success. The feeling of opposition only excited Amalia the more.

'Let him come!' she shouted. 'He shan't see me even if he wants to; I won't let myself be seen by him.'

Then Emilio had what seemed to him a good idea. 'Do you know,' he said, 'what has made Balli change towards you? Someone asked him in front of me whether he intended to get engaged to you.'

She stared at him fixedly, as if she were trying to discover whether he was to be trusted; she seemed not to have understood, and repeated the words as if it would help her to analyse them. 'Someone said that he was going to get engaged to me?' She laughed loudly, but it was only her voice which laughed. So he was afraid of having compromised himself, and of being obliged to marry her. But who could have put such an idea into his head? He didn't look as if he was as stupid as all that.

Had he supposed she was only a flapper who would fall madly in love the first time a man looked at her or spoke to her? 'I admit,' she went on, her admirable strength of will enabling her finally to speak in a tone of real indifference, 'I admit that Balli's company was not unpleasant to me, but it never occurred to me that it could be so dangerous as all that.' She tried to laugh again, but this time her voice broke and she burst into tears.

'I don't see in that case what you have to cry about,' said Emilio timidly. He would have preferred now to put a stop to the confidences he had so lightly provoked. But words did not relieve Amalia, they only made her grief more bitter. In that she was not like himself.

'Haven't I the right to cry when I am treated like that? He flies from me as if I had run after him.' She had begun shouting again, but the effort used up all her strength. Emilio's words had taken her by surprise, for she had not, even after all this time, decided what her behaviour should be. She again tried to soften the impression which the whole scene must have produced on Emilio. 'It is my lack of strength which makes things upset me so easily,' she said, resting her head on both her hands. 'You must often have seen me cry over something much less important, haven't you?'

Without admitting it to each other the thoughts of them both were carried back to the evening when she had burst into tears only because Angiolina had taken her brother away from her. They sat looking gravely at each other. She was thinking that at that time she had cried about nothing, and just because she had not experienced the hopeless despair which weighed on her now. He, on the contrary, was thinking how much that other scene had resembled this one, and he felt a fresh weight on his own conscience. This scene was clearly a continuation of the other.

But Amalia had made up her mind. 'I think it is your duty to defend me, don't you? I don't see how you can go on being friends with someone who has insulted me without any reason.'

'He has not insulted you,' Emilio protested.

'You are free to think as you like about it. But he has got to come back to this house, otherwise you will be obliged to turn your back on him. For my part, I promise you that he will find no change in my behaviour; I shall make a great effort to treat him much better than I think he deserves.'

Emilio was obliged to acknowledge that she was right, and said that even though he could not admit the matter was so important as to lead him to break off all contact with Balli, he would see that he understood that he was expected to come to the house as before.

But even this promise did not satisfy the mild Amalia. 'So an insult to your sister seems a mere trifle, does it? Do as you think fit then, but I also shall act as seems best to me.' She was cold and disdainful and threatening. 'To-morrow I shall apply to the agency over the way for a post as housekeeper or servant.' She spoke so coldly that he could not doubt that her intentions were serious.

'But did I ever say that I would not do what you want?' asked Emilio in alarm. 'I will speak to Balli to-morrow and if he doesn't come and see us that very day I shall see less of him in future.'

That 'less of him' again roused Amalia's anger. 'Less of him? You can do exactly as you like.' She got up, and without saying good night went to her room, where the candle was still burning which she had taken in the first time she sought refuge there.

Emilio argued that she probably went on showing anger because it made it easier for her to keep herself under control. The moment she began to soften, to the extent of saying a word of thanks or even of agreement, she would again be overcome by emotion. He wanted to follow her into the room, but he heard she was undressing, and wished her good night through the door. She replied in a low voice, and in a tone of hard indifference.

But he admitted that Amalia was right. Balli ought sometimes to come to the house. The sudden cessation of his visits was insulting, and in order that Amalia should be cured it was necessary first of all to remove all sense of outrage. He left the house in the hope of finding Balli.

Outside, at the very door of his house, he came upon the most powerful of all distractions. By a singular chance he found himself face to face with Angiolina. He immediately forgot his sister, his own remorse and Balli. It was a surprise for him. In those few days he had actually forgotten the colour of her hair, which set off her face in such a halo of fairness, and her blue eyes which now really had something searching in their gaze. His greeting was brief and, in his effort to be cold, almost violent. He gave her at the same time such a penetrating look that if she had not herself been surprised and agitated she might well have been frightened by it. Yes! She was agitated. She blushed in confusion as she returned his greeting. She was with her mother, and when they had gone a few steps further she leaned over so much towards her companion as to be able conveniently to look behind her. He thought he read in her eyes that she expected him to speak to her, and it was just this which gave him the strength to pass on at a quicker rate.

He continued walking for some time without thinking where he was going, just in order to calm himself. Perhaps Amalia had been right, and his leaving her had been the best possible education for Angiolina. Perhaps she still loved him! As he walked he fell into a delicious dream. She loved him, she was following him, she was trying to attach herself to him, while he continued to fly from her and to repulse her. How gratifying to his feelings!

When he came to himself, the memory of his sister again weighed on his mind. During those few days his plight had become so much more desolate that the thought of Angiolina, which had hitherto been so painful to him, now became a refuge, though an uneasy one, from the idea that he had made his sister's fate more bitter.

He did not succeed in finding Balli that evening.

Quite late Sorniani stopped him, on his way back from the theatre. After the usual greeting he suddenly said that he had seen Angiolina and her mother at the theatre, in the upper circle. She was looking lovely, he said, with a belt of yellow silk, and a little hat of which you could only see two or three large roses against her golden hair. They were doing the 'Valkyrie', and Sorniani expressed surprise that Emilio, who among all his many other activities used to be considered one of their most advanced musical critics, had not been at the theatre.

So she had gone on to the theatre, in spite of the confusion and agitation she had shown on seeing him; and she had been sitting in a relatively expensive seat. It would be interesting to know who had paid for it. Another of his vain dreams shattered!

He told Sorniani that he intended to go the following evening, but he had really no such intention. He had missed the one evening when he could have got any pleasure from the theatre. Angiolina would never have gone two evenings running, however much one had paid for her seat. Wagner and Angiolina! It was surprising enough that those two should have met even once.

He passed a sleepless night. He was restless and could not find a comfortable enough position in bed to lie in for long. He got up to try and calm himself, and thought that he might find some distraction in his sister's room. But Amalia had given up dreaming; even her happy dreams had been stolen from her now. He heard her turning over and over in bed, as if she did not find it very comfortable either.

Towards morning she heard him at her door, and asked what he wanted.

He had returned there, hoping to hear her speak, and to learn that she had found some enjoyment, even for one short spell in twenty-four hours. 'Nothing,' he replied, deeply disappointed at finding her awake: 'I thought I heard you moving, and wondered whether you were wanting anything.'

'No, I don't want anything, thank you, Emilio,' she replied gently.

He felt he was forgiven and experienced such a keen, sweet sense of satisfaction that his eyes filled with tears. 'But why aren't you asleep?' It was such a happy moment for him that he wanted to prolong it, and make it more intense by letting his sister see that it was his affection for her which moved him so deeply.

'I have only just woken up; and you?'

'I have slept very little lately,' he replied; he still thought it must be some consolation to Amalia to know how much he suffered too. Then, remembering his conversation with Sorniani, he told her he had decided to go to the 'Valkyrie' to try and distract his thoughts. 'Would you like to come too?'

'Very much indeed,' she replied. 'If it is not too expensive for you.'

'I can easily afford it for once,' said Emilio. His teeth were chattering from cold, but he found such comfort in standing there that he could not bear to leave his post.

'Are you in your nightshirt?' she asked, and when she heard he was, she ordered him to go back to bed.

He did so, reluctantly, but when he was there he at once found the position he had been searching for all night in vain, and slept without interruption for several hours.

It was easy enough to come to an understanding with Balli. Emilio met him next morning walking behind the cart which took dogs away to be killed, and quite overcome by pity for the poor beasts. He was no doubt genuinely affected, but he admitted that he indulged in the emotion because it increased his artistic sensibility. He did not pay much attention to Emilio's words, for his ears were deafened by the howling of the dogs, the most melancholy sound in creation, especially when provoked by the sudden and unexpected pain of something drawn tightly round the neck: 'The fear of death is in them already,' said Balli, 'and an immense and powerless indignation as well.'

Brentani remembered with bitterness that the same

surprise, the same immense and powerless indignation had been audible in Amalia's lamentation. The presence of the dog-killer, however, made his task easier, for Balli listened to him absent-mindedly and said he had no objection to coming to see him that very day.

He felt, however, slightly more doubtful at mid-day when he went to call for Emilio at the office. He was already convinced that Amalia had confessed her passion to her brother and that the latter had at first thought it better to keep him away from the house; and now it seemed that Emilio wanted him to go back because Amalia could not understand why he no longer came there. 'I suppose they want me to go for propriety's sake!' thought Balli, with his customary facility in explaining everything.

They were well on their way when another doubt arose in Stefano's mind. 'I hope the Signorina doesn't bear me any ill will.'

Emilio reassured him, for he had already had Amalia's promise. 'You will be received just as usual.'

Balli said no more. He was thinking that he would take care, for his part, not to behave the same as usual, for he did not want to encourage her and be pestered by her falling in love with him a second time.

Amalia had been prepared for everything but this. She had made up her mind to treat him politely but coldly, and now it was he who was giving this tone to their relationship. She had nothing to do but accept his lead and follow it passively, and she was not even able to betray any resentment. He treated her like a young lady whose acquaintance he had recently made, ceremoniously and with respectful indifference. There were no more of those jolly talks in which Balli let himself go completely, leaving not a rag on the most respectable reputation among his acquaintance, and behaving generally with an *espièglerie* that only his most devoted friends could be trusted to appreciate. A stray sarcasm uttered at such a moment would have spoilt his oratory and probably reduced him to silence. But today he did not say a word about himself, he only talked in his most conventional manner about things which Amalia did not even take the trouble to listen to, so stupefied was she by his coldness. He said that he had been very bored at the 'Valkyrie', where half the public were trying to make the other half believe that they were enjoying themselves; then he talked about another nuisance, the carnival, which still had to drag out one more long month of agony. There was nothing to do but yawn at such boring methods of killing time. Oh, but he was a bore too when he was in that mood. Where had all that delicious gaiety fled which Amalia had loved so much because she thought it had existed for her delight?

Emilio felt how his sister must be suffering and tried to rouse some sign of interest in her on the part of Stefano. He said how pale Amalia was looking, and threatened to send for Dr Carini if her looks did not improve. He mentioned Dr Carini, who was a friend of Balli's, in the hope of inducing the latter also to show some interest in Amalia's health. But Stefano persisted with a childish obstinacy in refusing to take any part in the discussion, and Amalia replied to her brother's affectionate words with a curt and snubbing phrase. She wanted to be rude to someone, and she was not allowed to be rude to Balli. Soon after the meal she retired to her room and left them alone.

When they were in the street together Emilio returned to his unfortunate remark, trying to explain it away and to remove every shadow of blame from Amalia. He said he had spoken too lightly. He must have been mistaken as to Amalia's feelings; he gave his solemn oath that she had never said a word to him on the subject. Balli pretended to believe him. He said it was unnecessary to raise the question again; he, for his part, had forgotten it long ago. As usual he was quite satisfied with himself. His behaviour had been perfectly calculated to set Amalia's mind at rest and to save his friend from any sort of worry. Emilio saw that he was only throwing breath away, and said no more.

The brother and sister went to the theatre together that evening, and Emilio hoped that the treat, from being so unaccustomed, would be all the more beneficial to Amalia.

But no! Her eyes lit up scarcely once during the whole entertainment. She hardly even noticed who was present in the audience. Her imagination was so fixed on the injustice which had been done her that she could not even take the faintest interest in all the many women more fortunate and more elegant than herself whom she used so much to enjoy looking at and talking about afterwards. Formerly she had never missed an opportunity of hearing the latest fashions described; now she did not so much as look at them.

A certain Signora Birlini, a rich lady who had been a friend of Amalia's mother, was in a seat not far off, and waved a greeting to her. Formerly Amalia had been proud of the attentions of rich women like her. But now it was only with an effort that she could bring herself to reply to the greeting, and she took no further notice of the large, blonde, amiable lady, who was evidently pleased to see Amalia in the theatre.

But Amalia was not really there at all. Although she could not grasp its details she let that strange music lull her thoughts; its powerful rhythms reared themselves about her, huge and menacing. Emilio snatched her for a moment from her reverie to ask how she liked a *motif* which was continually recurring in the orchestra. 'I don't understand it,' she replied. In reality she had not heard it. Her pain, absorbed into the music, took on a fresh colour and a greater significance, though at the same time it became simpler and purified of all that had defiled it. She was little and weak, and she had been beaten; how could she have hoped to survive? She had never before been so resigned, so free from all anger. She felt she wanted to go on crying quietly and make no sound. Here in the theatre, of course, the solace of tears was denied her. But she had been wrong to say she did not understand the music. That magnificent stream of sound signified the whole of human destiny; she saw it pouring down an incline, its path shaped by the unequal conformation of the ground. Now it would flow in a single cascade, now it would be divided into a thousand smaller ones, all coloured by an ever-changing light, and by the reflections which objects cast upon it. There was the harmony of sound and colour which held the epic fate of Sieglinde, but also, insignificant though it was, her own, the end of a part of life, the withering of a single twig. Her fate was no more to be wept over than that of the others; it deserved the same tears – no more; and the ridicule which had so cruelly oppressed her found no place in that picture which yet was so complete.

Her companion was familiar with the music, he knew how all those sounds were produced and how they were put together, but he did not succeed in getting so near to them as Amalia. He thought that his own passion and pain would immediately have clothed itself in the imagination of the composer. But no. For him, those who moved upon the scene were gods and heroes who transported him far away from the world of his sufferings. During the intervals he sought in vain among his memories for some experience which would have merited such a transformation; he could not find it. Had he perhaps found a cure in art?

When he left the theatre after the opera was over he was so full of this hope that he did not notice his sister was more cast down than usual. Filling his lungs with the cold night air, he said that the evening had done him a great deal of good. But as he went on chattering in his usual way about the strange calm which had pervaded him, a great sadness filled his heart. Art had only given him an interval of peace, and it would not be able to give it to him again, for now certain fragments of the music which had remained in his mind were already adapting themselves too perfectly to his own sensations, his self-pity, for example, and the sympathy which he felt for Angiolina or Amalia.

In his present state of excitement he would have liked to calm himself by urging Amalia to confide in him still further. He should have realized that their mutual explanations had been useless. She continued to suffer in silence, not even admitting that she had ever made any confession to him at all. Their suffering, which had been so similar in its origin, had not brought them nearer to each other.

One day he came upon her unexpectedly on the Corso, while she was taking a mid-day walk there alone. She was wearing a dress which she could not have worn for a considerable time, for Emilio had never seen it before. It was made of some rather thick material trimmed with bright blue, and looked very out of place on her poor thin little body.

She became confused on seeing him, and was ready to return home with him at once. Who knows what sad thoughts had driven her out there in search of distraction? He could readily understand it when he remembered how often his own desires had chased him out of the house. But whatever mad hope could have led her to put on that dress? He firmly believed that she had put it on, hoping to please Balli. What an amazing idea to spring up in Amalia's mind! In any case, whether she had had it or not, it was for the first and last time, for after the walk she returned immediately to the dress she always wore, which was grey like herself, and like her destiny.

10

His pain and his remorse had both become much milder. The elements of which his life was made up remained the same, but they had become attenuated, as if seen through a dark lens which robbed them of light and violence. A great calm, an endless ennui lay like lead upon him. He could see clearly now what a strange exaggeration his feelings had undergone, and he thought he was being quite sincere when he said to Balli, who had been observing him with some anxiety: 'I am cured.'

He thought it was true because he could not claim to remember exactly the state of mind he had been in before knowing Angiolina. The difference was so small after all! He had yawned less and he had not experienced the painful embarrassment which now seized him whenever he found himself alone with Amalia.

It was a gloomy season too. For weeks they had not seen a ray of sunshine, and as, when he thought of Angiolina, he always associated her sweet face and the warmth of colour in her fair hair with the blue sky and the sunlight, it seemed to him that all these things had disappeared together out of his life. None the less he had come to the conclusion that his leaving Angiolina had been a very good thing for him. 'It is better to be free,' he said with conviction.

He made an effort to profit by his newly acquired liberty. He felt that his mind had become inactive, and the idea pained him, for he remembered how years ago art had given colour to his life, lifting him out of the inertia into which he had fallen after the death of his father. It was then that he had written his novel, the story of a young artist whose intellect and health are ruined by a woman. He had portrayed himself in the hero, his own innocence and gentleness of nature. His heroine he had pictured after the fashion of the time as a mixture of woman and tiger. She had the movements, the eyes, the sanguinary character of the wild beast. He had never known a woman and that was how he imagined her, an animal whom it was hard to conceive ever being born or prospering in this world. But with what confidence he had described her! He had suffered and enjoyed with her and sometimes even felt that he harboured in himself that monstrous hybrid of tiger and woman.

He took up his pen again and wrote in one evening

133

the first chapter of a new novel. He discovered a new law of art to which he wished to conform, and he wrote the truth. He described his first meeting with Angiolina and his own feelings, but followed this almost immediately by his violent, angry feelings of the last few days; he described the appearance of Angiolina, which in his book he at once perceived to be spoilt by her base, perverse soul, and finally the magnificent landscape in which their idyll had at first been set. Worn out at last he stopped working, very pleased to have written a whole chapter in one evening.

The next evening he began working again, with two or three ideas in his head which were to be developed by him in the following pages. But first of all he re-read what he had already written. 'Incredible,' he murmured. The man was not in the least like him, the woman, it is true, retained something of the woman-tiger heroine of the first novel, but none of her life or reality. He found that the truth he had wanted to relate was less credible than the dreams which years ago he had taken for true. He felt that his mind had become dreadfully sluggish, and the discovery caused him acute anguish. He laid down his pen and put all he had written away in his desk, saying to himself that he would begin it all over again, perhaps on the following day. The idea was enough to quiet his mind; but he never resumed his writing. He wanted to spare himself all possible pain, and he did not feel strong enough to study his own incapacity and to overcome it. He could no longer think with a pen in his hand. When he wanted to write he felt his brain growing rusty, and he remained in a state of ecstasy in front of the white paper, while the ink dried on his pen.

He wanted to see Angiolina again. He could not make up his mind to go in search of her; he only said to himself that there could be no danger now in his seeing her again. If indeed he had wished to adhere exactly to what he had said when he left her, he ought to have gone to her at once. Surely he felt calm enough now to stretch out the hand of friendship to her?

He told Balli of his intention, and in the following terms: 'I only want to see if I can behave like an intelligent person when I meet her again.'

Balli had laughed too often at Emilio's love not to believe that he was perfectly cured now. Besides, for some days past he had himself felt the keenest desire to see Angiolina again. He had imagined sculpturing a figure just like hers and dressed in the same way. He told Emilio this, who promised to get her to sit for Balli directly he saw her. There could be no doubt whatever that he was cured. He was not even jealous of Balli any longer.

It soon appeared that Balli's thoughts were quite as much set on Angiolina as Emilio's own. He had been obliged to destroy a model on which he had spent months of work. He was going through a period of exhaustion too, and he was unable to discover any other idea in himself but the one he had given birth to that first evening when Emilio had introduced him to Angiolina.

One evening, when the two friends were about to separate, he asked: 'Haven't you seen her again yet?' He did not want to be the one to reunite them, but he did want to know whether perhaps Emilio had become reconciled to Angiolina without telling him. That would have been treason!

Emilio's calm had still further increased. Now that everyone allowed him to do exactly what he wanted, he did not really want anything, anything at all. The reason why he wanted to try and see Angiolina again was that he might try to acquire a certain warmth of thought and speech which was lacking within himself, and which he must supply from outside, and he hoped to live the novel he found himself unable to write.

It was only laziness which prevented him going to look for her. He would have preferrred that someone else should have undertaken the task of bringing them together again, and he half thought of inviting Balli to do so. Indeed it would all have been easier and simpler if

Balli had got her for himself as a model and had then handed her over to him as a mistress. He thought of suggesting it. He only hesitated because he did not want Balli to play an important part in deciding his fate.

Important? Yes, there was no doubt that Angiolina still remained a very important person for him, at least in comparison with everything else. Everything else was so insignificant. She dominated it all. He thought of her continually as an old man thinks of his youth. How young he had been that night when he wanted to kill her in order to calm himself! If he had written then instead of pacing about the streets like an angry lion, and afterwards tossing wearily in his bed, he would surely have discovered a new artistic road which later he had sought in vain. But it was all over for ever. Angiolina still lived, but she could never give him back his youth.

One evening, close to the Giardino Pubblico, he saw her walking along in front of him. He recognized her at once by her familiar step. She was holding up her skirt to protect it from the mud, and by the light of a dim street lamp he saw the shine of Angiolina's black shoes. He was troubled at once. He remembered how at the height of his passion he had thought that the possession of this woman would have cured him. Now he only thought: 'She would give me life!'

'Good evening, Signorina,' he said with what calm he could muster, so overwhelming did his desire become directly he saw her rosy childish face, and her wide-open eyes, so clear cut that they seemed to have been set that moment in her face.

She stopped and took the hand he held out to her, replying brightly and readily to his greeting: 'How are you? It is such a long time since we met.'

He said something in reply, but his attention was distracted by the force of his desire. Perhaps he had done wrong to display such serenity, worse still not to have thought what his behaviour ought to be in order to arrive at once at what he wanted, at the truth – physical possession. He walked beside her holding her hand, but after they had exchanged the first few words of people who are glad to meet each other again, he felt some hesitation as to how he should address her, and said nothing. The elegiac tone which he had used quite sincerely on other occasions would be out of place here, and if he allowed himself to appear too indifferent he would never reach his goal.

'Have you forgiven me, Signor Emilio?' she said at last, stopping in front of him and holding out her other hand for him to take. Her intention was of the best and the gesture was surprisingly original for Angiolina.

He managed to say: 'Do you know there is one thing I can never forgive you; that you made no effort at all to see me. Did you care so little about me?' He spoke sincerely, and he realized that it was useless for him to try and play a part. Perhaps sincerity would answer his purpose better than any pretence.

She was a little flustered, and stammered out that if he had not spoken to her she had meant to write to him the very next day. 'After all, what have I done?' she asked, forgetting that she had asked his pardon just before.

Emilio thought it politic to express some doubt. 'How can I believe you?' And then he said reproachfully: 'With an umbrella-maker!'

This made them both burst out laughing. 'You jealous thing,' she cried, squeezing the hand which she still held in hers, 'fancy being jealous of that wild man of the woods!' And it was true that however right he perhaps was in breaking off his relation with Angiolina he had certainly been wrong in making use of that stupid story as an excuse. The umbrella-maker was not the most formidable of his rivals. And this reflection gave him the strange feeling that he ought to lay at his own door all the evils which had befallen him since he had abandoned Angiolina.

She was silent for a long time. It could not have been on purpose, for this would have been too subtle for Angiolina. She was probably silent because she could think of nothing else to say to excuse herself, so they walked on in silence side by side through the dark, mysterious night; the sky was covered all over with clouds lit up only at one point by the light of the moon.

They reached Angiolina's house and she stopped, perhaps to take leave of him. But he made her walk on. 'Let us go on walking, on and on without speaking!' To please him she naturally continued to walk beside him in silence. And he loved her again from that moment, or at least he was conscious of it from that moment. He had walking beside him again the woman who was ennobled by his uninterrupted dream of her, and by that last cry of anguish which broke from her when he left her, and which for long had personified her wholly for him; ennobled too by art, for now his desire for her made Emilio feel that he had beside him a goddess capable of every lofty dream and sentiment.

Beyond Angiolina's house they came to a dark and lonely road shut in on one side by a hill, on the other by a low wall bounding the fields. She sat down on it and he leaned against her, trying to recover the position he had liked best in the past, during the first days of their love. He missed the sea. The one shining thing in this damp, grey landscape was Angiolina's fairness; she was the one warm, luminous note.

It was so long since he had felt her lips on his own that he was violently excited by it. 'Oh, my sweet! my dear one!' he murmured, kissing her eyes, her throat, her hands, her dress. She let him do just what he wanted, and he was so deeply moved by such unexpected docility and tenderness that he wept, at first silently, and then breaking out in sobs. He felt as if it was in his power to make that blissful moment last for ever. Everything was explained now, all doubts were solved. His life would consist henceforward of his love alone.

'Do you really love me so much?' she murmured, touched and wondering. There were tears in her eyes too. She told him how she had seen him in the street, looking pale and worn, and with evident signs of suffering on his face, and that her heart ached with pity for him. 'Why didn't you come before?' she asked him reproachfully.

She supported herself against him in getting down from the wall. He could not understand why she wanted to cut short that delicious explanation, which he would have liked to continue for ever. 'Come home with me,' she said firmly.

He felt dizzy with delight and took her in his arms and kissed her again and again, not knowing how to show his gratitude. But Angiolina's house was some way off and Emilio had time, while walking along, to fall a prey to all his old doubts and misgivings. How if he were to bind himself to her for life, then and there? He began to mount the stairs slowly, and turned on her suddenly with the question: 'How about Volpini?'

She hesitated, and stood still. 'Volpini?' Then she came firmly up the few stairs which divided her from Emilio. She leaned against him and hid her face on his shoulder with an affectation of modesty which reminded him of the old Angiolina and her melodramatic seriousness, and said:

'No one knows, not even my mother.' One by one all the old properties were coming back, and now it was her dear mother. She had given herself to Volpini; he had insisted on it, he had even made it a condition of continuing their relationship. 'He felt I did not love him,' whispered Angiolina, 'and wanted a proof of my love.' The only guarantee she had received in reward was a promise of marriage. With her usual lack of consideration for Emilio's feelings she named a young solicitor who had advised her to satisfy herself with that, since the law punished seduction under those conditions.

With their arms round each other they mounted the stairs which seemed as if they would never end. Every fresh step made Angiolina more like the woman he had fled from. For now she had begun chattering again, as a first step towards giving herself to him. Now she could at last be his because – she kept on repeating this – it was for his sake that she had given herself to the tailor. He could not escape that responsibility even if he gave her up altogether.

She opened the door and went along the dark passage towards her room. From another room the nasal voice of her mother was heard to call: 'Is that you, Angiolina?'

'Yes,' replied Angiolina, smothering a laugh. 'I am going straight to bed. Good night, Mother.'

She lit a candle and took off her coat and hat. Then she threw herself into his arms, or rather, clasped him in hers.

Emilio was able to test that evening the importance of possessing a woman whom one has long desired. On that memorable evening it seemed to him as if he had been twice transformed in his most secret soul. The deplorable inertia which had driven him again to seek out Angiolina had disappeared, but so had also the enthusiasm which had made him sob from mingled joy and sadness. The male was satisfied, but beyond that satisfaction he had really felt nothing at all. He had possessed the woman he hated, not the woman he loved. Oh, deceiver! It was not the first nor, as she would have him believe, the second time that she had slept with a man. It was not worth while being angry about it, because he had known it for a long time. But possession of her had set him free to judge the woman who had given herself to him. 'I shall dream no more,' he thought as he left the house. And then, as he looked at her, lit up by the pale moon-rays, he thought: 'Perhaps I shall never come here again.' He had taken no decision. Why should he? The whole thing was entirely without importance.

She had gone down with him to the street door. She had not been conscious of any coldness on his part, for he would have been ashamed to show any. On the contrary he had made haste to ask her for an appointment for the following evening, which she had been obliged to refuse, as she was busy all day and till late in the evening with Signora Deluigi. They agreed to meet the next day but one. 'But not in our house,' said Angiolina, suddenly growing crimson with indignation. 'How can you imagine such a thing? I don't want to run the risk of being killed on the spot by my father.' Emilio promised to provide a room for their next rendezvous. He would send a note tomorrow letting her know the address.

Was possession the truth after all? Her lying continued as shamelessly as before, and he saw no means of freeing himself from it. With her last kiss she begged him to be discreet, especially with Balli. She set store by her reputation.

Emilio was immediately indiscreet with Balli, that very evening. He did it on purpose, as the best way he could devise of reacting to Angiolina's lies, and without any regard to her recommendations to secrecy, which he was sure were intended only to deceive himself and not to keep others in the dark. But it gave him great satisfaction that every cloud was lifted from his brow.

Balli sat listening to him with the air of a doctor about to make a diagnosis. 'I think I really can take it upon myself to say that you are cured.'

Then Emilio felt a desire to confide in him still further and said how indignant Angiolina's behaviour made him, for she still wanted him to believe that she had given herself to Volpini in order to be able to belong to him. But he allowed himself almost at once to speak too warmly. 'She is trying to cheat me even now. It is so painful to me to see that she is just the same as ever that I almost feel I don't care whether I see her again or not.'

Balli at once saw through him and said: 'You are just the same as ever too. Not a single word you have said suggests indifference.' Emilio hotly protested, but Balli was not to be convinced. 'You have made a great mistake, a very great mistake, in getting to know her again.'

Emilio had plenty of opportunity that night for proving to himself that Balli was right. Indignation, and an angry unrest which demanded instant action, kept him awake. He could no longer deceive himself into believing that it was the indignation of a pure man shocked by an obscenity. He knew that state of mind too well. It was exactly like what he had experienced before the incident

of the umbrella-maker and before he had possessed
Angiolina, and now he had fallen into it again. His
youth was returning to him! He no longer wanted to
commit murder, but he would gladly have destroyed
himself in his shame and anguish.

His suffering was increased now by the burden on his
conscience, the remorse he felt at having tied himself
again to that woman, and his fear of finding his own life
still more compromised by her. Indeed, how was it
possible to explain the fellness with which she laid on
him all the blame of her connexion with Volpini, if it
were not that she intended to attach herself to him, to
compromise him and to suck dry the little blood he had
left in his veins? He was for ever bound to Angiolina by
a strange contradiction of his own heart: by his senses
(for alone in bed his desire for her had awakened again)
and by the very indignation which he attributed to hatred.

That indignation procured him the most delightful
dreams. Towards morning the tumult of his senses subsided, leaving only an emotional anxiety about his own
fate. He did not fall asleep, but lay in a curious state of
physical weakness which deprived him of the sense of
time or place. He thought he was ill, seriously, hopelessly
ill, and that Angiolina had come to look after him. He
read in her face the gravity and sweet self-devotion of the
good hospital nurse. He was conscious of her moving
about the room, and whenever she came near him she
brought him refreshment, touching his burning brow
with her cool hand or kissing him on the eyes and forehead with a touch so light as to be scarcely perceptible.
Could Angiolina kiss like that? He turned heavily in his
bed and returned to consciousness. If that dream should
come true then he could feel he had really possessed her.
And to think that a few hours before he believed himself
to have lost all capacity for dreaming. Oh, surely his
youth had returned! It coursed powerful as ever through
his veins and annulled whatever resolution his senile
mind had made.

He rose early and went out. He could not wait; he

must see Angiolina immediately. He sped along, all impatience to embrace her, but resolved not to chatter too much. He would not lower himself by declarations which would have put their relationship on a wrong footing. The truth could not come to one by possession, but possession itself, neither embellished by dreams nor words, was actually the pure and bestial truth.

But this was just what Angiolina with admirable obstinacy refused to hear of. She was already dressed to go out and she again gave him clearly to understand that she did not intend to dishonour her own house.

He had meanwhile made an observation which led him to feel that perhaps he ought to change his plan. He noticed that she was examining him curiously in order to see whether his love had diminished or increased in consequence of his having possessed her. She was betraying herself with touching ingenuousness; she had no doubt known some men who felt a repugnance for the woman they had slept with. It was easy for him to prove to her that he was not one of them. Resigning himself to the abstinence she imposed upon him, he contented himself with the kisses he had lived on for so long. But soon kisses were not enough for him and he again began murmuring in her ear all the tender words he had learned during the long period of his love for her. *Ange! Ange!*

Balli had given him the address of a house where they let out rooms for a certain purpose. He told her how to find it. She made him describe the house to her at great length, so that she should make no mistake, and also the exact position of the room, which was rather embarrassing to Emilio, who had never seen it himself. He had been too busy kissing her to notice at the time, but when he was alone in the street he perceived, to his great surprise, that it was only now he would really have been capable of finding his way to that room for himself. There could be no doubt about it! He had been directed by Angiolina.

He went there immediately. The woman who let out

the room was called Paracci, and was a disgusting old creature dressed in a dirty garment beneath which one could divine the contours of a swelling bosom, the one vestige of youth left in her flabby old age; a few scanty curls covered her head and between them one could see her red, greasy skin. She received him very politely and at once agreed to let him a room, saying at the same time that she only let to people she knew very well – therefore of course to him.

He wanted to look at the room and went in, followed by the old woman, through a door leading off from the stairs. Another door, which was always kept shut (Paracci said the words as if she were taking an oath), communicated directly with the street. It was furnished, or it would be more true to say it was encumbered, by an enormous bed, which looked clean, and two big cupboards; in the middle was a table, a sofa and four chairs. There would not have been room for a single other piece of furniture.

The widow Paracci stood watching him, her arms resting on her great swelling hips, and the smile on her face – an ugly grimace, displaying her toothless mouth – of someone who awaits a word of applause. She had in fact made certain attempts at decoration in the room. A Chinese umbrella was open above the top of the bed and some photographs were hanging on the wall, as in Angiolina's room.

A cry of astonishment escaped him when he saw, hanging beside the photo of a half-naked woman, the photo of a girl he used to know, a friend of Amalia's, who had died a few years ago. He asked the old woman where she had got those photographs and she replied that she had bought them to decorate the walls. He gazed for some time at the sweet face of the poor girl, who had posed before the camera all dressed up in her best – perhaps just that once in her whole life – only to serve as an adornment for that sordid little room. And yet he dreamed of love as he stood there in that sordid little room, while the disgusting old woman eyed him with satisfaction, delighted to have secured a fresh client. It was precisely under those conditions that he found it most exciting to picture Angiolina coming to bring him the love he longed for. He thought to himself with a thrill of delight: Tomorrow I shall have my love!

But when she came he felt he had never loved her less than he did that day. He had been rendered unhappy by long separation; he felt as if it had robbed him of all powers of enjoyment. An hour before going to the appointment he decided that if he did not experience the joy he expected he would tell Angiolina that he never intended to see her again, and he would tell her in the following words: 'You are such a loose woman that I am disgusted by you.' He had thought these words out while sitting with Amalia, whom he envied for her tranquillity although she looked so sad. And he had thought that for her love still remained a pure and spiritual desire; it was its realization which sullied and debased our poor human nature.

But that night he was happy. Angiolina made him wait more than half an hour, a century to him. He thought that anger was the only emotion he felt, an impotent rage which increased the hatred he had persuaded himself he felt for her. He thought he should strike her when she did come. There was no possible excuse, for she herself had said she was not going to work that day, and that therefore she would be able to be punctual. Wasn't it just because she had not wanted to keep him waiting that she had refused to make an appointment for the evening before? And now she had made him wait a whole day as well as an endless age besides.

But when she came he, who had already despaired of seeing her, was astonished at his own good fortune. He whispered reproaches on her lips, in her neck, but she did not attempt to answer them, they had so much the sound of an entreaty, a murmur of adoration. In the dim light widow Paracci's room became a temple. For a long time no words broke his dream. Angiolina was far better than her word. She had undone her wealth of hair and his head lay on a pillow of gold. He pressed his face into it like a child, to drink in the perfume of its gold. She was a complacent mistress and divined all his desires with exquisite intelligence; in that bed at least he need not complain of the quickness of her intuitions. There all was pure pleasure and delight.

It was only later that the memory of that scene made him grind his teeth with rage. Passion had for a moment freed him from his painful habit of observation, but had not prevented every detail of the scene from being impressed on his memory. Now for the first time he felt that he could say he knew Angiolina. Passion had left him indelible memories and from these he was able to reconstruct the feelings which Angiolina had left unexpressed, which she had even carefully concealed. In cold blood he could not have succeeded in doing so. But now he knew, knew with the most absolute certainty, that Angiolina had known men who had given her more pleasure. Several times she had said: 'Now that is enough. I can't bear any more.' She had tried to say it in a tone of admiration which she had not succeeded in finding. He felt the evening could be divided into two halves: during the first half she had loved him, during the second she had been obliged to make an effort not to repulse him. When they got up she betrayed that she was tired of being there. It naturally did not require then great powers of observation to read her real feelings – for seeing that he still hesitated she pushed him out of bed with the joking remark: 'Now come along, my beauty.' My beauty! She must have thought out that ironic word quite half an hour before. He had read it in her face.

As usual he would have preferred to remain alone so as to have time to put in order his own observations. For the moment he only dimly perceived that she no longer belonged to him; it was the same sensation he had had that evening when he was together with Angiolina in the Giardino Pubblico, waiting for Balli and Margherita. He suffered atrociously from it, a mixture of wounded vanity and the bitterest jealousy. He wanted to free himself from her altogether, but felt he could not leave her without having tried to win her again for himself.

He accompanied her to the main road, then, although she was in a great hurry, he persuaded her to walk home by the route he had taken the evening she had been seen with the umbrella-maker. The Via Romagna looked exactly the same as on that memorable evening, with its bare trees outlined against a clear sky, and underfoot an uneven surface covered with dense mud. But there was one great difference between now and then. Angiolina was at his side. Beside him, yet how far away! He was seeking her for the second time along that road.

He described to her his walk of the previous occasion. He told her how the desire to see her had made him fancy he saw her several times in front of him, and how the slight wound caused by a fall had made him cry, because it was the last drop in his cup of bitterness. She listened to him willingly, flattered to think that she had inspired such great love, and when he gave way to his feelings and complained that not all he had suffered had been sufficient to win for him the love he thought he deserved, she protested energetically: 'How can you say such a thing?' She kissed him to make her protest more efficacious. But then, as usual after thinking anything over, she made the mistake of saying: 'Didn't I give myself to Volpini for your sake?' And Emilio bowed his head, finally convinced.

That Volpini, all unknowingly, poisoned the pleasure which according to Angiolina he had procured for Emilio. Instead of suffering from Angiolina's indifference, directly he heard Volpini mentioned Emilio began to be afraid of her again, and of the plans he suspected her to be making. At their next meeting his first words were to ask her what guarantees Volpini had given her, that she should have abandoned herself to him.

'Oh, Volpini can't do without me now,' she said, smiling. For the moment Emilio's fears were set at rest; he thought it was probably a sufficient guarantee, for he himself, who was so much younger than Volpini, could not do without Angiolina either.

During the whole of their second rendezvous his powers of observation never slumbered for a single instant. He was rewarded by a most painful discovery; during the time he had made such an heroic effort not to see Angiolina someone else had filled his place, someone who evidently did not at all resemble any of the men he already knew and feared. It could not be either Leardi or Giustini or Datti. It must be he who had taught her certain new rather sharp and sometimes witty expressions, and some indecent puns. He was probably a student, for she flourished about some Latin words with all the ease in the world, generally with a coarse meaning. When pressed, she resuscitated the unfortunate Merighi, who would certainly have been surprised to know that he was still being laid under contribution; she said he had taught her those Latin words. As if she would have been capable of concealing her knowledge of Latin all this time; she would have been bound to display it. Probably the person who had taught her Latin was the same who had also taught her some very coarse Venetian songs. She made mistakes when she sang them, but even to know them as well as that she must have heard them a good many times, for she had always been unable to remember a single note of the songs which she had several times heard Balli sing. He was probably a Venetian, for she often used to amuse herself by imitating the Venetian pronunciation which she had evidently not known before. Emilio often felt him between them – a jolly *bon viveur*; he was able to reconstruct him up to a certain point, but then he escaped him, and he never succeeded in discovering his name. There was no new face among Angiolina's collection of photos. His new rival was not perhaps in the habit of giving away his photograph or perhaps Angiolina felt it more politic not to display the photographs which she had practically devoted her life to collecting. This was proved by the fact that even Emilio's was missing from her wall.

He was convinced that if he were to meet that individual he would have recognized him by certain gestures which she must have imitated from him. The worst of it was that he had only to ask her, as indeed he often did, from whom she had learned such and such a gesture or expression, for her to guess that he was jealous and denounce him. 'Jealous again!' she would cry, with astonishing intuition, whenever she saw him look grave and lowering. Yes, he was jealous. He suffered from all those echoes as much as if he had found himself face to face with his intangible rival. Worse still, with the excited fancy of a lover, he thought he could discover in Angiolina's voice certain intonations copied from the grave and slightly haughty tones of Leardi. Sorniani had probably taught her something too, and even Balli had left some trace of himself, for a certain rather affected manner he had of expressing surprise or admiration had been carefully copied. Emilio, however, failed to recognize himself in any single word or gesture of hers. He thought once with bitter irony: 'Perhaps there is no more room for me.'

His most hated rival was the one who remained unknown. It was strange how she contrived never to mention the man who must have come quite recently into her life, she who so much enjoyed boasting of her triumphs, even of the admiration she had seen in the eyes of men whom she had only met once in her life. According to her they were all madly in love with her. 'All the more credit to me,' she said, 'to have stayed at home all the time you were away, especially after I had been treated in such a way by you.' Yes, she actually wanted to make him believe that she had thought of no one but him during his absence. Every evening at home she had raised the question as to whether or not she should write to him. Her father, who had the honour of the family very much at heart, would not hear of it. When she saw Emilio laughing at the idea of that family council, she cried: 'Ask mamma and see if it isn't true.'

She lied obstinately, though she had not really mastered the art of lying. It was easy to make her contradict herself. But when the contradiction had been proved she would return with unruffled brow to her previous assertion, for in her heart of hearts she did not really believe in logic. And it was perhaps this simplicity of hers which redeemed her in Emilio's sight.

It was impossible, however, to trace the motives which had bound him so indissolubly to Angiolina. Any other small worry which came to him in the trivial round of his daily life, bounded by the office and his home, disappeared immediately at her side. Often when he had fled from home before the sad face of his sister he would fly to the Zarris, although he knew that Angiolina did not like his coming so often to the house whose honour she had so much at heart. He very seldom found her at home, but her mother would very politely invite him to wait till Angiolina came back, as she must be coming any minute now. She had been sent for only five minutes ago by some ladies who lived just round the corner – here she waved her hand vaguely from east to west – to try on a dress.

Waiting was inexpressibly painful to him, but he would remain for hours gazing as if in a trance at the old woman's hard face, for he knew that if he were to go home without having seen his mistress he should know no peace. One evening he lost all patience, and would wait no longer, though the mother, civil as usual, tried to detain him. On the stairs he passed a woman, who seemed to be a servant, with a handkerchief over her head, and covering part of her face. He stood aside to let her pass, but recognized her just as she was about to scamper up; his suspicions had been aroused by her evident desire to evade his notice, and also by her movements and figure. It was Angiolina. He felt better directly he saw her, and paid no attention to the fact that she pointed in quite a different direction from that indicated by her mother, to show where her neighbours lived, nor to the surprising fact that she evidently bore him no ill will for having compromised her again by coming to her house. She was very sweet and kind to him that evening, as if there was some sin for which she had to win forgiveness, but he, revelling in her kindness, had no time to think what it might be.

He only began to suspect her when she came to an appointment with him dressed in the same way. She said that as she was on her way home the night before after having been with him, she had been seen by some acquaintances, and she was afraid of being caught just as she was leaving that house, which had rather a bad name; that was why she had disguised herself. Too clever, alas! She did not realize that her ingenious story was merely a confession that the evening when he had met her on her own stairs she had also had good reasons for disguising herself.

One evening she arrived more than an hour late at their rendezvous. To save her knocking and so risk attracting the attention of the other lodgers, he used to wait for her on the dirty, winding staircase, leaning against a balcony on the landing and sometimes leaning out as far as he could in the direction from which she would have to come, so as to catch the first glimpse of her. When he saw some stranger coming up, he would retire hastily into the room, and this continual movement to and fro added enormously to the agitation he was in. It would in any case have been impossible for him to remain stationary. That evening, when he was several times obliged to shut himself into the room to let people pass on the stairs, he would throw himself on the bed and then get up again immediately, and he devised several ways of complicating the movement so as to lose more time over it. It seemed to him impossible later, when he was looking back over that time, that he could ever have been in such a state of mind. He had probably cried out in his anguish.

Even when she did come at last, the sight of her was not sufficient this time to calm him, and he reproached her violently. She did not take much notice, thinking that she could pacify him with a few caresses. She threw her handkerchief away and flung her arms round his neck; her wide sleeves fell back leaving her arms naked, and he noticed that they were burning hot. He looked at her more closely. Her eyes were shining and her cheeks crimson. A horrible suspicion dawned in his mind. 'You have just come from someone else,' he screamed. She let go of him, with the comparatively feeble protest: 'You are mad!' Then she began, without much show of indignation, to explain the reasons for her delay. Signora Deluigi had refused to let her go, then she had been obliged to run home to put on her disguise, and then her mother had made her do some work before she would let her go out again. There were sufficient reasons to explain ten hours delay.

But no doubt remained any longer in Emilio's mind. She had just come from the arms of another, and there rushed into his mind – as the only means of saving himself from all this filth – a plan of superhuman energy. He must not go to bed with her; he must drive her away on the spot, and never, never see her again. But he had already experienced the meaning of 'never again': one long agony, one continual regret, hours of endless agitation, hours of tormented dreams followed by hopeless languor, then a void, the death of imagination and desire, a state more painful than any other. He was afraid. He drew her to him and avenged himself solely by saying: 'I am not worth much more than you are.'

But it was her turn to rebel now, and struggling out of his arms she said emphatically: 'I have never allowed anyone to treat me like this. I am going.' She tried to put on her handkerchief but he prevented her. He kissed her and put his arms round her, begging her to stay; he was not coward enough to go back on his words by any profession of love, but when he saw her so full of determination he could not help admiring her, shaken as he still was by the mere idea of making such a resolution. Feeling herself completely reinstated she gave way, but only little by little. She said that if she stayed it would be the last time they would meet, and it was only just as they were separating that she consented to fix the day and hour of their next appointment. In the full consciousness of victory she had even forgotten the cause of their quarrel and was not interested in reviving the question.

He continued to hope that entire possession of her would in the end subdue the violence of his feelings. But he continued to go to their rendezvous with the same uncontrollable desire and he could not get rid of the tendency to reconstruct the *Ange* who was daily broken into fragments. His dissatisfaction led him to seek refuge in the sweetest of dreams; so Angiolina really gave him everything: the possession of her body and – since one gave birth to the other – the poet's dream as well.

He so often dreamed of her as a sick-nurse that he tried to continue his dream when she was actually beside him. Folding her in his arms with the passionate desire of the dreamer he said: 'I should like to be ill in order that you might tend me.'

'Oh, it would be lovely,' she said, for at certain moments she was ready to fall in with all his whims. The phrase naturally sufficed to banish any dream.

One evening when he was with Angiolina he had an idea which for that evening considerably relieved his state of mind. It was a dream which he continued to develop while with Angiolina, and regardless of her being there. He dreamed that they were very unhappy because of the unfair conditions of society under which they lived. He was so persuaded of this that he even imagined himself capable of performing an act of heroism in order to ensure the triumph of socialism. All their misfortunes were due to their poverty. His argument was based on the assumption that she was selling herself and that it was the poverty of her family which drove her to do so. But she did not perceive this implication and only regarded his words as a caress, and thought that he was blaming himself.

In another order of society he would at once have acknowledged her publicly without obliging her first to sacrifice herself to the tailor. He entered into Angiolina's lies in order to make her kinder to him and induce her to join in his ideas so that they might both dream together. She asked for some explanations and he gave them her, only too glad to be able to utter his dream aloud. He told her of the enormous struggle which had broken out between rich and poor, great and small. There could be no doubt as to the issue of the struggle which was to bring liberty to all, to them as well. He talked to her about the abolition of capital and the short hours of agreeable work which alone one would be obliged to do. Woman was to be the equal of man and love a mutual gift.

She asked for some further explanations which disturbed his dream, and finally concluded: 'If everything was to be divided there wouldn't be much left for anybody. The working classes are jealous good-for-nothings and will never succeed, however much you do for them.' He tried to discuss the question but gave it up at last. The child of the people was on the side of the rich.

He had the impression that she had never asked him for money. He could not deny, even to himself, that when he had discovered how poor she was and had accustomed her to accept money instead of sweetmeats and other presents, she had always shown herself extremely grateful, though always pretending to feel ashamed of taking it. And her gratitude was kindled anew at every fresh gift he made her, so that when he felt the need of making her more than usually sweet and loving he knew quite well how to set about it. He had felt this need so often that his purse was nearly empty. She never forgot to protest each time she accepted a present from him, and as the acceptance was only the simple act of holding out her hand while the protest consisted of a good many words, the latter remained more vividly in his mind than the former, and he continued to believe that their relationship would have been the same even without his gifts.

There was evidently great penury in Angiolina's

family. She had made every effort to prevent him paying her a surprise visit in her home. Those surprise visits did not suit her at all. But threats of not being there, or of having him thrown downstairs by her mother or father or brothers did nothing to deter him. Whenever he had time in the evening, however late it might be, he would go off to look for her, even if it often only meant his keeping old mother Zarri company. It was his dreams which drove him there. He was always hoping to find a changed Angiolina, and hastened thither to cancel the invariably sad impression of their last meeting.

Then she made one last effort. She told him that her father gave her no peace and that she had only succeeded with great difficulty in restraining him from making Emilio a scene. All that she had been able to obtain from him was the promise that he would abstain from using violence, but the old man was bent on giving him a piece of his mind. Five minutes later old Zarri came in. Emilio fancied that the old man, who was tall and thin and very shaky, and who was obliged to sit down directly he got into the room, knew quite well that his entrance had been announced. His first words were evidently intended to impress. He spoke slowly and with difficulty, but with an air of command. He said that he thought he was capable of advising and protecting any daughter of his who had need of it; for if she had not had him she would not have had anybody, for her brothers – not that he wanted to say anything against them – took no interest in family affairs. Angiolina seemed mightily pleased with this long preamble; suddenly she said she was going to dress in the room next door, and she disappeared.

The old man at once lost all his self-importance. He turned to look after his daughter, and at the same time took a pinch of snuff; there was a long pause during which Emilio thought over what he should say in reply to the charges which were about to be brought against him. Angiolina's father stared straight in front of him for some time, and particularly at his own boots. It was quite by chance that he raised his eyes again and saw

Emilio: 'Ah, yes,' he said with the air of a man who has just found something he had lost. He repeated the preamble, but with less emphasis; he was very absent-minded. Then he made a great effort to concentrate his attention and continue his speech. He looked at Emilio several times, always avoiding his eye, and only spoke when he could make up his mind to look at his empty snuff-box which he still held in his hand.

There were some bad people, he said, who persecuted the Zarri family. Had not Angiolina told him about them? It was wrong of her. Well then, there were people who were always on the lookout to find out things against the Zarri family. One had to be always on one's guard against them. Did not Signor Brentani know *Tic*? If he had known him he would not have come to the house so often.

Here the sermon degenerated into a warning to Emilio not to expose himself, young as he was, to such dangers. When the old man raised his eyes again to look at him, Emilio guessed the truth. In those strange blue eyes under their silver brows shone the light of madness.

This time the madman seemed to be able to endure Emilio's gaze. It was true that *Tic* lived up there at Opicina, but even from there he rained down blows on the legs and backs of his enemies. He added darkly: 'He even beats the little girl here.' The family had another enemy called *Toc*. He lived right in the middle of the town. He did not beat them but he did worse still. He robbed the family of all their jobs, he stole all their money and all their substance.

The old man had now worked himself into a fury and began to shout. Angiolina came rushing in, guessing at once what was the matter. 'Go along with you,' she said very crossly to her father, and pushed him out of the room.

Old Zarri stood hesitating in the doorway, and said, pointing to Emilio: 'He didn't know anything about *Tic* or *Toc*.'

'I will tell him,' Angiolina said, and burst out laughing. Then she called through the door: 'Mother, come and take father away,' and shut the door.

Emilio, terrified by the insane eyes which had been watching him for so long, asked: 'Is he ill?'

'Oh,' said Angiolina scornfully, 'he is an old waster, who never will do any work. There is *Tic* on one side and *Toc* on the other, and so he refuses ever to leave the house, and puts all the work on us women.' She suddenly burst into uncontrollable laughter and told him how, to please the old man, the whole family pretended to feel the blows which fell on the house from *Tic*. Several years before, when the old man's mania was just beginning, they were in a fifth-floor flat at Lazzareto Vecchio, *Tic* was at Campo Marzio and *Toc* on the Corso. They changed house hoping that the old man would venture out again into the street, when lo and behold! *Tic* moved up to Opicina and *Toc* to Via Stadion.

She said to him as he began to kiss her: 'This time you have been lucky to escape. You wouldn't have got off so easily if he had not remembered his enemies just at that moment.'

So they were becoming more and more intimate. He had now discovered all the secrets of the house. Even she felt that there was nothing left for Emilio to find out about her which might disgust him, and she used one day this charming expression: 'I tell you everything, as if you were a brother.' She felt she had him completely in her power, and though she was not tyrannical by nature and only wanted to make use of her power in order to enjoy herself and have as good a time as possible, she no longer treated him with any consideration. She would come late to appointments although she always found him with his eyes starting out of his head in the wildest state of excitement. She became more rough in her treatment of him. When she was tired of his caresses she would push him away with such violence that he said laughingly he was afraid she would whip him sooner or later.

He could not be quite certain, but he fancied that Angiolina and Paracci, the old landlady of the hired

157

room, had known each other before. The old woman used to look at Angiolina with a motherly eye, and admired her fair hair and beautiful eyes. Angiolina denied that she had ever known her before now, but betrayed a most exact knowledge of the house even in its remotest corners. One evening when she had come late as usual, old Paracci heard them quarrelling and intervened firmly on the side of Angiolina. 'I can't think how anyone can have the face to scold an angel like her.' Angiolina never refused homage, from whatever direction it came, and said, smiling complacently, 'You heard what she said. It ought to teach you a lesson.' He had indeed heard, and was horrified by his mistress's vulgarity.

As he had now made up his mind that there was no hope of raising her to his own level, he sometimes felt an irresistible desire to descend to hers or even below her. One evening she repulsed him, saying that she had been to confession that day and didn't want to sin. His desire on this occasion was not so much to possess her as to prove that he could be, for once at least, baser than she was. He assaulted her with violence, fighting till the last breath. When he lay at last in a state of exhaustion, and was beginning to repent of his brutality, he was comforted to receive a glance of admiration from Angiolina. For that whole evening she was completely his, the female adoring the male who had mastered her. He decided to act in a similar way on many future occasions, but was not capable of it. It was not so easy to find a second excuse for treating Angiolina with brutality and violence.

I I

I T seemed to be decreed by fate that Balli should always intervene to make Emilio's situation more painful in regard to Angiolina. It had been agreed between them for a long time that Emilio's mistress was to sit for the sculptor. The only thing needed to get the work started was that Emilio should remember to speak to Angiolina about it.

As he readily understood the reason for such repeated forgetfulness Stefano made up his mind to say no more about it. He felt that he was unable at the moment to get on with any other figure except the one he had imagined with Angiolina as his model, and just to pass the time, and because it amused him to play about with the idea, he began to build the frame of a human figure and to cover it with clay. He wrapped it all up in wet rags and thought to himself: 'A death shroud.' Every day he uncovered his nude and looked at it, imagining it clothed, then covered it up again in its rags, and carefully wetted them.

The two friends spoke no more about the subject. But Balli, hoping to attain his end without having to make a formal request, said to Emilio one evening: 'I can't work. I should be in despair about it, if I hadn't still got that figure in my mind.'

'I quite forgot to speak to Angiolina again,' said Emilio, without, however, taking the trouble to feign the surprise of someone who has really forgotten. 'I tell you what. When you meet her, speak to her about it yourself: you will see that she is only too ready to oblige.'

There was so much bitterness in this last phrase that Balli took pity on him and said no more for the moment. He knew himself that he had not intervened very happily between the lovers and he did not want to have any more to do with their affairs. He could not intrude himself upon them as he had done a few months earlier in the hope of curing his friend, and it was evident that Emilio's recovery must be a matter of time. The beautiful statue he had dreamed of so long, the only one which at the moment he felt any desire to do, was being destroyed by Emilio's incurable sensuality.

He tried to realize his plan with another model, but after a few sittings he gave it up in disgust. In reality the sudden abandonment of long-cherished ideas was nothing new in his career. But on this occasion, whether rightly or wrongly, he laid all the blame on Emilio. There was no doubt whatever in his own mind that if he could have had the model he dreamed of he would have been able to throw himself whole-heartedly into his work, if only to destroy it all a few weeks later.

He refrained from saying any of this to his friend and it was the last scruple he had regarding him. It was useless to explain to Emilio how important Angiolina had become to him; it would only have made the poor fellow's disease much worse. Who could have explained to Emilio that the artist's imagination had fixed on that object just because he had detected in the extraordinary purity of line, though quite independent of it, an indefinable expression of vulgarity and coarseness which Raphael would no doubt have suppressed but which he, on the contrary, wanted to copy and to accentuate?

As they walked together in the street he said not a word about the desire of his heart, but Emilio gained nothing by the consideration shown him by his friend, for the desire which Balli was afraid to express was magnified by him into something greater than it really was, and he suffered torments of jealousy. Balli now desired Angiolina as much as he did himself. How could he defend himself from such an enemy?

He could not defend himself! He had already confessed his jealousy, but he did not want to speak of it again; it would have been too stupid to betray jealousy of Balli after having tolerated the umbrella-maker as a rival. His shame left him defenceless. One day Stefano went to fetch him at the office, as he often did, to walk home with him. They were walking along the sea-front when they saw Angiolina coming towards them, all lit up by the mid-day sun which was playing in her fair curls. She had screwed up her face a little in the effort to keep her eyes open in the strong sunlight. Balli found himself suddenly face to face with his masterpiece and, disregarding its outline, saw it for the first time in all its details. She advanced towards them with that firm step of hers which did not in the least diminish the grace of her upright figure. Youth incarnate, clothed, would have walked like that in the sunlight.

'Look here!' Stefano exclaimed, suddenly making up his mind. 'Don't let your idiotic jealousy prevent me from creating a masterpiece.' Angiolina returned their greeting with the serious air she had assumed for some time past. But all her gravity was concentrated in the greeting, and even that manifestation of seriousness must have been taught her recently.

Balli stood still and waited for a sign of assent from his friend. 'Very well,' said Emilio mechanically after a moment's hesitation, hoping that Stefano would see how painful it was for him to give his consent. But Balli saw nothing but his model, and that she was escaping him; the words were hardly out of Emilio's mouth before he was after her.

So Balli and Angiolina had met again at last. By the time Emilio rejoined them he found them in complete agreement. Balli had lost no time and Angiolina, scarlet with pleasure, had at once asked him when she was to come. Tomorrow at nine o'clock. She agreed, saying that fortunately she did not have to go to the Deluigis next day. 'I will be punctual,' she said as they parted. It was her custom to say a great deal, the first words that came to her lips, and it never occurred to her that her promise to be punctual might give offence to Emilio as drawing a distinction between the appointments she made with Balli and those she made with him.

Directly he had done the deed, Balli's thoughts returned to his friend. He was at once conscious of having wronged him and affectionately asked Emilio's pardon: 'I really couldn't help it though I knew you would not like it. I assure you I won't take advantage of the fact that you pretend not to mind. I know it gives you pain. You're wrong, you know, quite wrong, but I am not altogether right, all the same.'

Emilio replied with a forced smile: 'Then I have nothing to say.'

Balli thought that Emilio was treating him more severely than he deserved.

'The only thing that remains for me then, if I want you to forgive me, is to tell Angiolina not to come? Very well, I will, if you want me to.'

It was impossible to accept the proposal because the poor woman – Emilio knew her as well as if it were he who had been her creator – was always specially drawn towards anyone who repulsed her, and he did not want to give her fresh reasons for loving Balli. 'No,' he said, in a more friendly voice. 'Leave things as they are now. I trust you, and only you,' he added, smiling.

Stefano warmly assured him that he deserved his confidence. He promised, he even swore that the very first time he found himself forgetting art even for a single moment during his sittings with Angiolina, he would turn her out. Emilio was weak enough to accept the promise, even to make Balli repeat it.

Next day Balli came to Emilio to report on the first sitting. He had worked like one possessed, and he had found nothing to complain of in Angiolina, who had held out as long as possible in her not very comfortable pose. She did not quite understand yet how to take up a pose, but Balli did not despair of teaching her. He was more than ever in love with his own idea. For nine or ten sittings he would not so much as have time to exchange a word with Angiolina. 'If I come to a point at which I have to stop for a while I promise you I will only talk about you. I bet you she will end by loving you with all her heart.'

'In any case, and that won't be a bad thing, you will bore her so much by talking about me that she will begin to take a dislike to you!'

He was not able to meet Angiolina during those two days, so he made an appointment with her for Sunday afternoon in Balli's studio. He found him hard at work.

The studio was really only a large warehouse. Balli did not want it to be elegant, so he had left it in its former rough condition, with every sign of the purpose for which it had been used. The stone pavement was as irregular as when the bales of merchandise had been dumped there; but in the winter a large carpet was put down in the middle to preserve the sculptor's feet from contact with the floor. The walls were roughly white-washed and little clay figures or plaster casts stood about on brackets, evidently put there at random, not in order to be admired, for they were piled up rather than arranged in groups. There was, however, a certain amount of comfort. The temperature was kept warm by a pyramid-shaped stove. A number of chairs and easy-chairs in every variety of size and shape, many of them very elegant, robbed the studio of its warehouse-like character. Balli said all his chairs were a different shape because he always needed one to sit on which matched the dream he was indulging in at the moment. But he said he still felt the need sometimes of shapes which he had not yet been able to find. Angiolina was perched on a stand, propped up with luxurious white cushions; Balli was standing on a chair beside another revolving stand at work upon his figure, which was only just sketched in.

When he saw Emilio he jumped down and greeted him warmly. Angiolina abandoned her pose too, and sat down among the white cushions; she seemed to be lying in a nest. She gave Emilio the kindest of welcomes. It was so long since they had met. She thought him looking a little pale. Wasn't he well? Brentani did not feel any particular gratitude to her for such a fond demonstration. She probably wanted to show him how grateful she was for being left alone so long with Balli.

Stefano was standing in front of his own work. 'Do you like it?' Emilio looked at it. A semi-human figure with its shoulders covered was kneeling on a rough and shapeless mass; in line and attitude the shoulders resembled Angiolina's. Up to that point there was something tragic in the figure. It seemed as if it were buried in the clay and were striving to free itself. The head too, of which the temples had been hollowed and the brow smoothed by the sculptor's thumb, looked like a skull carefully covered with earth so that it should utter no sound. 'You see how the thing is coming out,' said the sculptor, throwing a glance which was almost a caress over the whole work. 'The idea is not all there yet; it lacks form.' But the idea was only visible to him, something delicate and intangible. A prayer was to rise from that clay, the prayer of someone who believes for one moment and perhaps never will believe again. Balli explained too the form his idea was to take. The base was to remain rough and the figure was to go on becoming finer and finer right up to the hair, which was to be arranged with all the sophistication of the most up-to-date coiffeur. The hair was intended to contradict the prayer expressed by the face.

Angiolina took up her pose again, and Balli returned to his work. For half an hour she posed very conscientiously, imagining to herself that she was praying, just as the sculptor had told her, so as to have a prayerful expression on her face. Stefano was not satisfied with the expression and made a gesture of disgust, unseen except by Emilio. That nun didn't know how to pray. She had no idea of looking devout; she might throw her eyes up, but only to utter an impertinence. She was flirting with God the Father.

Angiolina's heavy breathing began to betray her weariness. Balli did not even notice, for he had reached an important point in his work; he made her bend her poor head, pitilessly, over her right shoulder. 'Are you very tired?' Emilio asked her, and as Balli could not see him he stroked her chin and gave it a support. She moved her lips to kiss his hand, but did not change her position. 'I can hold out a little longer.' How admirable she was, to sacrifice herself like that for a work of art! If he had been the artist he should have regarded her sacrifice as a proof of her love.

Soon afterwards Balli allowed her a short rest. He certainly did not need any himself and filled up the time by doing something to the base of his statue. In his long linen coat he took on almost a sacerdotal air. From her place beside Emilio, Angiolina gazed at the sculptor with ill-concealed admiration. He was a splendid man to look at, agile and strong, with shapely beard, slightly tinged with grey, but with golden lights in it still. He leaped lightly from his stand and back again without ever shaking the statue, and seemed the perfect embodiment of the intelligent worker, with an elegant shirt-cuff sticking out below the rough sleeve of his coat. Even Emilio could not help admiring him in spite of what he suffered just on that account.

Balli soon returned again to work. The sculptor punched the head a little more, without seeming to mind that he thereby made it lose the small amount of shape it had already. He put on a little clay in one place and removed it in another. It was to be supposed that he was copying, since he kept looking at the model, but the clay did not seem to Emilio to reproduce one single feature of Angiolina's face. When Stefano had finished working he told him so, and the sculptor taught him how he ought to look at it. For the moment there was no likeness except when you looked at the head from only one point of view. Angiolina could not recognize herself, and was vexed that Balli imagined he had portrayed her face in that shapeless mass of clay; but Emilio saw the obvious likeness. The face seemed to be asleep, immobilized by its clinging envelope of clay; the eyes, as yet unsculptured, seemed to be shut, but one felt that the vital breath was about to animate the lifeless clay.

Balli wrapped the figure in its damp shroud. He was satisfied with his work and excited by it.

They went out together. Balli's art was really the only point of contact between the two friends; they came together again in talking over the sculptor's idea, and during the whole of that afternoon their relationship recovered an intimacy which had long been lacking to it. For this reason the one who was least amused of the three was Angiolina, who almost felt herself *de trop*. Balli, who did not care to be seen about in such company during the daytime, insisted on her walking on in front of them; which she did, holding herself disdainfully erect, with her nose in the air. Balli went on talking about the statue while Emilio followed the girl's every movement with his eyes. There was no room for jealousy during all those hours. Balli was dreaming, and when he thought at all about Angiolina it was only to keep her at a distance, neither joking with her nor bullying her.

It was cold, and the sculptor proposed going into a tavern to drink some warm wine. As there were a great many people inside and a strong smell of food and tobacco, they decided to sit outside in the courtyard. At first Angiolina protested, saying she would catch cold, but when Balli said it would be an original thing to do she wrapped herself up in his cloak and enjoyed seeing herself admired by the people who came out of the hot inside room, and by the waiter who hurried to serve them. Balli did not notice the cold and kept gazing into his glass as if he were reading his own ideas there. Emilio was busy warming Angiolina's hands, which she willingly gave him to hold. It was the first time she had allowed him to caress her in Balli's presence and it gave him intense pleasure. 'Sweet creature,' he murmured, and went so far as to kiss her cheeks which she pressed against his lips.

It was a clear, blue night; the wind was whistling above the tall house which protected them from it. Fortified by the warm, aromatic drink which they swallowed in great quantities, they resisted the chilly temperature for about an hour. It was for Emilio another unforgettable episode in his love-story: the dark courtyard under the blue night sky and their little group at one end of the long wooden table. Angiolina definitely given over to him by Balli and showing herself a docile, more than docile – a tender mistress.

On the way home Balli said that he was obliged to go to a masquerade that night; he was horribly bored at the thought, but had arranged to meet a doctor-friend of his who said he could only go to the masquerade if he was in respectable company like that of the sculptor, so that his clients might the more readily excuse his presence in such a place.

Stefano would have preferred to go early to bed, so as to return fresh to work next morning. He felt shivers go through him at the idea of passing all those hours at a bacchanal.

Angiolina asked if he had a stall for the season and wanted him to tell her its exact position. 'I hope,' Balli said laughing, 'that if you are masked you will come and speak to me.'

'I have never been to a masquerade,' Angiolina emphatically protested. Then she reflected a moment and, as if she had just discovered that such a thing existed, she added: 'I should like so much to go to one.' It was agreed on the spot that they were to go to the masquerade which was to be given the following week for a charity. Angiolina jumped for joy and seemed so sincere that even Balli smiled amiably at her, as if she had been a child whom at small cost to oneself one has made happy.

When the two men were alone together Emilio confessed that he could find nothing to say against the sitting. Balli, however, poisoned all the pleasure he had felt that day by saying as they parted: 'So you are pleased with us? You must acknowledge that I did my best to give you satisfaction.'

So he owed Angiolina's show of affection to Balli's recommendation! The idea mortified him profoundly. Here was a fresh and important ground for jealousy. He determined to tell Balli that he did not care to owe Angiolina's tenderness to the influence of someone else. And he resolved to take the first opportunity to show less gratitude for demonstrations of affection which had so lately raised him to the seventh heaven of happiness. Now he understood why she had allowed herself to be caressed so willingly in Balli's presence. How submissive she was to the sculptor! For his sake she was willing to sacrifice her affectation of virtue and the lies from which Emilio could never escape. She was quite different with Balli. She would unmask herself for Balli who had not possessed her, but for him what would she do?

Next morning, early, he hastened to Angiolina, anxious

to see how she would treat him when Stefano was not there. Perfectly! She opened the door to him herself, after making sure that it was he. She was lovelier still in the morning. The night's rest had restored her blooming, virginal air. Her white wrapper striped with blue, a little faded, followed the firm lines of her body, leaving her white neck bare.

'Do I intrude?' he asked gloomily. He refrained from kissing her, preferring to save that up till after the quarrel which he meant to have with her.

But she did not seem to notice his sulks. She took him to her room: 'I must dress quickly,' she said, 'for I have to be at Signora Deluigi's at nine. You can be reading this letter while I dress.' She took a letter nervously out of a basket: 'Read it carefully and give me your advice.' Her face clouded over, and the tears came to her eyes. 'Read what is happening. I will tell you all about it. You are the only person who can help me. I have told mother all about it too, but she, poor soul, can't do anything but cry.' She left the room, but at once looked in again and said: 'If mother says anything to you about it, remember that she knows everything except that I have given my-self to Volpini.' With that she threw him a kiss and went out again.

The letter was from Volpini, a formal letter of fare-well. He began by telling her that he had always be-haved honestly towards her while she, he knew now, had been false to him from the first. Emilio began reading the almost illegible writing again more carefully, fearing to find himself mentioned as the motive for Volpini's desertion. But his name was not mentioned in the letter. Volpini had been informed that she was never Merighi's fiancée but his mistress. He had always refused to believe it, till a few days ago he had had absolute proof that she had been seen at several masquerades, always in the company of a fresh young man. There followed a few insulting phrases, badly put together, which gave the impression that the poor man was perfectly sincere, though one could not help laughing at a long word put in here and there which he must have looked up laboriously in a dictionary.

Old mother Zarri came in. With her hands as usual hidden under her apron she leaned against the bed and waited patiently till he had finished reading the letter. 'What do you think of it?' she asked in her nasal voice. 'Angiolina says no, but it seems to me it's all over with Volpini.'

Only one of Volpini's assertions had caused any surprise to Emilio. 'Is it true,' he asked, 'that Angiolina has so often been to the masquerades?' All the rest, such as her having been the mistress of Merighi and of a great many others too, was nothing new to him. He knew it was absolutely true, and the fact that others had been deceived as much as, and more, than himself, aroused his anger less than those lies of hers which he had always so hated. But even for him there was something new to be learned from the letter. She could act even better than he thought. The day before she had taken in Balli with her expression of joy at the thought of going to a masquerade for the first time.

'It is a pack of lies,' said the old woman, with the calm air of someone saying what she is sure will be believed. 'Angiolina comes straight home every evening directly she has finished her work, and goes to bed at once. I see her into bed myself.' Clever old woman! She had certainly not been taken in herself, and she would not admit that anyone should think they were being taken in by her.

Directly the mother had gone out, in came the daughter.

'Have you read it?' asked Angiolina, sitting down beside him. 'What do you think of it?'

Emilio replied coldly that he thought Volpini was quite right, for a girl who was engaged ought not to go to masquerades.

Angiolina protested vigorously. She go to the masquerades? Hadn't he seen how happy she had been the evening before at the thought of going to one, the first she had ever been to?

Quoted in such a way her argument lost all its force; the very joy she mentioned as a proof of her innocence must have cost her a great effort for it to have been so deeply impressed on her memory. But she brought forward many other proofs as well. She had spent every evening with him, when she had not been obliged to go to the Deluigis; she hadn't got a single rag to dress up in for a masquerade, and she had been counting on his help for the one they had planned to go to together. Emilio was not convinced; he felt certain now that she had frequented all the masquerades during that carnival, but he could not help being softened by the seductive eloquence with which she offered him her many proofs. She was not offended with him for having insulted her by doubting her veracity. She clung to him, trying to convince him and soften his heart, even though Balli was not there!

But he soon realized that she needed his help. She did not want to let Volpini off so easily, and she counted on Emilio's advice as to how she could hold him, for she had in him the boundless confidence which the uneducated always have in a writer. This fact did not, however, deprive Emilio of the satisfaction her endearments gave him; it was anyway better than being indebted for them to Balli. He wanted to show himself worthy of them and set about seriously studying the problem she had put before him.

He was obliged at once to confess that she understood it better than he did. She very acutely observed that in order to know how she ought to behave she must first of all know whether Volpini himself really believed the things he stated or whether he had written that letter to try and get her to clear up certain vague rumours which had reached him; also, whether he had written it with the firm intention of breaking with her or whether it was only a threat and he was ready to give way at the first move Angiolina might make. Emilio, when he read the letter again, was obliged to confess that Volpini mixed up his proofs too much for him to be able to disentangle any single good one. He quoted no name except

Merighi's. 'As to that, I have a very good answer,' said Angiolina with great display of anger. 'He can't deny that I gave myself to him first.'

Once put on the track, Emilio made a discovery which corroborated Angiolina's point of view. In the grandiloquent close of his letter Volpini declared that he was leaving her first of all because she was false to him, and secondly because she was very cold to him and he was sure she did not love him. Was it the moment to complain of a defect which lay perhaps in her nature, if the other charges he brought against her were as serious as the writer wanted to make out? She was immensely grateful to him for that point, which proved the truth of her own interpretation, and it did not occur to her that it was she herself who had put him on the track. Oh, she knew she was not lettered like him, and she didn't want to get credit for it! She was in the thick of the fight and girded on with equal energy every arm that was offered her which she thought would serve her purpose, without troubling to see who had forged it.

She could not write to Volpini immediately because she was obliged to run off at once to Signora Deluigi, who was expecting her. But she would be home at midday and begged Emilio to come then as well. She would be waiting for him, and between now and then they must both spend all their time in thinking over that one question. She wanted him to take the letter with him to his office to study it at his leisure.

They went out together, but she told him that they must part before they got into the town. She was sure now that Volpini had employed people to spy on her in Trieste. 'The cad!' she exclaimed emphatically. 'He has ruined me.' She hated him for having promised to marry her; it was that which had ruined her, she said. 'Now, of course, he would be glad to get out of fulfilling his promise, but he will find he has me to deal with!' She admitted that she detested him. He disgusted her, he was a filthy beast. 'It is your fault that I ever gave myself to him.' When she saw that Emilio looked surprised at such a charge, which she had never brought so violently before, she corrected herself, and said: 'Well, if it wasn't your fault, I did it for your sake.'

With these soft words she left him, and he remained convinced that she had brought the charge against him for the sole purpose of inducing him to support her with all his might in her impending struggle with Volpini.

He followed her for a short distance, and when he saw the impudent way she exposed herself to the gaze of every passer-by in the street, he was seized again by his old malady, which with him dominated every other feeling. Forgetting his fear that she would attach herself to him again, he felt intensely happy at what had happened. She needed him now because Volpini had deserted her, and at mid-day he would be able to have her entirely to himself for another whole hour, to feel that she really belonged to him.

In the commercial part of the town, in which at that hour no one was walking for pleasure, Angiolina with her supple, picturesque figure and firm step, and her eye which had attention to spare for so much beside her own actual passage through the street, attracted everyone's attention. And he felt that every man who saw that seductive figure in the street must at once think of going to bed with her. He could not escape the whole morning from the excitement produced in him by that picture.

He proposed at mid-day to make Angiolina appreciate to the full the value of his help and to enjoy all the advantages which such an exceptional position seemed to bestow on him. The door was opened by old Signora Zarri, who invited him in with the utmost warmth and asked him to walk into her daughter's room. He was glad to sit down after his rapid climb upstairs, and expected every moment to see Angiolina appear. 'She has not come in yet,' said the old woman, looking towards the passage as if she also were expecting to see her daughter arrive.

'She is not here?' cried Emilio, so bitterly disappointed that he felt he could hardly believe his own ears.

'I can't understand her being so late,' the old woman

went on, still looking out of the door. 'She must have been kept by Signora Deluigi.'

'How late do you think she will be?' he asked.

'I don't know,' she replied, in a tone of the utmost innocence. 'She ought to be coming any minute now, but if she has stayed to dinner with Signora Deluigi she might not come back till this evening.' She was silent for a moment, as if thinking things over, then she added, more confidently: 'But I don't think she is likely to have her dinner out, because it's all ready for her here.'

Emilio, who was an acute observer, saw at once that all her doubts were feigned and that the old woman knew there was no likelihood of Angiolina coming back soon. But as usual, his power of observation was not of much use to him. His desire chained him to the spot, while Angiolina's mother kept him company in silence, and with an expression of such complete gravity that, looking back on it, Emilio decided it must have been ironical. The youngest daughter came and stood by her mother's chair and kept rubbing herself against her back like a cat against a door-post.

He went away at last discouraged, after the kindest of farewells from the old woman and the little girl. He stroked the little girl's hair, which was the same colour as Angiolina's. In fact she was very much like Angiolina except that she had not her healthy appearance.

He thought it would probably be wiser of him to avenge himself on Angiolina by not going to see her unless she sent for him. Now that she needed his help she would very soon come and look for him. But in the evening, directly he came out of the office, he set off again on the road to her house, saying to himself that he should just like to find out the reason for her unexplained absence. It was very possible that this really had been a case of *force majeure*.

He found Angiolina dressed exactly as she had been when he took leave of her in the morning. She had only that second come in. She let him kiss and embrace her with the docility she always showed when she wanted him to forgive her for something. Her cheeks were flaming and her breath smelt of wine.

'I drank rather a lot,' she said, bursting out laughing. 'Signor Deluigi, who is quite an old man, over fifty, tried to make me tipsy; but he didn't succeed, not he!' He must, however, have succeeded rather better than she thought, judging by her uncontrollable mirth. She rocked with laughter. She was adorable with that unusual flush in her cheeks and her shining eyes. He kissed her open mouth, her bright red gums, and she let him do just as he liked, passively, as if she did not know it was herself he was kissing. She told him in broken phrases, amid her laughter, that it was not only the old man but all the family who had undertaken to make her drunk, and that though there were so many of them, still they had not succeeded. He tried to restore her to reason by talking about Volpini. 'Oh let me alone with that stuff!' cried Angiolina and, seeing that he persisted, she made no answer but began kissing him just as he had done to her, in the mouth and on the neck, with an initiative which she had never shown before, so that they ended up on the bed, she still in her hat and coat. The door was ajar, and it was unlikely that the sounds of their struggle should not have reached the kitchen where her father and mother and little sister were assembled.

They had made her completely drunk. A curious house the Deluigis' must be! He did not bear Angiolina any grudge himself because his own pleasure that evening had indeed been perfect.

Next day they met at mid-day, both in an excellent humour. Angiolina assured him that her mother had noticed nothing at all. Then she said she was very sorry indeed that he had seen her in that state. It wasn't her fault, it was that horrible old Deluigi!

He set her mind at rest, telling her that if it depended on him he would make her drunk once a day. Then they composed the letter to Volpini with a care of which they would hardly have seemed capable in their existing state of mind.

Angiolina might have appeared to show superior intelligence in her interpretation of Volpini's letter; the reply flowed entirely from Emilio's accomplished pen.

She would have liked to write him an insulting letter; she wanted it to give vent to an honest girl's righteous indignation, when she is falsely accused. 'And if Volpini was here,' she observed with lofty anger, 'he should just have a good box on the ear, and no reason given. That would soon teach him who is in the wrong.'

Her idea was all right, but Emilio wished to proceed with greater caution. Without it occurring to her to be offended, he made out an ingenious case, saying that in order to study the problem with greater facility he had asked himself the following question: How would an honest girl have acted in Angiolina's place? He did not add that he had embodied the honest girl in Amalia and asked himself how his sister would have behaved supposing she had had to reply to Volpini's letter, he only communicated to her the result he had arrived at. The honest woman would first of all have experienced enormous surprise; then doubt as to whether it were not a misunderstanding, and at last, though scarcely even then, the horrible suspicion that the whole letter was to be attributed to the lover's desire to escape from his responsibilities. Angiolina was charmed by this reconstruction of a whole psychological process, and he at once set to work.

She sat down beside him as quiet as a mouse, and with one hand resting on his knee and her head almost touching his so that she could follow what he was writing, she made her presence felt without in the least getting in his way while he wrote. Her being so near deprived the letter of all air of rigid preparation and, if it had not been destined for a man like Volpini, probably of its efficacy too, for it had quite lost the dignified character which he had meant to give it. Something of Angiolina leaked through into the phrases. Coarse words began to flow from his pen, and he let them flow, rejoicing to see her ecstatic admiration, the same expression she had worn a few days before when watching Balli in his studio.

Then without re-reading it she began to copy his prose, enchanted at being able to sign her own name to it. She had seemed much more intelligent when she was reasoning about how one ought to behave than she did now in her uncritical approbation. She could not indeed pay much heed to the contents of the letter, because the actual calligraphy absorbed all her attention.

With her eyes on the outside of the envelope, she suddenly inquired whether Balli had said any more about the masquerade to which he had promised to take her. The slumbering moralist in Emilio did not awake, but he strongly dissuaded her from going to the masquerade for fear Volpini should hear about it. But she had an answer ready for every objection. 'Oh yes, now I certainly shall go to the masquerade. Hitherto I haven't been, because of that wretch, but now! Let him hear of it, I don't care.'

Emilio pressed to see her that evening. She was to sit for Balli in the afternoon, then she had got to run to the Deluigis for a few moments, so she would not be able to come till quite late. She made an appointment with him for, as she said, she could refuse him nothing at the moment, but not in Paracci's house because she wanted to be home early. They would go for a walk to Sant' Andrea as they used to in those happy days when they had first met, and then he would walk home with her. She was still tired – she had drunk so much the day before – and she needed rest. The proposal pleased him too. It was one of his essential characteristics to delight in evoking the sentiment of the past. That evening he would analyse again the colour of the sea and sky and Angiolina's hair.

She said good-bye, and as a last injunction begged him to post the letter to Volpini. So he found himself in the middle of the road with that letter in his hand, a tangible proof of the basest action he had ever committed in his life, but of which he only became conscious now that Angiolina was no longer sitting beside him.

12

H E had just shut the door of his flat behind him and was standing hat in hand in the dining-room, uncertain what to do next, and wondering whether he could after all face an hour of boredom in his sister's mute society. Suddenly there came from Amalia's room the sound of two or three unintelligible words, and finally a whole phrase: 'Get away, you ugly brute!' He shuddered. Her voice was so changed by fatigue or emotion that it resembled his sister's only as an inarticulate shout proceeding from the throat can resemble the modulated speaking voice. Was she asleep at this hour and dreaming by day?

He opened the door noiselessly, and a sight presented itself to his eyes which till his dying day he could never forget. For ever afterwards one or other of the details of that scene had only to strike his senses for him to recall the whole of it immediately and to feel again the appalling horror of it. Some peasants were passing in a road near by, and for ever afterwards the monotonous air they were singing at that moment brought tears to Emilio's eyes. All the sounds which reached him were monotonous, without warmth or sense. In a neighbouring flat someone who could not play at all was strumming a vulgar waltz. Played like that the waltz sounded to him like a funeral march – how often it recurred to him afterwards! Even the cheerful day outside became sad for him. It was not long after mid-day and a dazzling sunlight was reflected from the windows of the opposite house into the lonely room. Yet his memory of that moment was always associated with a sensation of darkness and of frightful cold.

Amalia's clothes lay scattered all over the floor and a skirt prevented him from opening the door completely;

there were a few garments under the bed, her bodice was shut between the window-panes, and her boots had been arranged with evident care in the middle of the table.

Amalia was sitting on the edge of the bed, clothed only in a short chemise. She had not noticed her brother's entry, and continued gently to pass her hands up and down her legs, which were as thin as spindles. Emilio was surprised and shocked to see that her naked body resembled that of an ill-nourished child.

He did not realize at first that she was delirious. He did not see that she was physically worn out; he attributed her noisy breathing and the difficulty she had in drawing each breath to the tiring position she was sitting in. His first feeling was of anger; he had hardly escaped from Angiolina before he found this other woman ready to annoy him and cause him fresh anxiety. 'Amalia! What are you doing?' he said reprovingly.

She did not hear him, though she seemed to be conscious of the sounds of the waltz, for she marked its rhythm with her hands as she continued to pass them up and down her legs.

'Amalia!' he repeated in a faint voice, overwhelmed by this obvious proof that she was delirious. He put his hand on her shoulder. Then she turned. She looked first at the hand whose touch she had felt, then she looked him in the face; but there was no recognition in her eyes, only a feverish glitter and the effort to see. Her cheeks were flaming, and her lips purple and dry and shapeless like an old wound which refuses to heal. Her eye passed to the window flooded in sunlight but, hurt perhaps by the glare, returned at once to her naked legs which she continued to gaze at with curious intentness.

'Oh Amalia!' he cried, letting all his horror find vent in that one cry which he hoped might recall her to herself. A weak man dreads delirium and insanity as if they were contagious diseases; Emilio's loathing was such that he had to put great restraint upon himself in order not to fly from the room. Overcoming with an effort his violent repulsion, he again touched his sister's shoulder and cried: 'Amalia! Amalia!' It was a call for help.

It was a slight relief to him to notice that she had heard him. She looked at him again, thoughtfully, as if she were trying to understand the meaning of those cries and of the repeated pressure on her shoulder. She touched her chest as if she had suddenly become conscious of the weight upon it which tormented her. Then, forgetting Emilio and her own exhaustion, she shouted again: 'Oh, still those horrible creatures!' and there was a break in her voice as if she were going to burst out crying. She rubbed her legs vigorously with both her hands; then bent down with a swift movement as if she were about to surprise an animal in the act of escaping. She seized one of her toes in her right hand and covered it over with her left, then carefully raised both her closed hands as if she were holding something in them. When she saw they were empty she examined them several times, then returned to her foot, ready to stoop down again and renew her strange chase.

A shivering attack reminded Emilio that he ought to induce her to get into bed. He approached her, horrified at the thought of having perhaps to resort to force. His task was however quite easy, for she obeyed the first firm pressure of his hand; she lifted one leg after the other on to the bed, without any shame, and allowed him to pull the bedclothes over her. But she showed an inexplicable reluctance to lie down altogether, and remained leaning on one elbow. Very soon, however, she could no longer hold out in that position, and abandoned herself on the pillow, uttering for the first time an intelligible sound of grief. 'Oh, my God! my God!'

'But what has happened to you?' asked Emilio who, at the sound of that one sensible cry, thought that he could talk to her like a reasonable person. She made no reply, for she was intent on discovering what it was that still went on tormenting her, even under the bedclothes. She hunched herself all up together, sought out her legs with her hands, and in the deep plot she was evidently meditating against the things or creatures which tormented her, she even contrived to make her breathing less noisy. Then she drew up her hands again and gazed at them in incredulous surprise when she found them empty. She lay for a while beneath the sheets in a state of such distress that she seemed even to forget her terrible bodily fatigue.

'Are you better?' Emilio asked, in a tone of entreaty. He wanted to console himself by the sound of his own voice, which he modulated softly in an effort to forget his recent dread that he might have to restrain her by violence. He bent over her, so that she might hear him better.

She lay looking at him for a long time, while her quick, feeble breath rose towards him. She recognized him; the warmth of the bed seemed to have revived her senses. However far she wandered afterwards in her delirium, he never forgot that she had recognized him. She was evidently getting better. 'Now let us leave this house,' she said, pronouncing each syllable with care. She stretched out a leg as if she were meditating getting out of bed, but when he restrained her, with perhaps unnecessary force, she at once resigned herself and forgot what it was which had prompted her to the act.

She repeated it again soon afterwards, but without the same energy; she seemed to remember that she had been ordered to lie down, and not to get out of bed. Now she was speaking again. She thought they had changed house and that there was a great deal to do, that she would have to work desperately to put it all in order. 'My God! how dirty it all is here. I knew it was, but you would come to it. And now? Aren't we going away?'

He tried to calm her by playing up to her fancy. He caressed her gently, saying that it didn't look to him so dirty, and that now they were in the house they would do better to stay there.

Amalia listened to all he had to say, but she seemed also to be listening inwardly to other words beside his; then she said: 'If you want it I must do it. We will stay here then, but ... so much dirt...' Two tears flowed down her cheeks which had been dry till that moment;

they rolled like two pearls down her flaming cheeks.

Soon after she forgot that grievance, but her delirium soon produced another source of distress. She had been out fishing, and could not catch any fish: 'I can't understand! What is the good of going out fishing if there are not any fish? One has to go such a long, long way, and it is so cold.' The others had taken all the fish and there were none left for them. All her grief and fatigue now seemed to be due to that fact. Her fevered words, to which her exhaustion gave a kind of tired rhythm, were continually interrupted by some sound of distress.

He had ceased to pay any attention to her; he must find some way out of the situation, he must devise some means of fetching a doctor. Every idea which his despair suggested to him was examined in turn, as if it would have been possible to act on them. He looked round to see if he could find a cord to bind the sick woman to the bed and leave her alone; he took a step towards the window, to call for help from there, and at last, forgetting that it was impossible to make himself intelligible to Amalia, he began talking to her, trying to get her to promise to stay quiet during his absence. Patting the bedclothes gently down on her shoulders to show her that she was to stay in bed, he said: 'Will you stay like that, Amalia? Promise me you will!'

But now she was talking about clothes. They had enough to last a year, so they would not have to spend anything on them for a whole year. 'We are not rich, but we have everything we need – everything.' Signora Birlini might look down on them, because she was better off than they were. But Amalia was glad she was better off, for she was fond of her. She went on babbling in this childish, contented way, and it wrung his heart to hear her say how happy she was amid so much suffering.

He must decide something, and at once. Amalia had shown no sign of violence in her delirium, either in speech or gesture, and when Emilio had recovered from the bewilderment into which he had fallen from the moment he had come in and found her in that state, he left the room and rushed to the front door. He thought of calling the porter, or that he would run and fetch the doctor himself, or that he would go and ask Balli's advice. He had not made up his mind yet what he should do, but he must make haste and get some help for his unfortunate sister. He could not bear to remember her pitiful state of nakedness.

He stood hesitating on the landing. He felt a strong impulse to return to Amalia to see if she had taken advantage of his absence to commit some act of madness. He leaned against the banister to see if anyone was coming up. He bent right over, so as to see further, and for a single instant, only for a second, his thoughts wandered; he forgot his sister and remembered that this was just the position in which he used to wait for Angiolina. Even in that brief flash the image was so clear that, as he strained to see further, he was conscious of seeking not only the help he needed, but also the living form of his mistress. He straightened himself again, sick at the thought.

A door on an upper floor opened and shut again. Someone – salvation – was coming down the stairs. He sprang up a flight at one bound and found himself face to face with the tall, strong figure of a woman. Tall and strong and dark; that was all he saw, but he at once found the words he needed: 'Oh, Signora,' he entreated. 'Help me! I would do for any human being what I am asking you to do for me.'

'Is it Signor Brentani?' inquired a sweet voice; and the dark lady, who had already made a backward movement as if to retreat, stood still.

He told her that he had come home a short while ago and found his sister in such a state of delirium that he did not dare to leave her alone while he went to fetch a doctor.

The lady came down the stairs. 'Signorina Amalia? Poor dear! I will come with you at once, gladly.' She was dressed in mourning. Emilio thought she was probably religious and after a moment's hesitation said: 'May God bless you for it.'

The lady followed him into Amalia's room. Emilio

took those few steps in a state of indescribable anguish. Who could tell what fresh sight might await him! In the next room there was no sound to be heard, though it had seemed to him as if Amalia's breathing must be heard all over the house.

He found her with her face turned to the wall. She was talking about a fire now; she saw the flames; they could not touch her, they could only make her terribly hot. He bent over her, and kissed her flaming cheek, in order to draw her attention to himself. When she turned to him he was anxious, before going away, to see what impression the companion he was leaving with her made on her. Amalia looked at the newcomer for a moment, with complete indifference.

'I entrust her to you,' said Emilio to the lady. He felt he could safely do so. She had a sweet, motherly face; her little eyes rested on Amalia with great tenderness. 'The Signorina knows me,' she said, sitting down at the bed-side. 'I am Elena Chierici and I live on the third floor. Do you remember the day you lent me your thermometer to take my son's temperature?'

Amalia looked at her, and said: 'Yes, but it burns, and it will always go on burning.'

'Not always,' said Signora Elena, bending over her with a kind, encouraging smile, her own eyes moist with compassion. She asked Emilio to give her, before he went out, a jug of water and a glass. It was a serious business for him to find these things in a house where he had lived with as little regard for domestic details as if he had been in an hotel.

Amalia did not at once understand that refreshment was being offered her in that glass; then she drank eagerly in little sips. When she let herself fall back on the pillow she found a fresh support; Elena's soft arm was lying there, and her little head rested upon it with delightful ease. A wave of gratitude surged up in Emilio's breast, and he pressed Elena's hand warmly before leaving the room.

He rushed to Balli's studio, and ran into his friend

who was just coming out. He thought he might have found Angiolina there, and breathed freely when he found Balli alone. He had never any need to feel remorse for his own conduct during the few hours of that day in which he still imagined it possible to do something to save Amalia. During those hours his sole thought was of his sister, and if he had met Angiolina he should have trembled with pain solely because the sight of her would have reminded him of his own sin.

'Oh, Stefano! Such a terrible thing has happened to me.' He entered the studio and sat down on the chair nearest the door, and hiding his face in his hands burst out into despairing sobs. He would have found it hard to explain why he had burst into tears at that moment. He was just beginning to recover from the severe shock he had received and his grief pressed to find an outlet; or perhaps it was the neighbourhood of Balli, who must have had some part in Amalia's illness, which caused his sudden outburst of emotion. It is certain that he soon experienced satisfaction at having indulged in this violent expression of grief – for himself and for Balli too. His fit of weeping had soothed and calmed him; he felt a sense of moral restoration. He would devote the rest of his life to Amalia, and even if, as he feared, she were to become mad he would keep her with him, not as his sister but as his own child. And he found such solace in weeping that he forgot how urgent it was to send for a doctor. This, he felt, was his proper place, it was here that he could really work for Amalia's good. In his present state of excitement every exploit seemed easy to him, and he felt as if it were possible for him to wipe out the past and all its memories both for him and for Balli simply by that outburst of grief. He would teach him to know Amalia as she really was, so tender and good and unfortunate.

He related in great detail the scene which had just taken place; her delirium and exhaustion; and how for a long time he had not dared to leave her alone, till providentially Signora Chierici had intervened to help him.

Balli had the air of someone surprised by bad news – not at all the air Emilio felt he ought to have – and with the swift decision which came naturally to him in that state of mind he advised sending for Dr Carini. He had been told he was a good doctor; he was also a friend of his, and he would make him take an interest in Amalia's case.

Emilio still wept, and showed no sign of moving from the spot. He felt he had not yet finished all he had to say; he would not give in, and sought for a phrase by which he might move his friend. He found one which made him shudder with horror himself. 'Mad or dying!' Death! It was the first time he had imagined Amalia dying, disappearing and leaving him alone, just as he had succeeded in giving up Angiolina; he saw himself alone, overwhelmed by remorse because he had not profited by the happiness which up to that moment had been his for the asking, the happiness of devoting his life to someone who needed his care and self-sacrifice. With Amalia every hope of comfort vanished from his life. He said in a low voice: 'I don't know which is worse, my grief or my remorse.'

He looked at Balli to see if his friend had understood him. Stefano's face expressed genuine surprise. Remorse? He had always thought of Emilio as a model brother, and he told him so. He remembered however that Amalia had been slightly neglected of late for Angiolina, and added: 'Of course it wasn't worth your while to take up your time with a woman like Angiolina, but it was one of those misfortunes which happen to us.'

Balli had so little understood Emilio that he said he could not understand why they were wasting so much time. He must run off and fetch Carini, and Emilio was not to give up hope before hearing what the doctor said about Amalia. It might easily be that symptoms which seemed so alarming to the inexperienced eye would not frighten the doctor.

It was a breath of hope and Emilio clung desperately to it. They parted in the street. Balli thought it advisable not to leave Amalia alone with a stranger longer than

185

was necessary; Emilio was to go straight home, and he would go off and fetch the doctor.

They both set off at a run. Emilio's haste was caused by a great hope which had lately sprung up in his breast. It was not altogether out of the question that he might find Amalia restored to health, and greeting him with an affection equal to that which she would read in his own face. His quick step accompanied and spurred on his audacious dream. Never had Angiolina given birth to a dream inspired by so eager a desire.

He did not notice the cold wind which had lately started blowing, making one forget the warm spring-like day which had seemed in such violent contradiction to his grief. The streets were darkening rapidly; the sky was covered with great clouds driven along by a strong current of air, only perceptible on the earth in a sudden lowering of the temperature. In the distance Emilio saw against the dark sky a mountain peak all yellow in the dying light.

Amalia was still delirious. Directly he heard her tired voice, with its same soft tone, the same childish modulation dying away sometimes from exhaustion, he realized that while he outside had been indulging in mad hopes, the invalid on her sick-bed had not found a moment's respite.

Signora Elena was tied to the bed because the sick woman's head was resting on her arm. She said, however, that shortly after Emilio had gone out Amalia had become restless and rejected its proffered support; now she had settled down again.

The good creature's work was actually over now, and he told her so, expressing at the same time his infinite gratitude.

She looked up at him with her kind little eyes and made no attempt to remove her arm, on which Amalia's head was shifting from side to side uneasily. She said: 'And who will take my place?' When she heard that he intended to ask the doctor for a paid nurse, she begged earnestly to be allowed to stay there, and thanked him when he said with real emotion that he had never

186

dreamed of sending her away, but was afraid it would be tiresome for her to stay. He asked her if she did not want to warn anyone of her absence. She answered simply: 'There is no one in the house to whom my absence could cause surprise. A new servant has started work for me only today.'

Soon afterwards Amalia moved her head on to the pillow and the lady's arm was set free. She took off her hat and Emilio thanked her afresh, for he looked on that act as confirming her decision to remain at the bedside. She looked at him in some surprise, as if she did not understand. No one could have behaved more simply.

Amalia began talking again without changing her position and without calling for anyone, as if she were under the impression that she was relating all her dream aloud. She said the beginning of certain sentences and the end of others; some words she gabbled incomprehensibly, others she pronounced quite clearly. Sometimes she would exclaim aloud, sometimes ask questions. She would inquire anxiously, always satisfied with the reply, which perhaps she did not fully understand. Of Signora Elena, who had bent over her to try and understand a wish she seemed trying to express, she asked: 'But aren't you Vittoria?' 'No, I am not,' said the lady somewhat surprised. Amalia seemed satisfied with this reply and was quiet for some time.

A little later she began coughing. She struggled against her cough and her face took on an appearance of childish desolation; she seemed to be suffering great pain. Signora Elena made Emilio notice that expression, which her face had also worn during his absence. 'We must speak to the doctor about it; that cough shows that your sister has something wrong with her chest.' Amalia had another violent fit of coughing, and fought for breath. 'I can't bear it,' she moaned, and began to cry.

But before the tears were dry on her cheeks she had forgotten her pain. She began feebly talking about the house. There was a new discovery for making cheap coffee. 'They invent everything in these days. Soon we shall be able to live without any money at all. Give me a little of that coffee just to try. I will bring it back. I love justice. I told Emilio so too.' 'Yes, I remember you did,' said Emilio, to keep her quiet. 'You always loved justice.' He bent over her and kissed her on the forehead.

There was one moment of her delirium which he never forgot. 'Yes, we two,' she said, fixing him with her eye, and speaking in that tone of people in delirium which makes it doubtful whether they are merely crying out or asking a question, 'We two, here together alone, in peace.' The serious and anxious expression on her face echoed the seriousness of her words, and one felt that her anxiety expressed a burning grief. However, a short time after she was talking quite quietly of the two of them alone in the house they could run so cheaply.

There was a ring at the bell. It was Balli and Dr Carini. Emilio knew him already; he was a man of about forty, dark and tall and thin. It was said that his time at the Univeristy had been more full of amusements than study, whereas now that he was well off he made no effort to get paying patients, but preferred a subordinate position at the hospital so as to continue the studies he had neglected earlier. He loved medicine with the ardour of an amateur, but he alternated his studies with every sort of pastime, so that he had a good many more artist than doctor friends.

He stopped in the dining-room, and remarking that Balli had been able to tell him no more about Amalia's illness than that she had had a sharp attack of fever, he asked Emilio to give him some more details about it.

Emilio told him of the state in which he had found his sister a few hours before, alone in the house where she had probably been behaving very oddly all the morning. He described her delirium in detail, how it had shown itself first in an unrest which drove her to hunt for insects on her legs, and then in a ceaseless babble. He was deeply moved as he described and analysed all the anguish she had suffered that day, and wept as he told of her exhaustion and her cough which rang so false and thin, like the sound produced by a broken vessel, and of the intense pain which each fit of coughing produced in the sick woman.

The doctor tried to encourage him with a friendly word, then, returning to the subject, asked a question which caused Emilio considerable distress: 'And up to this morning?'

'My sister has always been delicate, but quite sane.' He had committed himself by that sentence, and it was only after he had said it that he was seized by doubt. Those dreams which she had had aloud, and which he had surprised, were not they indications of a disordered state of mind? Ought he not to mention them? But how could he do so in Balli's presence?

'Was your sister quite well up till today?' asked Carini, with an air of incredulity. 'Even yesterday?'

Emilio felt awkward and did not know what to reply. He could not remember having seen his sister at all during the last few days. When had he really seen her last? Months ago, it seemed; perhaps it was the day he had met her in the street dressed so strangely. 'I don't think she had been feeling ill. She would have told me,' he said.

The doctor and Emilio went into the sick-room, while Balli, after a moment's hesitation, remained behind in the dining-room.

Signora Chierici, who was sitting by her pillow, rose and went to the foot of the bed. The invalid seemed to be half asleep, but as usual went on talking as if she were keeping up a continuous conversation, and was obliged to reply to questions or to add a word or two to something which had already been said. 'In half an hour's time. But certainly not before.' She opened her eyes and recognized Dr Carini. She said something which seemed like a greeting.

'Good day, Signorina,' replied the doctor aloud, evidently with the idea of adapting himself to her delirium. 'I wanted to come and see you before, but I have not been able to.' Carini had only been to the house once before and Emilio was glad she had recognized him. She

189

must have got much better during those few hours, for at mid-day she had failed even to recognize her brother. He remarked this in a low voice to the doctor.

The latter meanwhile was studying the patient's pulse attentively. Then he uncovered her chest and applied his ear to it in various places. Amalia remained silent, and lay looking up at the ceiling. Then the doctor raised her in bed with Signora Elena's help and examined her back in the same way. Amalia resisted for an instant, but when she grasped what he wanted to do she tried to support herself.

She was looking towards the window now, where the light was rapidly becoming obscured. The door was open and Balli, who had stopped on the threshold, was seen by Amalia. 'Signor Stefano,' she said, without any show of surprise and without altering her position, for she had understood that they wanted her to keep still. Emilio, who had feared a scene, made an emphatic sign to Balli to retire, and his gesture alone marked the importance of the encounter.

But it was impossible now for Balli to retire, so he advanced, while she made repeated signs of the head to encourage him, and even called to him. 'Such an age,' she stammered, evidently meaning that it was such a long time since they had seen each other.

When they let her lie back on the bed, she continued to look at Balli, whom even in her delirium she clearly regarded as the most important person in the room for her. The fatigue they had caused her by forcing her to sit up had increased her exhaustion, and a slight attack of coughing made her face contract with pain, but she went on looking at Balli. Even while drinking rapturously the water which the doctor offered her, she never took her eyes off Balli. Then she closed her eyes and seemed as if she wanted to go to sleep. 'Now all is well,' she said aloud and quieted down for a few moments.

The three men left Amalia's room and assembled in the room next door. Emilio inquired impatiently: 'Well, doctor?'

Carini, who had not much practise in dealing with clients, expressed his opinion simply. It was inflammation of the lungs, he said, and the condition of the patient was extremely grave.

'Is there no hope?' asked Emilio, and awaited the reply with intense anxiety.

Carini looked at him compassionately. He said there was always hope and that he had known similar cases which had suddenly taken a turn for the better, and in which the patient had recovered completely, so that even the most experienced doctor had been taken by surprise.

Emilio's feelings at once swung in the opposite direction. Oh, why should not that astonishing phenomenon present itself in this case? It would suffice to make him happy for all the rest of his life. Was not this the unhoped-for joy, the generous gift of providence which he had desired for himself? For an instant hope reigned supreme; if he could have seen Amalia get up and walk, if he could have heard her talking reasonably, he would never have desired a greater joy than that.

But Carini had not finished talking. He said it was impossible that her illness should have broken out in a day. It had already reached a stage which made it clear that it had started one or even two days before.

Emilio was again obliged to take up the burden of that past which already seemed so far away. 'It is possible,' he admitted, 'but it is hard to see how. If it broke out yesterday, it must have been so slight that I did not notice it.' Then, offended by a reproachful glance from Balli, he added: 'It seems to me quite impossible.'

Then Balli broke in roughly, in the tone of voice which everyone accepted from him: 'Look here doctor, we don't know anything about medicine, you know. Is this fever going on the whole time, as long as the illness lasts? Or will there be some intervals?'

Carini replied that he was unable to say anything about the course which the illness would probably run. 'I find myself before an unknown quantity. All that I know about the illness is what I see at the present moment.

Whether there will be crises, and when they will be, whether tomorrow or this evening or in three or four days' time, I know absolutely nothing.'

Emilio thought that this justified him in entertaining the most daring hopes, and allowed Balli to go on questioning the doctor. He pictured himself at Amalia's side, cured, with her reason restored to her, and again become capable of appreciating his affection.

Carini said that the worst symptom he noticed was neither the fever nor the cough, but that continual restless babble. He added in a low voice: 'She does not seem to have a physique capable of resisting high temperatures.'

He asked for some writing materials, but before making out the prescription he said: 'I should give her wine and seltzer water to quench her thirst. Every two or three hours I should let her drink a glass of good wine. The young lady' – he hesitated slightly – 'the young lady is evidently accustomed to taking wine.' And he wrote the prescription with a few rapid strokes of the pen.

'Amalia is not used to taking wine,' Emilio protested. 'In fact she can't bear it; I have never been able to induce her to take any.'

The doctor made a gesture of surprise, and gave Emilio a look which implied that he could not altogether believe what he said. Balli also cast a scrutinizing glance at Emilio. He had already seen that the doctor had argued from Amalia's symptoms that he had an alcoholic to deal with, and he remembered noticing before that Emilio was capable of false and altogether misplaced shame. He determined to induce him to speak the truth, since it was impossible to hide such a thing from the doctor.

Emilio guessed the meaning of his look. 'How can you possibly believe such a thing? Amalia drink? Why, she can't even drink a glassful of water. I assure you she takes a whole hour to drink a glass of water.'

'If you give me your word for it,' said the doctor, 'so much the better, for the most delicate physique can sur-

vive a high temperature if it is not weakened by alcohol.'
He looked doubtfully at the prescription, then left it as
it was, and Emilio saw that he had not believed him. 'At
the chemist's they will give you a medicine of which you
must make her take a spoonful every hour. And now I
should like to speak to the lady who is looking after her.'

Emilio and Balli followed the doctor into the other
room, and introduced him to Signora Elena. Carini explained that he wanted her to try and persuade the
invalid to bear ice compresses on her chest, and said that
they would be of very great assistance in her cure.

'Oh, she will bear them!' said Elena, with a fervour
which surprised the two men.

'Go slowly!' said the doctor with a smile, glad to see
his patient in such compassionate hands. 'I don't want
you to force her, and if she shows too great a dislike of
the cold you must give up the attempt.'

Carini went away, promising to come at an early hour
next day. 'Well, doctor?' asked Emilio again in a tone of
entreaty. Instead of replying the doctor said a few words
of comfort, and promised to give him a fuller opinion on
the following day. Balli went away with Carini, promising to return immediately; he wanted to have the doctor
to himself, and to hear if he had told Emilio the truth.

Emilio clung to hope with all the strength of his
nature. The doctor had been mistaken in believing
Amalia to be a drunkard, so perhaps his whole diagnosis
was wrong. As his dreams never knew any limit Emilio
even thought that Amalia's health must still depend on
him. She had fallen ill in the first place because he had
failed in his duty as her protector; but now he was there,
and ready to procure her every satisfaction and every
comfort; and that the doctor could not know. He went to
Amalia's bedside as if he were already bringing her this
satisfaction and this comfort, but there he felt suddenly
helpless. He kissed her on the forehead and stood for a
long time watching her while she wore herself out in the
struggle to breathe a little air into her poor lungs.

When Balli came back he sat down in a corner, as far

from Amalia's bed as possible. The doctor had only been able to repeat to him what he had said to Emilio. Signora Elena asked if she could go to her flat for a few moments to give some instructions to her maid; she said she would send her to the chemist. She left the room, accompanied by an admiring glance from Balli. There was no need to give her money, for the Brentani's had long been accustomed to have an account at the chemist.

Balli murmured: 'Simple goodness like that moves me more than the loftiest genius.'

Emilio had taken the place which Elena left empty. It was some time since the patient had said a single comprehensible word; she murmured indistinctly, as if she were trying to give herself practice in pronouncing difficult words. Emilio rested his head on his hand and sat listening to that weary flow of dizzy sound. He had been listening to it since the morning till it seemed to have become a quality of his own ear, a sound from which he would never again be able to free himself. He remembered getting up one evening in his nightshirt, in spite of the cold, to wait on his sister who was suffering in the room next to his; and how he had offered to take her to the theatre the next evening. The gratitude in Amalia's voice on that occasion had been very consoling to him. Then he had forgotten the incident and had never tried to revive it. Oh, if only he had known that his life contained such a precious mission as to guard and cherish this life which was entrusted solely to him, he would never have felt the need of approaching Angiolina again. Now, when it was perhaps too late, he was cured of his unhappy love. Sitting there in the shadow he wept silently, bitterly.

'Stefano,' called the patient, in a low voice. Emilio started and looked at Balli, who was sitting in a part of the room on which the light from the window still faintly shone. Stefano apparently had not heard, for he made no movement.

'If you want to, I do too,' said Amalia. They were the identical words, and with them the same dreams sprang to life again, stifled though they had been by Balli's sudden desertion. The patient had opened her eyes now and was staring at the wall opposite her. 'I am ready,' she said. 'Do it, but quickly.' A fit of coughing made her face contract with pain, but immediately afterwards she said: 'Oh, what a perfect day! I have waited for it so long.' And she shut her eyes again.

Emilio thought he ought to send Balli out of the room, but he had not the courage to do so. He had done so much harm the only other time when he had interfered between Balli and Amalia.

Amalia again started to babble incomprehensibly, but just as Emilio was beginning to be reassured, she said aloud and clearly, after a fresh fit of coughing: 'Oh Stefano, I feel so ill.'

'Is she calling me?' asked Balli, getting up and coming to the bedside.

'I couldn't hear,' said Emilio, uncomfortably.

'I don't understand, doctor,' said Amalia, with her face turned towards Balli: 'I am lying quite still, I am looking after myself, but I still seem to be ill.'

Surprised that she had not recognized him after calling for him, Balli spoke to her as if he had been the doctor; he advised her to go on being good, and said that she would soon be quite well again.

She went on talking: 'What do I need all this for – this – this – this?' She touched her chest and her side. Her exhaustion became more apparent when she was silent, but she paused in search of a word, and not for lack of breath.

'This pain,' suggested Balli, supplying the word which she had been seeking for in vain.

'This pain,' she repeated gratefully. But soon after her doubt returned as to whether she had expressed herself badly, and she made a painful effort to continue. 'What did I need this ... for, today? What shall we do with this ... this ... on such a day?'

Only Emilio understood her. She was dreaming of her wedding.

But Amalia never gave expression to such a thought. She repeated that she did not need it, that nobody needed it, especially now ... especially now. But the adverb was never defined more clearly than that, and Balli could not understand what she meant. When she was lying back on her pillow and looking straight in front of her, or keeping her eyes shut, she was at once completely at home with the object of her dreams; when she opened them again she did not see that the person himself was there in flesh and bone beside her bed. The only one who could understand the dream was Emilio, for he alone knew all the real facts as well as all the dreams that had led up to this delirium. He felt that his presence by the bed was more than ever useless. Amalia did not belong to him in her delirium; she was still less his than when she was in possession of her senses.

Signora Elena returned, bringing the wet rags with her, and everything necessary to isolate them and prevent them wetting the bed. She uncovered Amalia's chest and protected it from the eyes of the two men by placing herself in front of the bed.

Amalia uttered a faint cry of terror at the sudden sensation of cold. 'It will do you good,' said Signora Elena, bending over her.

Amalia understood, but asked doubtfully, and struggling for breath: 'Will it really do me good?' She tried to escape from the painful sensation, pleading: 'Not today, please, not today.'

'I beseech you, little sister,' said Emilio, passionately, having at last found something in which he might be useful; 'please try to keep the poultice on your chest. It will cure you.'

Amalia's exhaustion seemed to have increased; her eyes filled with tears again. 'It is so dark,' she said, 'so dark.' It was in fact dark by now, but when Signora Elena hastened to light a candle Amalia did not seem to see it, and continued to complain of the dark. She was really trying to express quite a different sensation which was weighing upon her.

By the light of the candle Signora Elena perceived that Amalia's face was covered with perspiration; even her nightgown was soaked in it right up to the shoulders. 'Let us hope it is a good sign,' she exclaimed joyfully.

Meanwhile Amalia, who during her delirium was docility personified, tried to free herself from the weight on her chest, and at the same time not to disobey the orders she had heard ringing in her ears, by pushing the poultice round towards her back. But even there the cold gave her an uncomfortable sensation, and then, with surprising agility, she hid it under the pillow, content at last to have found a place where she could keep it without being made to suffer by it. Then she examined with an anxious eye the faces of her attendants, of whose help she knew she stood in need. When Signora Elena removed the poultice from the bed altogether she uttered a sound of surprise. This was the interval in which she showed most consciousness during the night, and even then her intelligence was only that of a mild, submissive beast.

Balli had got Michele to bring several bottles of red and white wine. By chance the first bottle they opened was *spumante;* the cork flew out with a loud detonation, touching the ceiling and fell on to Amalia's bed. She did not even notice it, while the others watched with terror the flight of the projectile.

The invalid drank the wine which Signora Elena poured out for her, but made various signs of disgust, which signs Emilio noted with profound satisfaction.

Balli offered a glass to Signora Elena, which she accepted on condition that he and Emilio should drink with her. Balli emptied his glass only after having drunk to Amalia's health.

But health was as yet very far away. 'Oh, oh, what do I see?' she called out soon after in a clear voice, looking straight in front of her. 'Vittoria with him? No, it cannot be, he would have told me.' It was the second time she had spoken of Vittoria, but Emilio understood now, because he had guessed who it was Amalia always meant by that emphatic 'he'. She was showing signs of jealousy. She continued to talk, but less clearly. Emilio could however follow her dream from her inarticulate murmuring, and realized that it went on longer than the preceding ones. The two persons she had created in her delirium had come together and poor Amalia pretended that she liked seeing them, and seeing them together. 'Who says I don't like it? I do.' Then followed a longer period during which she only muttered some indistinct words. Perhaps the dream had been over for some time and Emilio was still looking for signs of jealousy in those feeble cries of pain.

Signora Elena had again taken her accustomed seat by the pillow. Emilio went to join Balli, who, with his arms resting on the window-ledge, was looking down into the street. The storm which had been threatening for some hours was coming nearer and nearer. Not a drop of rain had yet fallen on the street. The last rays of sunset, dyed yellow in the turbid air, threw on the pavement and the houses the glow of a conflagration. Balli was watching it through half-shut eyes, and revelling in the strange colour.

Emilio made another effort to attach himself to Amalia, to protect and defend her, although she had repulsed him in her delirium. He said to Balli: 'Did you notice what a face of disgust she put on when she drank the wine? Do you think that was the face of someone who drinks habitually?'

Balli agreed, but desirous of defending Carini, he replied with his usual candour: 'But perhaps her illness has spoilt her palate.'

Emilio was so angry that he felt a lump rise in his throat. 'So you still believe what that imbecile said?'

When Balli heard the note of passion in his friend's voice he withdrew: 'I understand nothing about it; it was only Carini's conviction which made me feel a little doubtful.'

Emilio wept again. He said that it was not Amalia's illness or even her death which drove him to despair, but the thought that she had always been misunderstood and maligned. And now when a cruel destiny took delight in distorting her good, kind, gentle face with agony, it was interpreted as the result of a vicious life. Balli tried to quiet him; he said that when he thought it well over, it seemed to him impossible that Amalia should have indulged in a vice like that. But in any case he had never dreamed of wishing to insult the poor girl. Turning towards the bed, he said in a tone of deep compassion: 'Even if Carini's supposition were correct I should not have despised your sister in the smallest degree.'

They stood by the window for a long time in silence. The yellow glow on the street had long been blotted out by the darkness, which was advancing rapidly. Only the upper sky, across which clouds were still galloping, remained clear and yellow.

Emilio wondered whether Angiolina had gone to the appointment, and suddenly, forgetting in a moment what he had decided that morning, he said: 'I am going to keep my last appointment with Angiolina.' And why not indeed? Living or dead, Amalia would now for ever separate him from his mistress, but why should he not go and tell Angiolina that he wanted finally to break every relationship with her? His heart expanded with joy at the thought of this interview. His presence in this room did no one any good, whereas if he went to Angiolina he could bring back with him a sacrifice to lay at Amalia's feet. Balli, astounded by his words, tried to dissuade him from his plan, but he replied that he was going to the appointment because he wanted to profit by his state of mind to free himself for ever from Angiolina.

Stefano could not believe him; he thought he heard the familiar tones of the old, weak Emilio, and hoped to strengthen his resolution by telling him he had been obliged that very day to chase Angiolina from his studio. He said it in such a way as to leave no possible doubts as to the cause.

Emilio grew pale. His adventure was not dead yet. It was coming to life again, by his sister's bedside. Angiolina had betrayed him again in an unheard-of way. He felt as if he had been suddenly seized by the same agony from which Amalia was suffering; at the very moment of his realization that he had forsaken all his duties for Angiolina she was betraying him with Balli. The only difference between the indignation he had often felt before and that which cut his breath short now, was that his only means now of avenging himself on that woman was to abandon her. His shattered mind could no longer grasp the idea of vengeance. Events would have developed exactly the same if Balli had told him nothing. He could not succeed in hiding his painful surprise. 'I implore you,' he said, with a warmth which he made no effort to hide, 'to tell me exactly what happened.'

Balli protested: 'Besides the shame of having been obliged for once in my life to play the part of chaste Joseph I don't want to have to bear that of handing down to history all the details of my adventure. But if on a day like this you can still go on busying your thoughts about that woman, I tell you that you are hopelessly lost.'

Emilio defended himself. He said that he had made up his mind that morning to give up Angiolina, and that therefore what Balli had said could only in so far distress him as he the more regretted having devoted so large a part of his own life to such a woman. He would not have Stefano believe that he was going to his appointment with the intention of making Angiolina a scene. He smiled feebly. Oh, he was far indeed from that! In fact Balli's words had had so little effect on him that he hardly thought his purpose was any firmer now than before to break off his relations with Angiolina. 'All these things only move me because they carry my thoughts back to the past.'

He was lying. It was the present which had again become passionately alive. Where was the discouragement under which he had laboured during the long hours he had sat there vainly trying to help Amalia? The excitement he now felt was not a disagreeable feeling.

He would have liked to escape on the spot, in order to make the moment come more quickly when he could tell Angiolina that he never meant to see her again. But he felt it necessary first to obtain Stefano's consent. This was not difficult, for Stefano felt such extreme pity for him that day that he had not the courage to oppose any wish of his.

After a moment's hesitation, he asked Balli to stay and keep Signora Elena company. He had said, had he not, that he should be back very soon. So Angiolina was once more the cause of Stefano and Amalia being brought together.

Balli advised Emilio not to stop and make Angiolina a scene. Emilio wore the calm smile of a superior person. Even if Balli had not asked it of him, he could assure him that he should not discuss with Angiolina that last instance of her unfaithfulness. And it was sincerely his intention not to do so. He pictured his last conversation with Angiolina, friendly and even perhaps affectionate. He needed that it should be so. He would tell her that Amalia was dying and that he was giving her up without making her any reproach. He did not love her, but neither did he love anything else in the world.

He approached Amalia's bedside with his hat in his hand. She studied him for a long time. 'Have you come to dinner?' she asked. Then she seemed to be trying to look behind him, and asked him again: 'Have you both come to dinner?' She was still looking for Balli.

He said good evening to Signora Elena. He felt one last hesitation. Fate seemed always to enjoy placing Amalia's misfortunes in some bizarre connexion with his love for Angiolina, so might it not easily happen that his sister would die just when he was with his mistress for the last time? He went back to the bed; the poor creature seemed to him to be the very image of anguish. She was lying uncomfortably on one side, with her head off the pillow, and even hanging over the edge of the bed. That head, with its poor, damp, ruffled hair, was vainly seeking a place to rest in It was evident that this state might immediately precede her death agony. For all that, Emilio left her and went away.

He had responded to Balli's fresh recommendations with another smile. The cold night air stung him, and chilled him to the bottom of his soul. He use violence to Angiolina? Because she was the cause of Amalia's death? But that sin could surely not be laid at her door. No, evil just happened, it was not committed. An intelligent being could not behave with violence, because there was no room for hatred. His old habit of turning his thoughts inwards and analysing himself led him to suspect that his state of mind was the result of his need to excuse himself and prove his innocence. He smiled as it were at something very comic. How wrong he and Amalia had been to take life so seriously!

He looked at his watch and stood for a while on the sea-front. The weather seemed worse here than it did in the town. The tremendous clamour of the sea, joined to the howling of the wind, made one vast uproar composed of many voices small and great. The night was dark; nothing could be seen of the sea but the white crest of a wave here and there, which had burst asunder before it could hurl itself against the shore. They were keeping watch on the boats anchored along the quay, and here and there he could see the figure of a sailor working in darkness and danger up aloft on the masts which were keeping up their ritual dance towards all the four winds in turn.

Emilio felt the confusion of the elements was attuned to his grief, and it helped him to attain a greater calm. His habit of always thinking in images made him read a comparison between the scene before him and the spectacle of his own life. In that tumult of the waves, where each transmitted to the other the movement which had roused it from its own inertia, where each in turn strove to rise from its place only to fall again into a horizontal postion, he read the impassivity of fate. No one was to blame for all the vast destruction.

Beside him a huge sailor, planted firmly on powerful

legs clad in sea-boots, shouted a name towards the sea. Soon another voice shouted back. Then he flung himself on a stone pillar near by, loosed a cable which was wound round it, paid it out and made it fast again. Slowly, almost imperceptibly, one of the largest fishing-boats moved away from the shore, and Emilio saw that it had been made fast to a neighbouring buoy, to save it from being bumped against the quay.

The big sailor had taken up a fresh position now; had lit his pipe and was leaning against the post taking his ease in the midst of the storm.

Emilio thought that it was the inactivity of his own fate which had been responsible for his misfortunes. If only once in his life he had had to untie a rope and knot it again at a given moment; if the fate of one fishing-boat, no matter how small, had been entrusted to him, to his care, to his courage, if he had been compelled to override with his own voice the clamour of the wind and sea he would have been less weak and less unhappy.

He went to his appointment. His grief would return immediately afterwards; for the moment he loved, in spite of Amalia. He could not feel pain at a time when he was able to do exactly what his nature required. He tasted with delight the calm feeling of resignation and forgiveness. He could think of no words in which to convey his state of mind to Angiolina, so that their last meeting would seem to her absolutely inexplicable; for he should act as if a being of greater intelligence were present to judge both him and her.

The weather had changed, and now a cold, continuous wind was blowing; there was no longer any war in the air.

Angiolina came to meet him down the Viale di Sant' Andrea. When she saw him she burst out in great irrita-tion – painfully discordant to Emilio's present state of mind – 'I have been here half an hour already. I was just on the point of going away.'

He led her gently to a lamp-post and showed her the hands of his watch, which pointed exactly to the hour appointed for their meeting.

'Then I must have been mistaken,' she said, not much more pleasantly. While he was turning over in his mind how to tell her that this would be their last meeting, she stood still and said: 'You had really better let me off this evening. We shall meet tomorrow. It is so cold, and besides...'

He was snatched suddenly from his interrogation of his own thoughts, and began examining her; he at once realized that it was not the cold which had made her want to get away. He was further struck by the fact that she was dressed with greater care than usual. A very smart brown dress, which he had never seen before, seemed to have been fetched out for some great occasion; her hat looked new too, and he even noticed that she had on thin little shoes which were quite unsuited for walking about at Sant' Andrea in weather like that. 'And besides?' he repeated, halting beside her and looking her straight in the face.

'Now listen. I am going to tell you everything,' she said, assuming an air of self-assurance which was quite out of place; and she continued imperturbably, without noticing that Emilio's look was becoming more and more grim: 'I have received a telegram from Volpini, announcing his arrival. I don't know what he wants, but he must have got to the house by this time.'

She was lying, there was no doubt about it. Only that morning they had written that letter to Volpini, and here he was arriving, before he had received it, full of apologies, and eager to beg her pardon. Sick at heart he said, smiling sadly: 'What? You mean to say that the man who wrote you a letter like that only yesterday has come here today to take it back again in person, and even sends you a wire to warn you that he is coming. Just the sort of thing he would be likely to wire about! And supposing you happen to have made a mistake and that you found someone else there instead of Volpini?'

She continued to smile, still sure of herself: 'Ah, I suppose Sorniani has been telling you that he met me the night before last in the street, rather late, with a gentleman? I had just left the Deluigis and as I was afraid to walk alone in the streets at night, I was very glad of his company.' He was not listening to what she said, but the last sentence of what she thought a very sufficient justification struck him by its oddity: 'That was a *deo gratias* if ever there was one.' Then she continued: 'It is a pity I forgot to bring the telegram with me. But if you don't believe me, so much the worse. Don't I always arrive punctually at all my appointments? Why should I have to invent all that nonsense today, to get out of one?'

'It is not very difficult to see why!' said Emilio, laughing furiously. 'Today you have got another appointment. Be off to it at once! Someone is waiting for you.'

'Well, if that is what you think of me, I had certainly better go!' She spoke with determination, but did not stir from the spot.

Her words had the same effect on him as if they had been immediately accompanied by the act. She was going to leave him! 'Wait a moment, I have something to say to you first.' Even under the influence of tremendous anger which pervaded his whole being, he wondered for a moment whether it were not still possible for him to return to the state of calm resignation in which he had been before. But wouldn't he be justified in striking her down and trampling on her? He seized her by the arm to prevent her getting away, supported himself against the lamp-post just behind him, and brought his own contorted face close to her calm, rosy one. 'This is the last time we shall ever meet!' he shouted.

'All right, all right,' she said, wholly occupied in trying to release herself from his grasp, which hurt her arm.

'And do you know why? Because you are a...' he hesitated a moment, then flung the word at her, which even in his rage had seemed to him too strong, shouted it triumphantly, triumphant over his own doubt.

'Let me go,' she screamed, shaking with anger and fear. 'Let me go, or I shall call for help.'

'You are a whore...' he repeated, ready to give over shaking her, now that he saw he had really roused her.

'But do you imagine that I haven't known for a very long time whom I had to deal with? When I met you dressed like a servant, on the staircase at your house' (he remembered every detail of that evening) 'with that common handkerchief tied round your head, and your arms still warm from bed, the name I have just called you by came into my head at once. I decided not to say it and went on amusing myself with you like all the others – Leardi, Giustini, Sorniani and Balli.'

'Balli!' she laughed scornfully, and raised her voice to a scream so as to be heard above the noise of the wind and Emilio's voice. 'Balli is boasting; there's not a word of truth in it.'

'Because he wouldn't, the fool, out of consideration for me, as if it could matter to me whether you have slept with one man more or less, you...' and for the third time he called her by that name. She redoubled her efforts to escape from his grasp, but the effort to hold her fast had now become an all-absorbing motive to Emilio; he dug his fingers voluptuously into her soft flesh.

He knew that the moment he set her free she would go away and leave him, that all would be over between them and in such a different manner from that which he had dreamed of. 'And I loved you so much,' he said, trying perhaps to soften his own heart, but adding at once: 'But all the time I knew what you were. Do you know what you are?' Oh, at last he had found some compensation; he must compel her to confess what kind of a woman she was: 'Speak up, now! Tell me what you are!'

And now, having apparently reached a point of complete exhaustion, she became terrified of him; the colour left her cheeks, she stared at him with a look which craved for pity. She let him shake her without any effort to resist, and he thought she was on the point of falling to the ground. He loosened his hold and supported her. Suddenly she broke free and began running for her life. So she had been lying again. He never even attempted to catch her up; he stooped down and looked for a stone, but when he could not find one he collected some small pebbles which he hurled after her. The wind carried them along, and one must have hit her, for she uttered a cry of terror. The others struck the dry branches of the trees and produced a sound which was ridiculously out of proportion to the anger which had raised his arm to throw them.

What was he to do now? The last satisfaction he craved had been denied him. In contrast to his resignation everything around him remained harsh and cruel, and he himself had behaved brutally. The blood hammered in his veins from over-excitement; cold though it was, he was burning with fever, burning with rage, as he stood there motionless, his legs refusing to move. Already the calm observer had come to life in him and condemned the part he had played.

'I shall never see her again,' he said, as if in response to a reproof. Never! never! And when he was able to walk again, that word kept echoing in the sound of his own footsteps, and in the wind which whistled over the desolate landscape. He smiled to himself as he went back over the same road by which he had come, and remembered the ideas which had accompanied him to that rendezvous. How astonishing reality was!

He did not go straight home. He could not have played the part of sick-nurse in his present state of mind. His dream still possessed him utterly, so much so that he could not have said which road he had taken to go home. Oh! if his meeting with Angiolina had been what he had intended it to be, he would have been able to go straight to Amalia's bedside without even having to alter the expression of his face.

He discovered a fresh analogy between his relation with Angiolina and that with Amalia. He was obliged to detach himself from both of them without being able to say the last word which would at least have softened his memory of the two women. Amalia could not hear what he said; and to Angiolina he could not say it.

13

HE passed the whole of that night by Amalia's bedside in one uninterrupted dream. Not that he was thinking the whole time of Angiolina, but between him and his immediate surroundings there was a veil which prevented him seeing clearly. A great weariness forbade him indulging in the hopes which had persisted in visiting him from time to time during the afternoon, no less than in the fits of despair from which he had sought relief in tears.

Everything at home appeared to be exactly as he left it. Only Balli had given up his corner and gone to sit at the end of the bed beside Signora Elena. Emilio gazed for a long time at Amalia, hoping to be able to weep again. He scrutinized her, he analysed her, so as to be able to feel her sorrow and to suffer with her. Then he looked away again, ashamed of himself; he had become conscious that in his emotion he had gone in search of images and metaphors. He again felt the need of doing something for her, and told Balli that he would release him now, thanking him warmly for the help he had given.

But Balli, who had not even thought to ask how the interview with Angiolina had gone, took him aside to tell him he had no intention of leaving. He seemed embarrassed and sad. He had something to say, and it seemed to him so delicate that he did not dare say it without a preliminary preamble. They had been friends for so many years, and any misfortune which happened to Emilio he felt to be in a measure his own. Then he said with decision: 'That poor girl often mentions my name; I must stay.' Emilio pressed his hand without feeling any great sense of gratitude; he was certain now – so certain that it gave him a great sense of tranquillity – that there was no longer any hope for Amalia.

They told him that for some minutes past Amalia had been talking continually about her illness. Might not this be a sign that the fever was diminishing? As he sat listening to her, he was quite convinced that they were mistaken. And in fact she was delirious. 'Is it my fault that I am ill? Come back again tomorrow, Doctor, and I will be quite well.' She did not appear to suffer; her face was small and pinched, the very face which was suited to such a body. Still looking at her, he thought: 'She will die!' He pictured her dead, at rest, freed from all her pain and delirium. Then he blamed himself for having entertained such a heartless idea. He went a short distance away from the bed and sat down at the table, where Balli also was sitting.

Elena remained by the bed. By the dim candle-light Emilio noticed that she was crying. 'I feel as if I were by the bedside of my son,' she said, perceiving that her tears had been seen.

Amalia suddenly said she felt quite well, very well indeed, and asked to be given something to eat. Time did not pass normally by that bedside for those who were following the course of her delirium. Every moment she seemed to be in a new state of mind or to be experiencing fresh adventures, and she made her attendants pass with her through phases which in everyday life take days and months to develop.

Signora Elena, recalling one of the doctor's prescriptions, made some tea and gave it to her, and she drank it greedily. Suddenly her delirium led her back to Balli; but for a superficial observer there was a lack of connection in that delirium. The ideas were all mixed up, one was swallowed up in another, and when it reappeared one could recognize it as being identical with the one she had apparently abandoned. She had invented for herself a rival – Vittoria; she had received her graciously, but then, according to Balli, a quarrel had developed between the two women in the course of which Balli had realized that he was the patient's *idée fixe*. Now Vittoria was coming back again, Amalia saw her coming and loathed her. 'I won't say anything to her! I will stay here like a mouse, just as if she wasn't here. I am not asking for anything, so leave me in peace.' Then she called aloud to Emilio: 'You are her friend, so tell her that she is inventing it all. I have done nothing to harm her.'

Balli tried to calm her by speaking to her. 'Listen, Amalia! I am here and I should refuse to believe it if anyone said anything against you.'

She heard him and gazed fixedly at him for some time. '*You*, Stefano?'* But she did not recognize him. 'Well, tell her then!' Her head fell back exhausted on the pillow and they all knew, by past experience, that the incident was closed.

During the interval which followed, Signora Elena pushed her chair up to the table at which the two men were sitting, and begged Emilio, who she saw looked quite worn out, to go and lie down. He refused, but the few words they interchanged started a conversation between the three which sufficed to distract them for a short while.

Signora Chierici, to whom Balli, with his usual indiscreet curiosity, had already put several questions, related that when Emilio had run into her on the stairs she had been on her way to Mass. Now, she said, she felt as if she had been in church ever since the morning, and experienced the same lightness of conscience as when one has prayed fervently. She spoke without hesitation, and in the tone of a believer who has no fear of the doubts of others.

Then she told them her own story, which was a strange one. Up to the age of forty she had lived without any close ties of affection, having lost her parents when she was very young; her days had passed in this way, solitary and serene. But then she had met a man who was a widower, and was marrying again in order to provide a mother for the boy and girl he had had by his first wife. From the very beginning the two children had treated

* She used the familiar *tu*.

her with antagonism, but she was so fond of them that she was confident of winning their hearts in the end. She was mistaken. They always insisted on regarding her as a stepmother, and hating her on that account. The family of their own mother kept on interfering between the children and their new mother and told them lying stories about her to turn them against her, and made them believe that the spirit of their mother would be jealous if they were to show any affection to their step-mother: 'I, however, grew fonder and fonder of them, so much so that I even loved my rival who had bequeathed them to me. Perhaps,' she added, with a certain subtlety of observation, 'it was just that disdainful expression on their baby faces which made me all the more fond of them.'

Soon after the father's death the little girl was taken away from her by an aunt who persisted in believing she was ill-treated.

The boy remained with her, but even after his mother's family were no longer there to influence him directly he continued, with astonishing obstinacy in one so young, to treat her with the same disdainful enmity, which showed itself in many unkind actions and rude words. He caught a malignant form of scarlatina, but continued to resist her even in his fever till, worn out at last, a few hours before he died, he flung his arms round her neck calling her 'mother' and begging her to save him. Signora Elena took pleasure in describing in detail the boy who had made her suffer so much. He was daring, vivacious and intelligent; he understood everything, except the love which was offered him. Now Signora Elena's life was passed between her empty house, the church in which she prayed for the child who had loved her for one single instant, and the grave, at which there was always plenty for her to do. Yes, she must go to-morrow without fail to see what success she had had with a young tree which would not grow straight, and to which she had put some supports.

'Then I shall go away if Vittoria is here!' shouted

Amalia, sitting straight up in bed. Emilio, terrified, lifted the candle to see her better. Amalia was deathly pale; her face was the colour of the pillow which formed a background to it. Balli looked at her with evident admiration. The yellow candle-light irradiated Amalia's damp cheeks, so that its light seemed to emanate from within herself. It was as if the cry came from her bright and suffering nakedness. It was like the plastic representation of a violent cry of pain. Her little face, on which firm purpose was imprinted for an instant, threatened majestically. It was only a flash; she fell back at once on her pillow calmed by words of which she could not understand the meaning. Then she resumed her solitary murmuring, accompanying by a word here and there the dizzy course of her dreams.

Balli said, 'She looked like some mild good fury. I have never seen anything like it.' He had sat down, and remained gazing into space with that visionary look he wore when pursuing an idea. It made Emilio glad to see him; he felt that Amalia in dying had become the object of the noblest love which Balli could offer.

Signora Elena took up the conversation again at the point where she had left it. Probably in quieting Amalia she had never for a moment detached her mind from the thought which was dearest to her. The resentment she felt towards her husband's relatives was another element in her life. She said they had looked down on her because she was the daughter of an ironmonger. 'In any case,' she added, 'the name of Deluigi is a name to be respected.'

Emilio marvelled at the strange chance which had brought into his own house a member of the family so often mentioned by Angiolina. He at once asked Elena whether she had any other relations. She said no, and denied that there could be a family of that name in the town. She denied it so emphatically that he was obliged to believe her.

So his thoughts were drawn to Angiolina during that night as well. As in the period which now seemed so far away, before Amalia's illness, when he had only looked on her as a tiresome person whose company he must avoid as much as possible, he was seized again by a burning desire to rush off to Angiolina and reproach her for the new treachery of which he had just learned and which seemed to him the worst of all. Those Deluigis had sprung up at the very beginning of their relationship, and she had created each individual member of the family in turn according as she had need of them. First there had been the old Signora Deluigi, who loved Angiolina like a mother, then the daughter who was her dearest friend, and finally the old father who had tried to make her drunk. This lie had been repeated at every single meeting, and the thought of it robbed his memory of Angiolina of all its sweetness. Even those rare signs of love which she had been clever enough to feign were now shown up by the clearest possible evidence for what they really were – lies, lies. And yet he soon felt that fresh act of treason to be a new link between them. Amalia was moving about, wearily, on her bed of suffering; for a long time he forgot all about her. When he had recovered a little calm he was obliged to recognize with sorrow that directly Amalia's illness should have disappeared, or Amalia herself, he would rush off again at once to Angiolina. In order to exercise pressure on himself he sat for a long time stiffly in the same position, and swore that he would never again fall into her snare. 'Never again, never again.'

Even that interminable night, the most painful he had ever watched through, and which in its turn became a subject of regret, was slowly passing. A clock struck two.

Signora Elena asked Emilio to give her a soft towel to wipe Amalia's face. So as not to have to leave the room, he looked for his sister's keys and opened her wardrobe. He was at once struck by a strange medicinal smell. The little linen there was, was folded away in big chests which were filled up with bottles of various sizes. He could not at first quite make out what they were and brought the candle nearer in order to examine them. Several chests were filled to the brim with bottles which shed a mysterious golden ray as if they held some treasure enclosed; in other chests there was still some room and the bottles were distributed in such a way as to leave no doubt that it was the collector's purpose to complete her strange hoard as soon as possible. Only one phial was out of place, and it still contained the remains of a transparent liquid. The smell of the liquid no longer left any doubt in Emilio's mind; it was scented ether. Doctor Carini was right then; Amalia had sought forgetfulness in drugs. He did not bear any ill-will against his sister at this discovery, not even for a moment; his mind at once jumped to the only possible conclusion: Amalia was lost. The effect of that discovery was to send him back at last and finally to her.

He shut the door of the wardrobe and locked it carefully. He had not succeeded in keeping guard over his sister's life; he would try now to keep her reputation intact.

Dawn was beginning, dark, hesitating, sad. It was whitening the window-panes but left the interior of the room in darkness. One ray, however, seemed to have penetrated, for the daylight breaking over the glasses on the table coloured them with faint and delicate shades of blue and green. The wind was still blowing in the street with the same even, triumphant sounds as when Emilio had left Angiolina.

But within the room there was a great stillness. For the last few hours Amalia's delirium had only betrayed itself in a half-spoken word now and then. She was lying quietly on her right side with her face close to the wall and her eyes wide open.

Balli had gone to rest for a while in Emilio's room. He had asked them not to let him sleep for more than an hour.

Emilio went and sat down again at the table. He started suddenly in affright; Amalia was no longer breathing. Signora Elena had noticed it too, and risen from her chair. Amalia was still gazing at the wall with wide-open eyes, and a few minutes later she began breathing again. The first four or five breaths seemed those of a healthy person, and Emilio and Elena looked at each other smiling and full of hope. But the smile very soon died on their lips, for Amalia's breathing became more and more rapid, then grew slower and slower, and finally ceased. The interval was so long this time that Emilio cried aloud with fear. The breathing began again, calm for a short time, and suddenly quickening to a dizzy speed. It was a period of agonizing suspense for Emilio. Although after an hour of the closest attention he had been able to verify for himself that the momentary cessation of breathing was not death, and that the regular breathing by which it was followed was not the prelude to health, he held his own breath with anxiety when Amalia ceased to breathe, gave himself up to mad hope when he heard her calm, rhythmic breathing begin again, and even shed tears of disappointment each time her painful breathing was resumed.

The dawn was shining on her bed now. The back of Signora Elena's grey head which, like a good nurse, she was only leaning on her chest, thus stealing a little superficial rest, was all silvered over. For Amalia the night would never end. Her head, with its clear contours, detached itself now from the pillow. Her dark hair had never seemed to clothe her head so well as during her illness. Her profile was that of an energetic person, with its prominent cheek-bones and pointed chin.

Emilio rested his arms on the table and leaned his head on his hands. The hour in which he had maltreated Angiolina seemed a long, long way off, for it again seemed to him impossible that he should be capable of such an action. He felt in himself neither the energy nor the brutality which would be needed to accomplish it. He shut his eyes and fell asleep. It seemed to him afterwards as if he had been conscious of Amalia's breathing even while he was asleep, as if he had continued to experience the same fear, hope and disappointment as before.

When he woke up it was full daylight. Amalia was looking at the window with wide-open eyes. He got up,

and hearing him move she looked at him. What a look!
No longer feverish, but of someone mortally tired who
has not complete control of it and cannot make the effort
to guide it in the right direction. 'What is the matter
with me, Emilio? I am dying.'

Intelligence had returned and, forgetting the observation he had just made on her eyes, all Emilio's hope
returned. He told her she had been very ill, but that now
she was getting better. The affection he felt in his heart
overflowed and he began shedding tears of consolation.
He kissed her tenderly and cried that from henceforth
they would always live for each other, they two alone,
and would never part. It seemed to him as if all that
night of agony had existed simply in order to prepare
him for such an expected happy solution. Afterwards he
looked back on the scene with shame. He felt as if he had
wanted to take advantage of that single flash of intelligence in Amalia to quiet his own conscience.

Signora Elena hurried forward to calm him and warn
him not to excite the invalid. Unfortunately Amalia
understood nothing. She appeared to be so entirely filled
by one single idea as to have all her senses occupied with
it. 'Tell me,' she begged, 'what has happened? I am so
frightened! I saw you and Vittoria and . . .' Her dream had
become mingled with reality and her poor exhausted mind
was incapable of disentangling the complicated skein.

'Try and understand,' Emilio passionately besought
her. 'You have dreamed without ceasing since yesterday.
You must rest now, and then you shall think again.' The
last words were said in response to another sign made by
Signora Elena, who thereby attracted Amalia's attention
to herself. 'It is not Vittoria,' she said, evidently reassured. Oh, this was not the kind of intelligence which
could be regarded as the envoy of health; it displayed
itself only in single flashes, which threatened to light up
her grief and make her more sensitive to it. Emilio was as
frightened as he had been before her delirium.

Balli came in. He had heard Amalia's voice and
wanted to be there too, to rejoice in her unexpected

improvement. 'How are you, Amalia?' he asked affectionately.

She looked at him with an expression of incredulous surprise. 'So it was not a dream then?' She gazed at Balli for a long time; then she looked at her brother, and again at Balli as if she wanted to compare their two bodies and see whether either of them lacked the appearance of reality. 'But Emilio,' she exclaimed. 'I don't understand.'

'When he knew you were ill,' Emilio exclaimed, 'he wanted to keep me company during the night. It is our same old friend whom you know so well.'

She was not listening. 'And Vittoria?' she asked.

'That woman has never been here,' said Emilio.

'He has the right to do as he likes, and you may go with them if you want to,' she murmured, with a sudden flash of resentment in her eye. Then she forgot everything and everyone and remained gazing out of the window.

Stefano said, 'Listen to me, Amalia! I have never known this Vittoria you keep talking of. I am your devoted friend and am staying here to help you.'

She was not listening. She was watching the light in the window, and evidently making an effort to revive her failing eyesight. She seemed to gaze in admiration and ecstasy. Her features wore an ugly grimace, which evidently took the place of a smile.

'Oh, she cried, 'what a lot of lovely children!' She gazed for a long time in admiration. Her delirium had returned. But she had now a respite from the dreams of the night in these luminous visions clothed in the colours of the dawn. She saw rosy children dancing in the sunshine. It was a delirium of few words. She only named the object she saw, and nothing else. Her own life was forgotten. She named neither Balli, nor Vittoria, nor Emilio. 'So much light,' she said, enchanted. She was lit up too. They could see the red blood mount under her transparent skin and colour her cheeks and forehead. She was changing, but she was not conscious of herself. She was looking at things which kept moving ever further and further away from her.

Balli proposed sending for the doctor. 'It would be useless,' said Signora Elena, who had realized from that sudden flush the point things had reached.

'Useless,' Emilio repeated, shocked at having his own thought expressed by others.

In fact, Amalia's mouth soon afterwards contracted itself in that strange effort whereby even the muscles which are not adapted to the purpose are forced to labour for breath. There was still vision in her eye, but she did not say another word. Very soon her breathing changed into the death-rattle, a sound resembling a dirge, the dirge of this gentle creature who was dying. It seemed the expression of a mild affliction, a humble but conscious protest. It was in fact the lament of matter which, already abandoned by the spirit, and beginning to disintegrate, was uttering the sounds it had learned during its long period of painful consciousness.

14

THE image of death is great enough to fill the whole of one's mind. Gigantic forces are fighting together to draw death near and to expel it; every fibre of our being records its presence after having been near to it, every atom within us repels it in the very act of preserving and producing life. The thought of death is like an attribute of the body, a physical malady. Our will can neither summon it nor drive it away.

Emilio nourished himself for a long time on this thought. The spring was over and he had only been conscious of it by seeing it flower on his sister's grave. It was a thought unaccompanied by any remorse. Death was death, and not more terrible than the circumstances which had led up to it. Death had passed by, the supreme misdeed, and he felt that his own errors and misdeeds had been utterly forgotten.

During that time he lived as much as possible alone He even avoided Balli, who after behaving so well at Amalia's bedside had already completely forgotten the brief enthusiasm with which she had been able to inspire him. Emilio could not quite forgive him for not being more like himself in this. It was now the only thing with which he had to reproach him.

When his own emotion became less violent, it seemed to him that he had lost his balance. He hastened to the cemetery. The dusty road, and above all the heat caused him unspeakable suffering. By the grave he adopted a contemplative pose, but he did not know how to contemplate. What he felt most was the burning sensation in his skin caused by the sun, dust and sweat. When he got home he washed himself, and in the refreshing water lost all memory of his outing. He felt himself utterly alone. He went out with the vague idea of attaching himself to somebody, but on the landing where he had one day found the help he sought, he remembered that a very short way off there was someone who could teach him to remember – Signora Elena. He had not forgotten Amalia, he said to himself as he mounted the stairs – he even remembered her too clearly, but he had forgotten the emotion caused by her death. Instead of seeing her in her last struggle with death he remembered her sad and downcast, her grey eyes reproaching him for his desertion, or desolately replacing in the cupboard the coffee cup she had put out for Balli, and finally he remembered her gestures, words, or tears of anger and despair. They were all memories of his own sin. He wanted to bury them all again in Amalia's death; Signora Elena would call it up for him. Amalia herself had been insignificant during her life. He could not even remember that she had shown any desire to draw nearer to him, when in order to save himself from Angiolina he had tried to make their relationship more tender. It was her death alone which had been of any importance to him; that at least had rescued him from his shameful passion.

'Is Signora Elena at home?' he asked the maid who came to open the door. In that house they were probably not very used to visitors. The maid – a fair, pretty girl – would not let him come any further, but called in a loud voice to Signora Elena, who at once came out into the dark passage from a side door and stood in the light which was shed from the room. 'What a good thing I came,' thought Emilio joyfully, feeling a sudden emotion at the sight of Elena's grey head which, faintly lighted from the room, shone with just those silver rays which had caught it on the morning of Amalia's death.

Signora Elena welcomed him with great warmth. 'I have been hoping to see you for such a long time. I can't tell you what a real pleasure you give me by coming.'

'I felt I should be welcome,' said Emilio, deeply moved. He was touched by the friendship offered him by this unknown woman at Amalia's deathbed. 'We have not known each other long, but a day like the one we spent together often brings one closer than many years of intimacy.'

Signora Elena led him into the small room she had just come out of, which was the same shape as Brentani's dining-room, and just above it. The furniture was simple, even bare, but everything was most beautifully kept, and one did not feel the need of any other furniture. Simplicity seemed almost carried to the point of excess on the walls, which were left entirely bare.

The maid brought in an oil lamp, ready lit, and wished them good evening in a loud voice. Then she went out again.

The signora looked after her with a kindly smile.

'I can't get her out of the countrified habit of wishing me good evening when she brings in the lamp. For that matter I think it is rather a charming habit. Giovanna is such a good creature, and so simple. It is strange to find anyone so ingenuous in these days. Sometimes I feel a desire to cure her of such an adorable complaint. You should see what eyes she makes when I tell her something about our modern customs.' She laughed heartily, open ing her eyes wide, in imitation of the girl she was telling him about; she seemed to be studying her in order to appreciate her the better.

The biography of the servant had interrupted Emilio's emotion. In order to solve a doubt which arose in his mind he told her that he had been to the cemetery that day. His doubt was immediately solved, for the lady said, without a moment's hesitation: 'I never go to the cemetery now. I have not been once since the day your sister was buried.' She went on to say that she knew now that one could not fight with death. 'The dead are dead, and comfort can only come from the living.' She added, without any bitterness: 'We may wish it otherwise, but so it is.' She then said that the short service she had rendered to Amalia had sufficed to break the charm of her memories. The grave of her little son no longer stirred her or helped her to renew her emotions, as it had done before. She was really expressing what was in Emilio's mind, especially when she summed it all up by saying: 'It is the living who have need of us.'

She again spoke about Giovanna, her maid. By good fortune she had recovered from an illness, and it was Elena who had helped to save her. They had got to know each other during that illness. When the girl recovered, her mistress had realized that it was the little dead boy who had come to live in her. 'But gentler and kinder and more grateful, oh, so much more grateful!' But this new affection was also a source of anxiety and even of sorrow, for Giovanna was in love. . . .

Emilio had ceased listening to her. He was entirely occupied by the solution of a serious problem. When he went away, he greeted the servant respectfully on the threshold, as one who had succeeded in saving a fellow-creature from despair. 'Strange,' he thought to himself; 'it almost seems as if one half of humanity exists to live and the other to be lived.' His thoughts returned at once to his own concrete case: 'Perhaps Angiolina only exists in order that I may live.'

He walked along quietly and refreshed through the

cool night which had succeeded that oppressive day. The example of Signora Elena had proved to him that even he might somewhere in life find his daily bread, his reason for living. This hope accompanied him for some time; he had forgotten all the elements of which his wretched life was composed, and thought that on the day he chose to begin again from the beginning, he would be able to do so.

His first attempts to put this to the proof were a failure. He had tried writing again and derived no sort of emotion from it. He had tried women and found that they did not interest him. 'I love Angiolina!' he thought.

One day Sorniani told him that Angiolina had run away with a cashier who had robbed his bank. The event had aroused a scandal through the whole town.

It was a most painful surprise to him. He said: 'My life has fled.' But on the contrary, Angiolina's flight restored him for a while to full vitality, plunged him again into the midst of his sufferings and resentments. He dreamed of vengeance and love, as on the first occasion when he had abandoned her.

When his resentment had died down he went to see Angiolina's mother, just as he had gone to see Elena when the memory of Amalia had threatened to become faint. This visit also was imposed on him by a definite state of mind which demanded that a fresh impulse be given it at that very moment, so much so that he paid his visit during office hours, unable to put it off even for a moment.

The old woman received him as kindly as usual. Angiolina's room had changed its appearance a little, for all the knick-knacks had been removed which she had collected during her long career. The photographs had disappeared too, and were now no doubt adorning the walls of a room in some other town.

'So she has run away?' said Emilio, in a tone of bitter irony. He savoured that moment as if he had been talking to Angiolina herself.

Old mother Zarri denied that Angiolina had run away. She had gone to stay with some relations of theirs who lived in Vienna. Emilio made no comment, but soon afterwards, yielding to an imperious desire, he assumed again the accusing tone which he had made an effort to lay aside. He said that he had foreseen everything. He had tried to correct Angiolina and to point out the straight road to her. He had not succeeded and he was deeply distressed about it; but it was far worse for Angiolina, whom he would never have deserted if she had treated him differently.

He would not have been able to repeat afterwards the words he said at that all-important moment, but they were evidently very efficacious, for the poor old mother burst out into a strange dry sobbing; she turned her back on him and went away. He followed her with his eye, rather surprised at the effect he had produced. The sobs were obviously sincere; they shook her whole body so much that she could scarcely walk.

'Good day, Signor Brentani,' said Angiolina's little sister, coming in at that moment with a pretty curtsey and holding out her hand. 'Mamma has gone in there because she doesn't feel well. But we hope you will come back another day.'

'No!' said Emilio solemnly, as if he were only now in the act of abandoning Angiolina. 'I shall never come back again.' He stroked her hair, which was less thick but the same colour as Angiolina's. 'Never again!' he repeated and kissed her on the forehead with profound pity.

'Why not?' she asked, flinging her arms round his neck. He was so taken aback that he allowed her to cover his face with kisses that were by no means childish.

By the time he succeeded in breaking away from that embrace, disgust had destroyed any kind of emotion he had felt before. He saw that it was unnecessary to go on with his sermon and went out, after having given the child an indulgent, fatherly caress, so as not to go away leaving her unhappy.

When he was alone again in the road a great heaviness took possession of him. He felt that the caress he had given out of pity to that child really marked the end of his adventure; but he himself could not have said exactly what important period of his life had ended with that caress.

For a long time his adventure left him unbalanced and discontented. Love and sorrow had passed through his life and, deprived of these elements, he had rather the feeling of someone who has had an important part of his body amputated. But the gap was finally filled. A love of quiet and of security sprang up again in him, and the necessity of looking after himself robbed him of every other desire.

Years afterwards he looked back with a kind of enchanted wonder on that period which had been the most important and the most luminous in his life. He lived on it like an old man on the memories of his youth. Angiolina underwent a strange metamorphosis in the writer's idle imagination. She preserved all her own beauty, but acquired as well all the qualities of Amalia, who died a second time in her. She grew sad and dispirited, her eye acquired an intellectual clarity. He saw her before him as on an altar, the personification of thought and suffering, and he never ceased loving her, if admiration and desire are love. She stood for all that was noble in his thought and vision during that period of his life.

Her figure even became a symbol. It was always looking in the same direction, towards the horizon, the future from which came those glowing rays, reflected in rose and amber and white upon her face. She was waiting! The image embodied the dream he had once dreamed at Angiolina's side, which that child of the people could not understand.

That lofty, splendid symbol sometimes seemed on the point of coming to life again as a warm-blooded woman, but always a sad and thoughtful one.

Yes, Angiolina thinks and sometimes cries, thinks as though the secret of the universe had been explained to her or the secret of her own existence, and is sad as though in all the whole wide world she could not find one single solitary *deo gratias*.